**Praise fo**

"Mystical and occult e ... t
make Lisa Renee
a fun an
—*Romanti*

**Praise for Olivia Gates**

"The profound emotions evident on every page
will thoroughly pull the reader into the lives
of these unforgettable characters."
—*Cataromance.com* on *Mortal Enemy, Immortal Lover*

**Praise for Linda O. Johnston**

"*Alpha Wolf* has mysteries, romance and thrilling
supernatural aspects, and they combine to tell an
enthralling love story."
—*Cataromance.com*

**Praise for Barbara J. Hancock**

"These are two people who complete each other
and, even with things like psychics and werewolves
and government conspiracies,
that's what romance is all about."
—*DearAuthor.com* on *Wilderness*

**Praise for Caridad Piñeiro**

"Piñeiro infuses her vampires with very human
feelings, making her paranormal story seem realistic.
It's a great read!"
—*Romantic Times BOOKreviews* on *Fury Calls*

**Praise for Lydia Parks**

"[With] sizzling sex between alpha vampires and
intelligent heroines, Parks delivers a deliciously
engaging bedtime story."
—*Romantic Times BOOKreviews* on *Addicted*

# AWAKENING THE BEAST

LISA RENEE JONES,
OLIVIA GATES,
LINDA O. JOHNSTON,
BARBARA J. HANCOCK,
CARIDAD PIÑEIRO AND
LYDIA PARKS

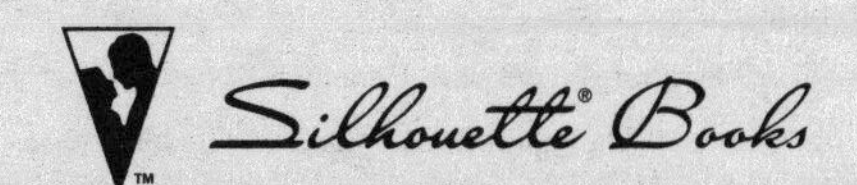


nocturne

Recycling programs for this product may not exist in your area.

AWAKENING THE BEAST

ISBN-13: 978-0-373-25094-3



This edition published by arrangement with Harlequin Books S.A.



Visit Silhouette Books at www.eHarlequin.com

**Printed in U.S.A.**

CONTENTS

# RETURN OF THE BEAST

*Lisa Renee Jones*

To Matt—the real reason my heart is still in Texas

***LISA RENEE JONES***

is an author of paranormal and contemporary romance. Having previously lived in Austin, Texas, Lisa now resides in New York. She has the joy of filling her days with the stories playing in her head, turning them into novels she hopes you enjoy! You can visit her at www.lisareneejones.com.

Dear Reader,

When my editor called me about writing a Nocturne Bites story, I was in a U-Haul truck, moving from Texas to New York. Leaving Texas behind was an emotional roller coaster, and during the drive, I was replaying in my head all the things I was going to miss about my home state. So it was easy to decide—I wanted my Nocturne Bites story to be *all Texas,* and it seemed only appropriate that my romance feature a *real* cowboy. I have learned they don't have many of them in New York.

"Return of the Beast" features a hero nicknamed Ryder, a name he was given for his ability to tame even the wildest of horses. Ryder works as the horse trainer at the Brownsville, Texas, horse ranch that the Knights of White use as a cover for their Demon-hunting operation. Something inside Ryder tells him to go home, back to Round Rock, Texas, where he first became a Knight of White, to the place he was attacked by a Demon. It is here that he finds the Demons are again preying on innocents, and one of those innocents is a woman who will change his life. Ryder is about to be tamed—if he dares allow such a thing!

The entire Knights of White series is based upon the Texas Legend of Matamoros Monsters, aka Demons. Texas is at the heart of the Knights of White, and that will never change, because much of my heart is still in Texas, as well.

Lisa Renee Jones

# *Chapter 1*

Chris Evans. That had been his name. A name he'd tried to forget. A life he'd left behind. But he wouldn't ever forget this day. Because today he had returned home, today he had returned to the place where he'd died and been reborn, an immortal Knight of White—a Demon hunter known only as Ryder.

Leaning against his black Chevy pickup, Ryder stared at the wooden stairs leading to the double doors of the small-town bar he'd visited that night—the night he'd been attacked by Demons. Rows of vehicles surrounded him; the full parking lot showed how busy the Double R Tavern was this night. Music poured from the doors and window of the popular nightspot with a blustering force extending beyond its panels. The plentiful crowd overflowed to the porch.

In the distance, thunder rumbled with ominous force,

lightning flickering across the black sky, a scent of rain lacing the air. In a gust of wind, dust lifted in the air around his well-worn boots. Almost as if Mother Nature shouted a warning—beware of danger approaching. Of darkness beyond a storm. Darkness that mimicked the ache in his chest, the painful memories of the past that chased him night and day. He scrubbed his jaw and told himself to go inside, that the ache would persist until he got this over with.

Those memories reached out to him, taunting him with a nagging insistence, as they had for weeks now. Reminding him of a night twenty-five years before in this very parking lot, when he'd been a man with a family, with people who had loved him, people he had loved.

Wrangling with his emotions, Ryder ran a hand through his thick, sandy-brown hair. Edgy still, he scrubbed his palms down the faded Levi's he wore. Finally, he shoved aside his thoughts, pushing off the truck in the same moment, and charged toward the porch. Charged from the past into the present.

But halfway to the steps and counting, he drew to an abrupt halt. The soft sound of a female's delicate voice lifted in the air, the impact of which set his nerve endings on fire. He swallowed hard against the intensity of the reaction, struggling to grasp how or why a simple voice could wreak havoc on his composure. But before he could delve deeper within himself, the voice sounded again, this time hinting at urgency, at a bit of fear—angry fear. Fear that spurred him into action.

Ryder followed the voice as it lifted in the air, traced the location to four vehicles down, behind a nineties-model Ford pickup. "Let go of her arm!" the voice demanded.

"Ouch," another female said, a choked sob bitten back with the word.

Fighting back the unnatural instinct to pounce before evaluating, Ryder forced himself to stop, to assess the situation before acting. He crept to the vehicle's edge, the nearby lights allowing him a decent visual of the scene unfolding. A brawny cowboy held the arm of an obviously distressed, petite blonde. A tall, leggy brunette stood in confrontation, her hands balled on her jean-clad hips. She didn't even have to speak for him to know that this was the one who owned the voice he'd heard moments before.

"I came to take her home," the brunette declared, "and that's what I am doing."

The cowboy snidely rejected her claim. "She doesn't want to go with you." He ran his hand down the blonde's hair, his touch possessive. "Do you, Kelly?"

Fear radiated off the blonde. "No," Kelly said, casting him a submissive, beaten look, and then turning her attention to her friend in explanation. "I…we just had a little spat. I shouldn't have called."

The brunette glared at the cowboy, dismissing the blonde's statement. "I know you hit her." Her voice was low, venomous. "And it's not the first time. I've seen the bruises. I'll call the police before I let her stay with you."

Sarcastic amusement laced his bark of laughter. "Go ahead," he said. "In case you didn't know, I own this joint. And the good ole Round Rock Police Department enjoys their free drink privileges. Call them. See if it will do you any good. In the meantime, we'll be inside enjoying ourselves." He sneered. "You should consider having a drink. Might make you likable for once."

The brunette didn't appear rattled by the insult. She grabbed Kelly's arm. "Come on. We're going home."

The cowboy shackled the brunette's arms, and Ryder felt the flare of his temper launch him into action. He didn't wait to introduce himself, he strode forward, intent on freeing both women. A heroic effort rendered unnecessary when the brunette landed a well-placed knee firmly in the cowboy's groin. Instantly, the man doubled over with a loud grunt, and the women were freed. Ryder slowed his progress, felt the urge to laugh—something he would have considered impossible in this place, on this day. The urge quickly washed away as the cowboy lashed out.

"Bitch," the man yelled at the brunette as she grabbed her friend and tugged. "I'll make you pay for that."

Ryder stepped in front of the ladies, sheltering them with his big body, his eyes briefly touching the heart-shaped face of the brunette before he focused on the critical matter at hand—the scumbag cowboy. "It's not nice to threaten the ladies," he admonished.

The man unfolded to a near-standing position, a good four inches below Ryder's six foot two, one hand still guarding his crotch. He sidestepped toward the brunette. "That one there isn't a lady. Not by a long shot. And mind your own business, buddy. This is private property, so walk your interfering ass outta here."

Ryder shrugged. "Not a problem. But the ladies go with me."

"You looking for trouble, man?" he challenged. "Because if you are, you come to the right place."

"I like trouble," Ryder drawled, deciding the man's straight nose and square jaw would make nice targets. "Care for a demonstration?"

The brunette stepped forward. "I'll demonstrate," she said, standing by Ryder's side, her attention fixed on the other man. "If you think for a minute, Hector, that I won't call the news stations and plaster flyers all over this city announcing you hit her, you're wrong. Let's see how long the police will support you once it's public."

A hiss slid from Hector's lips. "And I'll tell them all you're just a bitter lover. Bet some of your ranch hands will offer to comfort you."

She recoiled as if slapped. "You bastard."

"You betcha, baby," he said. "Now all of you get off my property."

He started to back away, and Ryder grabbed his shirt, used his supernatural strength to lift him off the ground. "Touch either of these ladies ever again, and I will show you the meaning of the word *bastard*." He dropped him, and the man stumbled, his jaw gaping with shock as he caught himself on his hands and then scrambled backward. A second later, he turned and ran away.

Ryder drew a long breath, somehow certain he would need a little fortification before facing the woman at his side. Slowly he turned, delaying their direct connection as he assured himself that Kelly was safe, finding her resting against the truck, nervously hugging herself.

Then, and only then, did Ryder let his gaze settle on the brunette, on the woman already under his skin, her dark eyes touching his with the same riveting force with which her voice had affected him. The contact danced along his nerve endings with an electric charge. And he knew…she was why he was here. She was the reason this place had called him home.

# *Chapter 2*

Alexis Wright had never been a woman to be blown away by any man, certainly not in the middle of a difficult situation. She'd grown up on a ranch surrounded by big, virile men who were often a bit too sure of their own masculinity. Her father—"Big W" to the rest of the world—had been one of those big virile men until six months ago, when a heart attack had stolen him away. And he'd taught her how to take charge of a situation, even when it overflowed with testosterone. But here, now, today, staring into the eyes of the sexy stranger who'd managed to come to her rescue—despite her best efforts not to need rescuing—she found herself feeling anything but in control. Hypnotized was more like it.

"Are you both okay?" the stranger asked, his voice low, sensual and good gosh, a bit too distracting for comfort.

Alexis inwardly shook herself and tore herself out of the

deep, dark depths of his eyes. Distractions were dangerous when you managed a ranch with debts the size of Texas. "Yes," she said, her voice cracking a bit, and she couldn't for the life of her say why. "Thank you." She glanced at her friend Kelly Parker. "You okay, Kell?"

Kelly nodded. "I'm fine." Which was a lie. Kelly hadn't been fine since her cheating husband had driven her into Hector's abusive arms and then into Alexis's spare bedroom. Kelly cast the stranger an appreciative look. "Thank you."

"No thanks needed," he said, offering a gentle smile that contrasted with the ruggedly masculine features of his face. Thick brows, strong jaw, high cheekbones. A full bottom lip that thinned as he added, "Guys like that one get under my skin." His gaze shifted and settled heavily on Alexis, heating with contact. His voice lowered. "It was my pleasure to help." His mouth curved upward again, amusement coloring his voice. "Though I have to say, you didn't need it all that much. That's a dangerous knee you got there."

"My secret weapon," Alexis said, laughing, realizing she liked this man way too much. "Works like a charm."

He grinned, approval in his expression as he offered her his hand. "I'm Ryder."

Alexis swallowed hard, her gaze somehow touching his mouth before she jerked it downward, across a broad forearm to his extended palm. "Alexis Wright," she said, sliding her hand into his. It closed instantly over hers, big, warm, possessive—as if he claimed her in some way. She swallowed hard as warmth spread up her arm. Her attention slowly traced the broad width of his shoulders and lifted to his face, to the strong chin with the tiny dimple in the middle. "Kelly is my friend."

"Nice to meet you both," he said, reluctantly releasing her hand. "Hate that it had to be under these conditions, though."

"We should go," Kelly said, interrupting with an urgent quality to her voice. "Before Hector comes back."

Which was true. Alexis wouldn't put anything past Hector. "She's right," she agreed. "We should go." The memory of Ryder lifting Hector off the ground flashed in her mind. "Somehow, I doubt Hector's ego is faring very well. You tossed the man around like a wet noodle. He might come back with baseball bats and some extra hands."

A baffled expression flashed across Ryder's face. He scrubbed his jaw, the rasp of newly formed whiskers scraping on his palm. "Like a wet noodle, huh?" he asked, appearing more interested in her silly words than the prospect of Hector's return.

"It was one of my father's million or so crazy sayings," Alexis explained.

His brows dipped, seriousness flickering in his gaze before fading, as if he caught the past tense but decided not to ask questions. "Sadly," he commented, "I am not sure how qualified I am at the particular craft of noodle whipping, but I've bred horses for years and wrestled a few stallions that make bullies like that guy look like kittens."

"You train horses?" she asked, surprised, but then not so surprised. He had a way about him, a soothing quality that seemed to fit such a calling.

"Yep," he said. "I oversee the breeding operation for Jaguar Ranch."

"Jaguar Ranch," she said, eyes going wide. "As in the Jaguar Ranch in Brownsville?"

He nodded. "You've heard of it?"

"Who hasn't?" she said. "Isn't it like ten thousand acres big or some insane size like that?"

"Twenty," he said. "And one of the biggest horse-breeding operations in the country."

"Twenty," she repeated. "Makes my little family-owned ranch look like a kiddie ride." Alexis would have said more, but a big drop of rain smacked down on her nose. She swiped at it, expecting another, but found none. "I guess that's our sign to depart before it really starts raining," she said, tossing the keys to Kelly so her friend could get inside the truck. "We really should go."

Ryder didn't immediately respond, his gaze lifting, scanning the area. Something in him seemed to change, shift, but she couldn't put her finger on what. "I'm going to be here a few weeks," he commented. "Hate to stay locked up in a hotel room. Don't suppose you'd have room and board at that ranch of yours, in exchange for an extra set of hands?"

Kelly called out, "Yeah, she does," as she unlocked the passenger's side of the truck.

Alexis would have glared at Kelly if her friend hadn't ducked into the vehicle to avoid her wrath. It wasn't Kelly's place to speak on her behalf, and Kelly knew full well Alexis was trying to downplay her struggles at the ranch since her father's death.

Intent on dismissing Kelly's words, Alexis opened her mouth to speak. Ryder interjected before she could, taking Kelly's claim and running with it. He held out his arms. "I'm your man," he declared. "Put me to work." He grinned. "Teach me how to give a proper noodle whipping, and I will teach your men how to tame a wild beast." He laughed. "Or I can rope and wrangle cattle. Whatever you need." He shook his head. "Well. I might draw the line at shoveling shit, but then, a good meal can convince a man to do a lot of things."

She tried not to read anything into the "I'm your man" statement, but it was hard not to. Maybe because he was the first man to get her attention in too long to remember. She was more than attracted to Ryder; something about him made her comfortable. But none of this changed the bottom line. She didn't have any extra money. Heck, she was barely keeping her current crew fed and housed.

"I couldn't pay you what you are worth," she said, unwilling to confess her inability to pay. She didn't need that getting around and spooking her men. If the ranch faltered in even the tiniest way, she was liable to lose it.

"Keep me away from the confines of the local motel," he urged, "and that's payment enough." She hesitated, and he added, "Save a cowboy, Alexis." His voice lowered. "Save me."

Awareness swirled in her limbs. Why did she feel as if they were talking about something more than keeping him out of a motel? Save him? Good gosh, his expertise might help *save her.* Still. As much as she needed help, this was too good to be true. "I doubt my little ranch even begins to compare to what you are used to. You might prefer a motel."

"Try me," he pressed. "You might be surprised."

She already was. Surprised she was entertaining this idea as seriously as she was. He reached for his cell phone, yanked it off his belt and punched a key. "Talk to my boss back at Jaguar. He'll tell you I'm trustworthy."

Her eyes went wide. "No. No. That's okay."

Ryder hesitated, studied her a moment. "You have a fax machine, right?" She nodded. "I'll have my references faxed over. I insist." She hesitated, and then gave him the number, watching as he punched it into his cell phone memory. "Save me from motel hell, Alexis. Give me a bunk with the guys and a big, wide-open sky. Make Round Rock bearable."

Alexis shook her head and smiled at his insistence. The man could be very persuasive. And Big W didn't raise no fool. The experience this stranger had gained working in an operation like Jaguar's might bring something they were missing to the table. And she needed that something before the bank foreclosed on the ranch. And bringing on a new hand would send a signal to the crew that things were good. "You're here for personal business, you said. Only a few weeks?"

"I won't outstay my welcome," he said. "If that's what you're worried about."

She wasn't worried he'd outstay his welcome. She was worried she'd start depending on him, and then he'd leave. She inhaled, her chest suddenly tight with emotion she didn't want to feel. Her gaze lifted to the sky as the rain began to fall. The rain she hoped would wash away the damn tears she didn't want Ryder or anyone else around her to see.

# *Chapter 3*

Ryder maneuvered his truck past the wooden gates of Big W Ranch, trailing Alexis as she drove the bumpy dirt path. He remotely remembered Big W Ranch. Remembered his father mentioning Big W's little girl—Alexis. She had been a toddler when he'd been attacked. An innocent child who might have been a victim as easily as anyone else. And now, life had come full circle. Demons—Darkland Beasts as they were known to the Knights—had found their way back to Round Rock, hunting innocents again as they had hunted him. Perhaps they'd find Alexis this time if he didn't stop them. He'd picked up their scent back at the bar, his senses raw with the taint of their presence, his nerves on edge ever since.

He reached up and flipped the windshield wipers on high; the rain pounding on his windshield created more unease within Ryder. Huge droplets melted into each other one after another, crashing over metal and glass, erasing his chances of properly evaluating his surroundings.

Following Alexis's lead, Ryder pulled into a circular drive in front of a two-story house, its beaming floodlights fighting the darkness of the storm. He killed the engine and watched Alexis and Kelly exit their vehicle. Alexis waved him forward, but he didn't move. Instead, he watched the two women run toward the high porch a few feet away, rain drenching their clothes and hair. At the top of the stairs, they paused under the cover of the overhang, glanced in his direction and talked together, both fumbling with wet hair and clothes as they did.

More than happy to give them space to talk, Ryder took a moment by himself to consider his next move. Because with each passing moment, the circumstances he'd come upon grew more complex, more in need of careful evaluation.

He could damn near taste the stench of Demons. They were close. His fingers tightened on the steering wheel, gripping so he wouldn't reach for the saber shoved beneath his seat. The Demons were here, inside this ranch, eating it away from the inside out—Demons that would not die without decapitation, without the use of his sword. Yet, to stay near Alexis, to keep her and her people safe, he could not make a rash move and scare her—and getting out of the truck with blades strapped to his body qualified as rash.

His gaze captured Kelly entering the house, leaving Alexis alone, waiting on him. Ryder quickly shoved open the truck door, no less reluctant to exit without his weapons than moments before, but accepting that he had no choice. And certainly he was not reluctant to be near Alexis again.

Alexis. She set him on fire; she called to him in a soul-deep way. He felt what she felt—ached from the loss of a father who she had not admitted losing, worried about the loss of a ranch that she had not admitted was in danger. She was his mate. There was no other explanation.

The wind thrust rain against his body, soaking him within moments of his feet touching the ground. Heaviness settled in his heart, even as the anticipation of being near Alexis made it pound faster, harder. There were Knights who were centuries older than he, Knights who struggled without a mate, slowly eroding from the inside out. For each Knight had been touched by a Beast, and that taint lived forever on his soul—until a mate bound the darkness within, the Beast within, and freed him forever. It was a struggle Ryder hadn't experienced yet, still young and in control. So what made him, a Knight only twenty-five years, worthy of salvation over them?

He knew nothing of the answer, but nevertheless, as he charged up the steps toward her, he could not deny the protectiveness she summoned from him, nor the fierceness of her emotions as they wrapped around him, flowed through him.

Only a few steps separated them as he drew to a halt under the lighted enclosure; her wet hair plastered to her lovely face, showing her true beauty. Long, dark lashes framed worried brown eyes. Only a foot separated them, and that was too much. He wanted to protect her, but he wanted more than her safety. He wanted her.

Alexis tilted her chin upward, her gaze searching his, heat sparking between them, borne of a connection that went beyond desire. Possessiveness flared in him, a primal burn that reached beyond the man and stirred the Beast within. "Come inside," she said, her voice barely above a whisper.

He didn't argue. Inside, close to her, was where he belonged. In her bed was where he belonged. Ryder followed her through the door, and forced down the Beast that pressed him to grab her and pull her close. To kiss those wet lips dry. Because making love to her might be as rash as getting out of that truck with swords drawn. She might pull him close now and push him away tomorrow.

And that wasn't an option. Not now. He hoped not later. But deep down he knew there were complications, reasons that might defy the bond of mates. Reasons she couldn't leave, reasons he couldn't take her with him.

Alexis was thankful to have Kelly home safely, but in the process of bringing her home, she'd also brought home Ryder. Growing up on a ranch, she'd certainly seen many a cowboy exchange labor for room and board. She'd learned not to ask questions, to be glad for the help. But Ryder wasn't one of those men; he was different in ways she had yet to understand.

Shoving open the front door of the house, Alexis walked inside, her hand resting on the door as she welcomed Ryder inside, her mind processing her intense reaction to him.

He hesitated on the doorstep, eyeing his boots and then her. "I'm pretty muddy."

"As am I," she said, waving her hand at her own feet and pointing out the trail of mud on the floor. "It appears Kelly was, too." She eased farther behind the door to allow his entry. Memories floated through her mind, an image of her father that stabbed painfully in her gut. She shoved it aside. "This house has seen far worse than a little mud."

Thunder rumbled directly overhead, the walls of the house shaking, as if urging him forward. "Come in," she encouraged, a chill making her shiver as the air conditioning kicked on, the vent above her head spraying her wet skin with chilly air.

Ryder obeyed, stepping into the narrow hallway leading to the rest of the house. The potency of his presence was instant, intense. Alexis inhaled, Ryder's big body close, his impact on her more devastating to her senses than she thought possible. She wanted him. God, how she wanted him. As if he somehow reached inside her and flipped a switch from off to on.

She swallowed hard and turned away from him to shut the door. Mentally she locked out the storm with her actions, realizing, with overwhelming completeness, how much she wished she could truly lock out the world. For just one night, she didn't want to be the Big W boss lady. She didn't want to worry about being judged by the men who worked for her, by the bank that threatened foreclosure. She didn't want to pretend she was Superwoman on the outside, when inside the steel was melting. Didn't want to miss her father so much. She wanted an escape. But she didn't dare allow herself such a thing. Not when this man would soon be among her crew.

Willing her body to calm, Alexis turned to face Ryder. "I'll go get some towels," she said, finding him only inches away from her. Anything further she might have said slid away, lost. Alexis stared into his eyes. *Green.* His eyes were green. She'd wondered, back at the bar. Wondered what color the eyes that drew her deep into their depths were. In all of her twenty-eight years, she couldn't remember ever being so enthralled by a man's face—with the strong jaw now forming a shadow of a dark beard, the scar slashed across his right brow, the sensual line of his mouth.

Damp hair fell over her face, jolting her back to reality. Alexis shook herself inwardly and shoved the wayward strands behind her ears. "Let me get those towels."

With those words, she sidestepped around him and started to depart, intent on escape to pull herself together. Instantly, his hand gently shackled her arm, his palm branding her with wicked heat that slid up her arm, and somehow managed to spread across her chest, her breasts aching with sudden awareness.

They were shoulder to shoulder, the air charged with attraction. She lifted her gaze to his, a question in her eyes. Why did she want him so much? What was he doing to her?

"Alexis," he said softly, an intimate rasp to his tone that promised he had more to say.

Her name, one word, that was all he said, yet that word hung in the air with a silky promise of something important to follow, a promise she found herself silently willing him to speak. Because for some inconceivable, completely irrational reason, this moment felt as if it might have a profound impact on her life. That this man, a complete stranger, held some secret she desperately needed to have revealed.

# Chapter 4

Alone in the hallway of Big W's ranch house, Ryder and Alexis stared into one another's eyes, heat swirled around them, blanketing them in awareness, in desire. Ryder wanted so many things in those moments. He wanted to kiss Alexis, to taste her, to touch her. He wanted to bury himself deep inside her body and claim her as his own. To tell her everything he was, everything he had been, to simply wipe away the secrets that would make protecting her a difficult task. And he wanted his sword.

But were the things he wanted the right choices?

Seconds ticked as they stared at one another, the moment of decision upon him. What would he do? What would he say?

"Oh. Ah, hi."

Kelly's voice came from behind Ryder, her presence bursting through the spell woven around Alexis and him.

Regret tore through Ryder, the loss of opportunity, of choice, gone with the intrusion.

Ryder quickly noted the flush of embarrassment coloring Alexis's ivory skin. He immediately let go of her arm, but he had to wonder why Alexis would react in such a way to Kelly finding them together. He pivoted to face Kelly, assessing her with a newfound interest about how she affected Alexis. She wore white sweats and a pink T-shirt, her blonde hair piled on top of her head. She was a pretty woman, perhaps mid-thirties, slender, curvy, nice facial features. But she lacked confidence. He could see it in her eyes, in the way she carried herself. Which explained why she put up with Hector's abuse.

"Sorry," Kelly said, shifting her weight from one foot to the other, as if the scrutiny made her antsy. "I..." She looked at Alexis, indicating the mop in her hands before resting it against the wall. "I was going to clean up the mess on the floor before you did." Her gaze swept Alexis and Ryder again, taking in their wet clothing. "Let me get some towels for you two." She rushed away, leaving no time for response.

"Thanks," Alexis murmured, sounding a bit baffled.

Before he could ask why, Ryder's text-message alert went off on his cell phone. He yanked his Nokia 8800 off his belt, surprised it still worked considering it was wet, and punched the receive button. His gaze lifted to Alexis. "My references are on your fax," he said, his voice lowering. "So you know you can trust me."

Her gaze caught his. "Your boss really went out of his way in the middle of the night."

"We take care of our own," he said, and added silently, *and now you are one of us.* Or at least destiny said she was. But even if she would have him, if she would walk away from her life to accommodate his pledge to the Knights, would the other Knights resent her presence, resent his reward of a mate?

"Here you go," Kelly said, reappearing in the doorway. She tossed Ryder a towel and then Alexis. "I'll mop up the floor."

Alexis rubbed the towel through her hair and then studied Kelly with a thoughtful expression. "Thank you, Kell. I know you'd prefer to be in a hot bath right now."

Kelly nodded, her eyes clouding over. "It's the least I can do, considering everything." Her lips lifted a bit. "And you have Ryder to attend to."

Ryder scrubbed his head with the towel, and bit back laughter at the obvious inference that they were attending to personal matters, not business. Alexis frowned, her brows dipping in an adorable way a second before she turned to him. "Let's go look at those references."

He smiled. "Lead the way," he said, following her to the end of the hall. To his left was a huge sunken living room, with wood paneling and brown carpeting. To the right, double wooden doors that she pushed open and walked through. Ryder found himself in the center of a den with an aged wooden desk in the far right-hand corner; books lined the walls.

"This reminds me of back home," he said.

Alexis draped her towel over an empty file folder rack before walking behind the desk to a credenza where the fax machine rested. She lifted the faxed pages, glancing across the desk at Ryder. "How so?" she asked.

"Jag's office looks a lot like this," Ryder said, tossing the towel he held over his shoulder and walking to one of the bookshelves. One war title after the next, fiction and non-fiction, lined the shelves. Humans were obsessed with war and fighting each other, when the real dangers lurked in shadows, hoping for their destruction. "He's a history buff."

"So was my father," she said, and looked up from reading the fax. "Jag," she repeated. "As in your boss, Jag?"

He nodded. "Right," he said. "You got the fax, I take it?"

"I did," she said, setting the papers back down on the fax machine and walking to the desk. "Your credentials are, well…they're amazing. You don't need to be here, helping me. Why would you?"

"Why do my reasons matter?"

She didn't answer his question; instead she inhaled deeply, seemed to battle within herself a moment before exhaling again. "Someone with your experience could go somewhere else and be paid a lot of money. Why come here instead?"

"I don't need the money," he said, which was true. He didn't have as much as the older Knights, but he'd done well enough. Like the other Knights, he was given an allowance and expected to spend little to nothing himself. He'd invested; he'd saved his money.

She laughed, the sound laced with disbelief. "Everyone needs money." Her pain lanced the air and ripped through his heart.

His hand still resting on one of the books on the shelf, afraid to say the wrong thing, his next words were a gentle prod. "How long has your father been gone?" he asked.

"Six months," she said, surprising him with the quick answer. "Massive heart attack. No warning."

His heart squeezed. "I'm sorry."

Her chin lifted. "I'm dealing with it."

Ryder crossed the room until he stood at the opposite side of the desk from her. "I can see that," he said, but he knew she wasn't as tough as she wanted the world to believe. He could see the pain in her eyes, feel it in the room, almost taste it in the air. His voice was low. "I'm sure his death impacted the ranch. That can't be easy to manage."

Her head turned to the side, her gaze going to the wall, then flickering back. "The ranch is fine."

He reached for common ground, a way to let her know he understood what she was living. "Were you familiar with Wild Rose Ranch?" he asked, referring to his family's ranch, certain she would remember it. Just as Big W's was remotely familiar to him. Ranching within close proximity brought familiarity and often friendship.

"The Evans place," she said, her brows dipping in thought. "B.J. Evans, right? Or was it Ivans?"

"Evans," Ryder offered.

"I remotely remember it, but it was sold off when I was a kid."

Sold five years after their son, Chris Evans, went missing—that son had been him. But she wouldn't know that. She'd been too young to remember much. Clearly, she barely remembered his family name. A sad thought. His past was gone, lost. "I was one of the Evans boys," he said quietly, implying there had been a son other than Chris when there had not been. "B.J. was my father," he said quietly.

She swallowed hard. "Was?"

He nodded. "He died ten years ago," Ryder said, remembering the funeral as if it was yesterday, remembered standing in the shadows, a ghost who didn't exist. "Lung cancer. My mother passed not long after." Broken heart. Lost her son. Lost her husband. Ryder ground his teeth and pressed past the painful memories, more determined than ever to win Alexis over. He rounded the desk, willing her to turn and face him.

He waited until she did, waited for the confirmation that she welcomed his nearness. Slowly, she turned, her eyes seeking his, compassion overflowing from their depths. Raw pain that she'd masked before now glistened in her eyes. A shared loss, a mutual understanding. "The place that replaced your family ranch, they breed horses. Is that what your family did?"

"Yes," he said.

"You learned about horses from your father?"

Ryder gave a quick nod. "He was a good man," he said. "And Wild Rose was a small ranch like this one. A family business where everyone mattered. So in answer to your question—why would I work here rather than somewhere else? The answer is simple. This ranch is as close to going home as I am going to get. And right now, I really needed to come home." There was a deep-felt truth behind those words he hadn't recognized until he spoke them. He did need to be here. He needed to deal with the past. And he was meant to find her.

Suddenly, though, he realized how much he needed what was forming between them to feel real, not just some fated matchup. That meant going slow, that meant earning trust through actions rather than a supernatural bond. "The ball is in your court, Alexis. Tell me to stay and I will. Tell me to leave and I'm gone."

# Chapter 5

Alexis replayed Ryder's words in her head. *Tell me to go and I'll go.* She inhaled the spicy male scent of him and felt her body heat. Space. She needed space before she did something insane, like tell him to stay, or…kiss him.

"Stay or go?" he urged softly, his voice a velvety caress along her nerve endings, creating deliciously provocative thoughts of what might happen between them if she allowed it to.

*Tell him to go.* "Stay," Alexis said, ignoring the voice in her head. The one that said an affair was a distraction she couldn't afford. So was depending on someone who would be gone in a short while—it would weaken her. Ryder was an emotional liability. He had a way of seeing past her walls, of unraveling little sections of the tightly spun ball that had become her life, and with little or no effort. And she wasn't sure she had the emotional fortitude to fall for him and then say goodbye. Not now. Not with everything she was going through.

But as surely as she warned herself of these things, she saw Ryder's eyes flicker with relief and knew that his desire to be here, to explore whatever was going on between them, matched her own. She studied him, her eyes searching his, finding pain and loneliness. He had some healing to do, as well. Healing they might do together. Yes. It made sense. He was the Evans' boy; he'd lived a life much like her own, experienced loss as she had. Her stomach fluttered with this knowledge, and confidence filled her. This was the right choice.

She acted before she could change her mind. "Follow me," she said, stepping around him, her arm brushing his. A jolt of reaction made her lashes flutter, her steps falter for a flash of a moment. She willed her heart to calm as she continued forward. When had she reacted like this to a man? Not for years. Maybe not ever.

With Ryder on her heels, awareness oozing from her every pore, Alexis crossed the living room and entered the box-style, outdated, yellow-toned kitchen, then opened the door leading to the basement. She flipped on the light and started down the stairs, her knees ridiculously weak. Every step came with excruciating, exciting awareness—of how she moved, of how close he was to her.

At the bottom of the stairs she pushed open yet another door, this one to a bedroom. She swallowed hard as she flipped on the light and stepped inside the room and to the left. Ryder joined her, his overpoweringly male presence shrinking the rather large room to small and intimate. For an instant their eyes connected, electricity zapping her limbs, a sweet ache low in her belly, tight across her chest.

At the same moment, they surveyed the room. Her gaze

swept the rose-colored decor, taking in what he, too, was seeing. A floral bedspread lay perfectly smoothed across a queen-size bed. Floral pictures were well-placed on the walls in gold-colored frames. A pink lampshade softened the lighting, its shadows playing on the the bedside table of vintage, stained-white wood.

"This was my housekeeper's room until a month ago," Alexis explained. "She married and moved about a mile down the road." She laughed. "Married my foreman." His brow inched upward in surprise, and she continued, "None of us had any idea. They'd known each other for years. The room is a little feminine." And small. Really small. "I thought you could stay here rather than in the bunkhouse with the other men. You'll be more comfortable. Well, as long as roses don't bother you."

His lashes lowered, lifted, eyes half-veiled. The bed. The room. Electricity charged the air. "It's perfect," he finally said, a husky quality to his voice that caressed her every nerve ending with excruciating perfection.

It was time to go—before she didn't. "There's a shower on the other side of the basement," she said, hesitating. "I'll get you towels. I guess your bag is in the truck?"

"Yes," he said. "I'll weather the storm and go get it."

"I hate that you have to do that," she said, thinking of how bad it was outside. "But there's a side door to the basement around back if you want to pull around. I can show you." She started for the door, and suddenly his hand was around her arm, her body pulled tight against his long, muscular frame. Her hands on that broad, perfect chest.

"I swore I wouldn't touch you," he said softly. "Not tonight, not yet." He inhaled. "You smell like heaven. Tell me to let you go. Tell me not to kiss you. Tell me and I won't."

For once, she didn't want to decide, she didn't want that weight on her shoulders. Damn it, it made her mad that he'd put this on her. "Fine. Don't. Let go." Then she melted into him. God, he felt good.

"That's not fair," he whispered.

"Life isn't fair," she answered, a moment before his lips came down on hers.

She tasted as good as she smelled, like salvation with sweet honey flavoring. Ryder's tongue slid past her teeth in a deep, passionate caress. His vow to go slow with Alexis had faded quickly the minute he'd entered that bedroom, diminishing to damn near zero with lightning speed. He told himself this was only a kiss, a sample of what pleasure they could share together. But the softness of her hands somehow ended up under his shirt, heating his skin. He barely remembered her pulling the shirt from his pants. He deepened his kiss, hungry now with the caress of her hand. She didn't resist; in fact, her tongue challenged his, seeking, stroking. The Beast in him, the primal side, clawed to life in a way he didn't remember ever feeling before now. It burned to have him pull her down on the bed, to take her, to claim her.

And somehow they were closer to that bed now, his legs hitting the mattress. He fell backward and took her with him, his hand on her backside, his lips hungrily moving over hers. His other hand slid into her hair. His teeth nipped her lips. They were on fire, hungry, needy. Both touching, exploring. His shirt was open, her hands on his chest. God, he wanted *her* shirt off. Black, V-neck—a skimpy shirt he couldn't wait to see removed. He pictured it in his mind. He wanted all of her. No barriers.

As if she sensed his thoughts, she suddenly pulled back

and looked at him. Her fingers drew his gaze to the hem of her shirt, and she started to pull it over her head. But her eyes caught his, her eyes filled with passion and…trust. God. Reality and guilt slammed into him, lancing the will of his inner Beast. His hands went to hers, stilling her actions. He wanted to deserve that trust. He needed that for reasons he couldn't explain. Needed something real in his life beyond a sword.

"Alexis," he whispered. "I don't want you to regret this tomorrow. This isn't why I'm here."

She shook her head. "This is about now." She leaned forward and pressed her lips to his before whispering, "Don't make me think about tomorrow."

With a low growl born of his struggle for control, Ryder rolled her onto her back. He slipped his legs over hers, rather than allowing himself inside the V of her body where he really wanted to be. His cock was thick, heavy with arousal, yet he would not give in to his desire. She was vulnerable right now, more so because of their mating bond. A bond she didn't even know existed. But he did. He knew, and he couldn't ignore the implications. Forever was a long time to begin with regrets.

He leaned his weight on his elbows. "You have to think about tomorrow, because I'm not going anywhere. I'll be here then, just as I am now."

She shook her head. "Sometimes tomorrow just doesn't matter," she whispered. "You have to know that."

There was raw emotion in her voice, an ache he wanted to erase. "Tomorrow matters," he said, and he kissed her—her need too much for him to ignore. It reached inside him, stroked him with emotion, fired him with desire. Desire to please her, to make love to her, to show her tomorrow mattered in ways she had yet to understand.

# *Chapter 6*

Ryder took his time and made love to her with that kiss, a message in each stroke of his tongue, a promise of passion beyond this moment. But passion turned quickly to fiery desire. Their hands traveled, explored. Desire building, second by second, caress after caress. He found his way into the V of her body, fit his cock to the center of her core, her hips arching into his. He drank in the soft sounds of pleasure that escaped her mouth into his as he molded her breast to his palm, stroked her nipple through the soft, black T-shirt. But it wasn't all of her and he needed all of her. Needed in a way he could never put into words.

He shoved her shirt upward and eased it off of her as she removed it. Standing up and giving her his back, he reached for enough control to undress before he kissed her again. When finally he turned around, he was naked, aroused, his hungry stare devouring the sight of her spread out on the bed, waiting for him, his gaze hungrily painting a trail along her naked body. She rested on her elbows, legs slightly parted. Her nipples a rosy pink, her breasts full, high. Her skin the most beautiful ivory he'd ever seen. Flawless. Perfect.

His knees hit the mattress, his eyes fixed on her face as he eased her knees apart. Her lashes fluttered, gaze sliding to his erection, the inspection arousing, erotic. His hands trailed up her shapely thighs, her lashes lifting, desire-filled eyes meeting his. He watched her expression as his fingers glided higher and higher, watching the pleasure in her eyes, in her face, until finally he slid his thumb into and through the silky wet heat of her body. Alexis sucked in a breath and shivered. Her reaction pleased him, and encouraged him to continue.

His lips followed where his palms had been, mouth trailing up one of those stellar thighs until his warm breath trickled over her clit, his tongue following. A gasp escaped her parted lips, her back arching. But he didn't give her more, didn't take her fully into his mouth. Not yet. Later. He wanted her first orgasm to be with him inside her, buried deep, the two of them as one.

Ryder trailed kisses upward again, over her stomach, palming her breasts and flicking one plump nipple to a stiff peak. He replaced his fingers with his mouth, suckling and licking, teasing, her hands in his hair, urging him to give her more pleasure. When finally she called his name, pleaded for more, he moved fully on top of her, bracing his weight on his arms and settling his hard length onto the wet heat of her body.

"I've figured out how to make tomorrow matter," he said softly, kissing her jaw, her lips, sliding his cock more snugly between her legs.

"How's that?" she asked breathlessly.

"I'm going to make love to you until tomorrow is already here," he promised near her ear. Ryder pulled back to look into her eyes, to search her face. "Is that okay with you?"

For several seconds Alexis simply blinked up at him, studied him, an unreadable expression on her face. Then suddenly she smiled, her eyes shimmering with a taunt. "Ask me tomorrow."

Her answer both surprised and pleased him. Ryder chuckled low in his throat, the sound absorbed by her lips as he kissed her. A gentle kiss filled with the warmth she created in his heart, with the realization she made him laugh easily, that she lightened the darkness within him. But the gentleness of the kiss quickly turned hot again. He wanted inside her, he wanted all of her. Needed all of her. Responding to that need, Ryder reached between them, wrapped his shaft in his palm. Teasing them both with delicious friction, he slid it back and forth, gliding along the silk folds of her body—setting every nerve ending in his body on fire.

Alexis clung to him, her fingers digging into his shoulders. "Ryder," she gasped, the word a demand, a plea.

He entered her then, but forced himself to retain control. Ryder inched deeper, deeper, slowly sinking to her core. For a moment, he buried his head in her shoulder, reveled in the warm heat of his mate surrounding him. Reveled in the perfection of the moment.

Seconds passed, and Ryder inhaled. He eased back, searching Alexis's face, wanting to know she felt what he did. Instantly, their eyes collided in a rush of pure white-hot fire the likes of which he'd never known. Something happened in that moment with Alexis—a bond formed, a connection he would never be able to put into words. It was as if she poured herself inside him. As if she became a part of his very existence. He could barely breathe.

Then, as one, they moved, their mouths connecting, bodies swaying. It was a rush of passion, a wild bonding of two people who had to have each other. Who needed to be close more than they needed air to breathe. Ryder was pumping into her now; each contact with her core rocketed fire through his veins. Each thrust a blast of riveting pleasure. He wanted to feel her all over. To be closer. And she wanted it, too. Her breasts were pressed against his chest, her calves wrapped around his legs, arms clinging to his back. This was the wildest of rides, the kind no one would dare try to tame. A ride that peaked when she suddenly called out his name, when she clung to him a second before her body spasmed around his cock.

And then it happened—out of nowhere, the Beast within him flared. Ryder stiffened with the primal demand that charged his body. His gums tingled with the promise of fangs, and he buried his head in her neck, desperate to hide his face. There was only one time a Knight bore fangs, and that was when they marked their mate—to finally say goodbye to their Beast forever. And God, how he wanted to mark her. To claim Alexis as his own. No! He pumped into her. Drove the primal urge into passion. He would not claim her like this. He would not. He pumped again and again. Pushed deeper, harder, until the urge for release prevailed. Until he exploded inside her in one hard thrust, shaking from head to toe. Until his muscles slowly eased to relaxed, his body gently covering hers.

Seconds passed, perhaps longer. Ryder climbed out of the haze that had overtaken him and realized Alexis was stroking his neck with her fingers. Calming the wildness inside him. He'd never felt anything like what he'd felt making love to her, never felt his Beast demand so much of him. What if he couldn't control it next time? He inhaled and raised his head, stared into her eyes, saw a sense of satisfaction and peace in her that was not there before. Something their lovemaking had created. And he knew he would and could control himself.

# *Chapter* 7

It was four o'clock in the morning, and Alexis sat on the end of the bed, dressed in Ryder's shirt, eating a piece of toast smeared with her favorite strawberry jam. She couldn't believe how relaxed she felt with him. How comfortable talking. And they'd talked a lot. For hours. Well, more than talked. Made love. Talked to recover. Made love again.

"It's good, right?" she asked, watching Ryder take a bite of the toast. He wore blue boxers with horseshoes on them, which she couldn't help but tease him about.

"It's great," he agreed, finishing off his third piece. "You said your housekeeper makes this stuff?"

She nodded. "Beverly is an amazing cook. She makes pancake syrup, too. It's *so* good. Everything she makes is." She laughed. "Good thing I work hard or I'd be fat. You should taste her muffins."

He studied her a moment. "What time does Beverly get in to work?"

Alexis reached for the glass of chocolate milk sitting on the nightstand, finishing off her last bite of toast. "Soon." She took a drink. Ryder covered her hand and the glass with his palm, long fingers wrapping around and sliding between hers. He tilted the glass to his lips. Heat curled in her stomach at the intimate act. God. She was so into this man. She'd never connected this completely with anyone. Neither female nor male. Never listened to someone talk for hours, hungry to hear more. His horse-training stories were completely enthralling; his suggestions for incorporating his techniques into their operation, exciting—if not impossible. She had no money to make changes. "My foreman, Rick, will come with her. You can meet him, and he can show you around." She'd already discussed Ryder being introduced as a hired consultant from Jaguar Ranch, evaluating their operation for possible improvements.

"I'd rather you show me around," he said.

If only she could. "I have to go to town today," she said, dreading the meeting she would be attending. A plea for more time to pay off the loans her father had taken on the ranch. "You'll like Rick, though. He's a good man."

Ryder took the glass from her hand and set it on the nightstand. "Are you worried Beverly and Rick are going to find us down here together?"

"Yes." Her reputation was all she had, her professionalism. "I've lost good men lately. Men I thought would never leave have up and disappeared. If they stop respecting me, I'll lose more. Bedding the newest cowboy in town won't give me respect."

His lips twitched. "And here I thought *I* bedded *you.*"

"Only because I let you," she teased.

He grinned. “So that’s how it is, is it?”

She nodded. “That’s right.”

His expression turned serious, his voice lowered. “Any regrets, Alexis?”

She touched his jaw, ran her palm over the dark brown stubble. “Not yet,” she whispered. “You planning on giving me any?”

“Not unless me making love to you again is going to give you regrets,” he whispered a moment before his lips found hers.

Alexis sighed, melting into the kiss. She wanted him now, and wanted to find solace in his arms as she hoped he did in hers. She’d seen the pain in his eyes, felt the comfort of knowing he understood what she was going through. Somehow, she could feel the healing they were delivering to each other. Somehow, she could see the path beyond the past to the present.

No regrets.

With their horses tied nearby and Alexis by his side, Ryder sat on top of a wooden fence and looked down a hillside, watching herds of cattle grazing the miles and miles of green pastures before them. This had been his family’s land, his home.

“It’s hard for you, being here,” Alexis said. It wasn’t a question. Simply an understanding she seemed to have of him. A way of knowing without words. She touched his leg, resting her palm there. A week had passed, and they had grown closer, talked more. But still she held back. Still she hadn’t told him how bad the financial situation was at the ranch. Not that she had to. He had been around long enough to know there were corners she was cutting, supplies that were short. He could see her stress, feel her worry. And she was scared—of her situation, of him, of herself. Afraid of counting on someone who would leave, as her father had. A natural reaction to death. But could he break through those fears before he was forced to face his duty again?

"It's hard to believe this place belongs to someone other than my family," Ryder said, refocusing on the land before him. He gave her an opening with those words, a chance to tell him she feared losing her family ranch. He wanted her to admit that to him. But another part of him wanted her to say she was ready to let it go. That she would consider a life away from here. She was his mate, and whether it was a creation of nature or simple attraction, the primal instinct to protect her and keep her close grew more intense with each passing moment.

Silence stretched in torturous minutes before Alexis finally spoke. "I can't imagine life away from Big W," she said, answering his silent question with painful clarity. She wanted to stay. He had to go. "It's a part of me." She glanced at him and back at the horizon. "I can't imagine how hard it is to see this land and know it's gone from you."

Her words cut like a knife on too many levels to analyze. He didn't want to think about them, didn't want to dig deep enough to feel their full impact. The sun was beginning to set anyway, his mood darkening with it.

A raw tingling began to form in his body, his senses alerting him of imminent danger—Beasts. "We should go," he said, keeping his voice nonchalant, his body relaxed, his eyes alert. Several cattle began to act uneasy; one began to run. *"Now."*

She nodded and eyed the area around them. "Why do I feel like we are being watched?"

Ryder jumped from the fence and grabbed Alexis,

pulling her against his body and then toward the horses. "Technically, we're trespassing," he warned, explaining away what she sensed—which was Demons and death. "Maybe someone isn't happy about that."

Alexis started to mount her horse, and it snorted, side-stepping with unease. "Easy, boy," he murmured, rubbing its neck. He'd dealt with many a horse around Beasts, trained them to face Beasts with calm composure. But that took time he didn't have. Again he spoke to the horse. "Easy." He eyed Alexis. "Talk to it."

She nodded and did as he said, her gaze skirting around nervously. Ryder mounted his horse a moment before a snarl sounded nearby.

"Wolves!" Alexis yelled.

Ryder reached over and patted her horse's hindquarters, and then they both launched into action. Not wolves, he thought. Hell Hounds and Demons. The Demons that had stolen his life. He wouldn't let that happen to Alexis. Not now. Not ever. He looked back over his shoulder, that vow repeated in his head over and over as they distanced themselves from danger. Alexis was safe, but for how long? And how did he save her without destroying what she called her life? Because he couldn't stay, and she didn't want to leave.

He'd thought that finding Alexis had been a blessing he didn't deserve. Instead, he was beginning to wonder if this was his eternal hell. To know his mate existed but have duty force him to destroy her life, create resentment or simply force him to walk away, to leave her behind.

# *Chapter 8*

The sun was setting, the night muggy. It was two weeks after Ryder had joined the Big W operation, and he stood on the front porch of the house and eyed the scene in the driveway. Alexis and Kelly stood by Kelly's red Volkswagen in heated debate. Again. Kelly was going to see Hector. Alexis was begging her not to. Kelly waved her hands in anger and then got into the car. Ryder waited as Alexis approached, looking shaken and upset.

This was the first time he'd seen her in twelve hours. He'd left early to work with Rick that morning. Alexis had gone into town to the bank, very closed-lipped about why, but he intended to find out tonight. Not that he needed much guesswork. The ranch was falling apart; the cattle were being attacked and killed by wolves—or so Rick thought. But it wasn't wolves. It was Hell Hounds. A little detail Ryder had been handling off the radar. He'd been hunting, killing as many Demons as he could. Telling Alexis he was scouting for wolves, checking traps. But there were too many. It was time to ask for help. He needed more men; he needed the Knights. He shoved the thought aside for the short term, as Alexis climbed the stairs and tried her best to give him a smile.

"Hi," she said.

"Hi." He wanted to pull her close, to hug away her frustrations, but he couldn't. She wanted their relationship off the radar. She saw him as temporary, and she didn't want her reputation with the men hurt. He didn't want to be temporary, but the complications were many. Yet he had a sworn duty as a Knight at Jaguar Ranch, she had a life here in Round Rock. Mixed emotions tormented him. How could he face the elder Knights suffering without a mate with one of his own? And even if he dared do such a thing, he would be asking Alexis to live in a world full of Demons, in a war zone. To leave behind Big W Ranch, the home she was fighting to save.

"She's going to see him again," Alexis said, her jaw clenched as she leaned on the railing beside him and watched the red car disappear. "She threw you in my face. Said she knew we were together. That I had a lot of nerve judging her when I'm sleeping with someone I've only just met."

"I wondered why you were so secretive with her," he said softly. "Considering she is a good friend and all. I guess I have my answer." She'd already shared their history, the way they'd grown up together, the way Kelly felt like a sister to her. "Friends and family know how to push our buttons more than anyone. And they usually push those buttons when deflecting from themselves."

Alexis sighed and nodded her agreement. "Yeah, well, friend or not, she doesn't have her head on straight. She can't be a good friend to someone else, because she isn't even a friend to herself right now."

Ryder turned to her then, taking in her profile, her dark brunette hair lifting as a lone breeze skirted across the porch. She was beautiful. Sincere. Hardworking. And he was falling in love. He opened his mouth to speak, not even sure what he was going to say, when the phone rang, the sound carrying through the screen door.

She pushed off the rail. "I have to get that. I'm expecting a call."

He followed her inside, lingering in the living room as she grabbed the phone in the den. He could hear her talking to the bank. *No, they would not give her more time.* She was going to sell the ranch, she promised the caller. Ryder had mixed feelings about that declaration. He wanted her with him, but more than anything, he wanted her to be happy. Her voice continued to echo off the walls, vibrating with desperateness.

Without any hesitation, he turned on his heels and headed for the door. He and Alexis needed to have a talk. But first he needed to talk to Jag—and do so in private. If Alexis wanted to keep the ranch, damn it, she'd keep it. Even if it meant leaving Round Rock without her. Even if that meant leaving his mate here, to happiness that didn't include him.

At the north end of the ranch, Ryder dismounted the stallion he'd ridden to the secluded hillside and tied it to a tree. He removed his cell phone and dialed Jag. A quick conversation later, and Jag materialized in front of him, the only Knight able to orb from place to place—his gifts as their leader were extraordinary.

Tall and dark, of Hispanic heritage, Jag wore jeans and

boots as another might wear a crown: regal and proud. Even without the sword strapped to his right leg, he was a lethal force, so powerful that one instantly sensed it in his presence.

"Beasts," Jag said instantly, a hiss to his voice. "They are here."

Ryder inclined his head, his expression grim. "Yes. Hell Hounds, too. They've been killing off the cattle."

Jag narrowed his eyes on Ryder. "Yet you tried to handle it on your own," he said flatly. "Why?"

The truth exploded from Ryder, the truth that had been eating him alive for days. "Because I can't face the other Knights," he said, staring at the clear night sky speckled with bright twinkling stars and a full moon. "Because—" he inhaled and looked at Jag "—I found my mate." He scrubbed his jaw and turned to Jag. "Why? Why am I given a mate when so many others are struggling to survive the Beast within them? I don't understand." He'd heard stories of Knights finding mates, afraid to claim them, afraid the Beast within would take control and hurt them. "I have control. Even with Alexis, I have control. They don't. How can I face them with a mate? How can I say I was somehow more important?"

"This isn't about importance, Ryder," Jag said, his tone even, certain. "It is timing. When your mate is ready, so must you be. Everything has to come together." He waved a hand through the air. "Clearly, yours is in danger. There is a purpose that you and she will serve. A reason you must find each other."

Ryder shook his head. "A purpose." Cynicism laced the words. "Right."

Jag laughed. "I know what you are feeling." He glanced at the sky, scanned the horizon. "I used to question things," he said, a calming quality to the sureness and confidence in his voice. "I used to ask why." He cut Ryder a sideways look. "I even resented that those above us knew things they wouldn't just come out and say. The 'purpose' answer I was given by my mentor really bit me smack in the ass."

His mentor. Salvador, the earthly guide to the Knights, the link to the Archangel Raphael. They all knew of him, but few had met him. "You doubted?"

"I did more than doubt. I resented Salvador. I second-guessed him. I tore myself up inside over the past and the present, and why I was chosen to lead the Knights."

"But not now?"

He shook his head. "Now, I accept rather than question. I've seen enough to be able to look out at the vastness of the world and be thankful something greater exists to keep the darkness in check. Evil exists and always will, Ryder. We're important. We keep the balance, so evil can never overtake humanity. This was your time to find your mate. And yes, curse me if you will, but there is a purpose, a reason. Her safety being one of them."

Ryder shoved his hands in his pockets. Even if he accepted, even if he stopped questioning, it wasn't so simple. "I can't take her away from her life."

"What makes you think she won't go willingly?"

Ryder didn't look at Jag. "I don't like this destined-mate crap."

"You want her to choose you." It wasn't a question.

His chest tightened. "Yes. I need to stay. For a while. Until I'm sure." He turned to face Jag. "I have a proposition for you."

Jag's lips lifted, and he turned to face Ryder, an intrigued look on his face. "A proposition?"

"The Beasts are heavily populating this region. We thought they were gone once, clearly they are not. They're infested, staking a claim we can't let them have. Why not bring a few of the newer Knights here? We'll operate out of this location and deal with the Demons targeting the area. It will be good training for them. And a good post for us." He paused before adding the punch line, the big idea he'd come up with on his way over here. The one he thought would never be accepted, but he had to try. "Indefinitely."

Jag arched his brow, and Ryder proceeded to unveil his whole plan. When he'd finished explaining what he proposed, he held his breath. Jag smiled and held out his hands; using the magic he alone possessed, he produced two swords and offered one to Ryder.

"Nothing like a good Demon-killing mission to seal a deal. Let's hunt."

Ryder's chest filled with relief as he accepted the saber, his plan now a reality except for one thing. He needed Alexis to say yes—to his plan to save her ranch, and to his proposal to stay around for long past tomorrow. He wanted to stay forever. Which meant she had to know the truth—she had to know he was a Knight of White, and that he had more than ghosts in his past. There were Demons.

# *Chapter 9*

Alexis sat on the edge of the tub, still fully dressed, watching the basin fill with water, the bubbles grow. She was upset. Upset on so many levels, Alexis didn't know if she was coming or going. Worried over Kelly and completely rattled over the ranch—afraid she was about to lose it. No. Certain. Absolutely certain that everything her father had worked for was going to end horribly. At least selling the ranch would have felt like a successful ending. Losing it was devastating. Adding to those things was a complication she'd warned herself not to create, but she had. She'd gone and fallen in love with Ryder. Head over heels in love. And tonight she'd been ready to tell him everything going on in her life, to spill the beans about how bad her circumstances were. No more talking in circles and telling him half the story. No more avoiding his ideas to help the ranch grow and prosper because she didn't have the money to implement any of the changes he suggested. She was going to trust him completely.

But as surely as she'd been ready to open up, he'd disappeared. Gone three hours without a word. The timing had been undeniably horrible. A silent promise that leaning on him was dangerous. He was leaving. He had never said anything about staying. Not once. Heck. Maybe he already had left. Maybe he'd heard her talking to the bank and had packed up and gone. She stood up and took off toward the door, determined to find out.

Turning off the water, she ran down the stairs as if she was on fire. She needed to know if she had trusted her heart to someone who didn't deserve it. Halfway down the stairs, she drew to an abrupt halt, her heart pounding like a drum in her chest. Ryder was standing at the bottom of the stairs. He was devastatingly handsome, his hair tousled, lithe muscle defined beneath soft denim. But it was his eyes that got to her, the soul-deep torment within them.

"Alexis." He whispered her name, softly, full of emotion.

"What?" she whispered. "What is it?"

He took a step upward, coming closer to her. She wanted him closer. "I don't want to leave you," he said.

Her heart squeezed. "But you're going to."

He shook his head slowly, his voice still low, his voice gravely. "I have obligations. Things I have to deal with."

She could barely swallow. "I understand. I knew this was temporary." She drew her spine stiff. "I appreciate all the help you gave us."

He looked at her in disbelief. "Just like that? You're ready to kick me to the curb?"

"What do you want me to say, Ryder? You just told me you're leaving."

"No, Alexis. You don't understand. I never said I was leaving. I said I have obligations. I have more than obligations. I have a duty."

"To Jaguar Ranch," she said flatly. It hurt. He had a real job, a real life. Damn it. Why did she do this to herself? And she had done it to herself. He'd never promised her anything. Before he came, she'd been fine on her own.

His hand was on the railing. "I thought about all kinds of ways to talk to you about this. Played it over and over in my head."

"Goodbye," she said. "It's simple." She crossed her arms in front of her body, feigning nonchalant cool when her insides were shredded. "It's okay."

He stared at her, his eyes dark, intense. Anger began to burn in their depths. "Is it okay?" he asked, a demand in his voice. "Is my leaving really okay with you?"

She wanted to tell him no. No, it wasn't okay. But she was scared. When had she become so scared? "I don't know what you want from me. I don't." Why did he have to push her beyond her comfort zone?

"I want you to *answer the question,*" he said. "Is my leaving okay with you?"

She wanted to answer. "You have obligations. What I want doesn't matter." She turned to walk up the stairs.

He grabbed her arm and pulled her around to face him, heat flickering up her arm with the touch. "I want you to believe in me enough to tell me to stay," he said. "I want you to say it. But if you do, I need you to mean it." His lashes lowered, lifted. He whispered her name. "Alexis. Tomorrow is here."

She was confused. No. She was done fighting. She wanted him. "Damn you, Ryder. No. No, I don't want you to go." Her eyes burned, stupid tears threatening to make her look weak and needy. "Are you happy now?"

He laced his fingers through her hair, framed her face. "I don't want to go, Alexis. I don't."

"Why do I sense a *but?* You don't want to, but what?"

The front door jiggled. Not now, Alexis thought desperately. "Kelly," she said. "It has to be."

"Alexis!" It was the housekeeper, Beverly. "Alexis!"

Before they could make it to the bottom of the stairs, Beverly was there, her short, dark hair wild, her expression flustered. "Rick is in jail. He saw Hector roughing up Kelly and he went after Hector."

"Oh, no!" Alexis said. "Is he okay?"

"Yes," she said. "Yes. He's fine. He's worried about Kelly. He thinks Hector is going to blame her for all the bad publicity at the bar."

"Let's go," Ryder said, grabbing Alexis's hand and tugging her with him.

Alexis saw Beverly glance at their connected hands, but she didn't care. She didn't care because something in the way Ryder held her hand, the way he claimed her crisis as his own, made her never want to let go of him.

Ryder whipped the truck into the parking lot of the Double R Tavern, thinking how profoundly ironic it was to end up here tonight, the place where he'd become a Demon hunter. He'd been only seconds from confessing who and what he was to Alexis when they'd found out about Kelly. And damn, how he'd wanted to tell her. Wanted to get the secrets dealt with, the past behind him, once and for all. But this situation with Kelly had to be handled first. More than once he'd thought he'd spotted evidence of Kelly being abused. More than once he'd wanted to come to this bar and beat that sorry bastard's ass. It was long past due.

Easing the truck into a graveled spot at the side of the bar, Ryder put the gear in Park and left the engine running. Alexis reached for the door, and Ryder grabbed her arm. "Stay here behind the wheel, ready to drive. I'll take care of Hector. You can count on it." She looked as though she might argue, but changed her mind, logic winning against her emotional need to see Kelly. He started to get out. "Lock the doors."

The minute he was out of the truck, he scented Beasts. Damn it! His swords were under his seat in the truck. Another little ironic twist of this night. Same bar he'd died at. Same enemy. No way to defend himself.

He started for the door when he heard Alexis call his name. "Ryder." She was running toward him. "The back parking lot. I just saw them go out the side door."

*Back parking lot*. The location of his attack. And Alexis was running in that direction. Ryder's gut twisted with warning. This moment was what he had come here for; this was where everything began and where it could end.

# *Chapter 10*

Alexis rounded the side of the bar to find the back parking lot empty except for one vehicle, Hector's, and only one small light illuminating the area, the shadows thick and threatening. Several yards away, she saw Hector and Kelly.

"Kelly!" Alexis screamed, trying to stop her from getting into Hector's pickup truck, but to no avail. Kelly got in; Hector didn't. He charged toward Alexis, and she felt the menace in him. She started to back away, certain Ryder would be there any second.

Hector was running toward her now, angry, ready to lash out. Probably blaming her for her foreman's actions, too. She turned and started to run, thankful for the sight of Ryder charging toward her. With…swords. He had swords in his hands. What in the blazes was happening?

Her question was absorbed by the growl that sounded behind her. A vicious snarl followed. A snarl like she'd heard in the wood with Ryder that day. Hector's horrid gasp came next. Instinct had her turning toward the noise, trying to see what might attack. "Don't!" Ryder yelled. "Don't turn! Run! Run!" She ran and he sped past her. The sound of blades connecting behind her was too much. She turned.

To her absolute shock, she found Ryder matching blades with not one but two men. Hector was on the ground bleeding from his neck. Dead. He was dead. Or close to it. Alexis backed away in horror as she fixed her attention on one of the *thing*s fighting Ryder. Because that was no man! *Monster.* The word repeated in her head over and over. She didn't know what to do. Was this a nightmare?

She inhaled, held her hand to her chest, tried to calm her racing heart. Think! Think! Help. They needed help. She screamed the word. "Help! Help! Help!" All the while, her eyes stayed focused on Ryder, praying his sword was the one to prevail. Music pumped from the walls of the bar; her cries were lost in its volume.

Her gaze caught abruptly on Hector's truck as the door popped open. Kelly was going to get out. "No! No!"

Alexis started running toward her, past the battle. From the corner of her eye, she saw another monster dart from the woods, and it was chasing her. She screamed and ran faster. But it was fast. Too fast. It was already practically on her. She stumbled. Her heart pounded against her chest, ready to explode. She scrambled, rotated to her back to try to see her attacker, certain she was about to die.

Suddenly, Ryder's sword swished through the air, and the monster's head came off. Alexis gasped, certain blood would splatter everywhere. Instead, flames erupted on the head and body, and moments later the monster was gone. Her gaze swept the area around her. The other monsters were gone. Hector was gone! His body was gone! Kelly. Where was Kelly? Frantically, Alexis turned to find her friend standing behind her. "Oh, thank you," she said in a sigh of relief. "Are you okay?"

"No," Kelly sat down. "Hector must have put something in my drink. I'm seeing things."

Ryder knelt down in front of Alexis, his focus on her, not Kelly, his swords by his side on the ground. He touched her face, hand skimming her hair. "Are *you* okay?" he asked, but gave her no time to reply, pulling her into his arms. He held her close, tight, as if he never wanted to let go.

"I'm okay," she whispered, the warmth of him surrounding her, making her believe those words. A thought rushed at her. She jerked back, urgent. "Hector. Hector was bleeding. We have to call 9-1-1."

Ryder stared down at her. "He's one of them now, Alexis. He's gone."

She shook her head, rejecting those words, rejecting the reality that included monsters. "What's happening?"

"I'll explain everything, I promise. But not here. Not when they could come back." His hand skimmed her hair. "At home."

*Home?* Alexis blinked at the underlying meaning that might lie in those words, unable to ask questions. Ryder was on his cell phone already, telling someone where to come, where to clean up. She squeezed her eyes shut. There were so many things she didn't understand. Things about Ryder she didn't understand.

Ending the call, Ryder pushed to his feet and offered her his hand. She stared up at it, at him. "Why do I trust you after all of this?" she asked, because she did. She trusted him more completely now than ever, yet she wondered if she knew him at all.

He knelt down again and looked into her eyes, the light nearby allowing her to see the tenderness in them. "Because I would die to protect you, and I think you can sense that. And because I love you, Alexis. I love you."

Doubt slid away with his emotional confession. Because she loved him, too.

Hours after the fight behind the bar, Alexis stood on her front porch with Ryder and Jag, Ryder's hand resting protectively on her back. She listened as they debated which Knights would soon be joining Ryder to hunt the nearby territory and deal with the Demon infestation. Her head was spinning with all she'd learned of Demons and Angels.

The Demons were apparently keen on claiming territory. They'd been here once, they'd always come back. Hector was now a Demon who'd been a random victim as Ryder had once been. Only Ryder wasn't a Demon. Ryder was a Demon hunter. She was his mate. She could save him from the Beast within him, bind it so it could never taint his soul.

She'd learned this from Marisol, the woman who had appeared with Jag behind that bar and orbed everyone back to the ranch. Orbed. Somehow, transported them in the blink of an eye from one place to the next. One minute they were in the parking lot behind the bar, the next at the ranch. It had been amazing. Even more amazing was the way Marisol had erased Kelly's memories and then, with a wave of her hand, sent her into a healing sleep. Kelly was resting, and before Marisol had left, she had assured Alexis that Kelly would be well the next morning. Alexis had every intention of making sure she was more than well. She was going to make sure Kelly had a fresh start.

Alexis narrowed her gaze on Jag as he spoke. He was

a man easy to like, impossible to ignore—and not because he was a hunky six foot plus of Hispanic male. It was an inner strength he possessed, a leadership presence you noticed immediately. Which was befitting since he was more than the owner of Jaguar Ranch. He was the leader of the Knights of White. And Ryder was a Demon hunter. She still couldn't fully get her mind around that fact but, having seen the Demons, acceptance came easy.

That Ryder had once been bitten by one of those creatures was horrifying. She'd seen Hector's neck, seen all the blood. She shivered just thinking about it, and Ryder pulled her under his shoulder, warmth filling her. Jag turned his attention to her as well. "Partners," Jag said, extending his hand to her.

Alexis smiled at Jag. "Yes. Partners." She'd agreed to an investment in the ranch which would allow horse breeding to become part of their operation. Ryder would stay and train Rick to run the operation. New staff would be hired with the experience needed. The ranch was saved. And *Ryder was staying.*

Jag released her hand and shook Ryder's. "Be safe, my man. Help will arrive soon."

"Thank you," Ryder said softly.

Jag smiled at Alexis. "Peace, Alexis," he said without any further explanation. And then he simply disappeared.

Alexis shook her head and turned to Ryder. "It's going to take a while to get used to that."

Ryder slid his hand around hers, gently leading her inside the house. "It does us all." Once they were inside he picked her up.

Alexis gasped. "What are you doing?"

"Taking you to bed."

She laughed. "I'm not sleepy."

"Neither am I," he said, casting her a heated look.

"I was hoping you'd say that," she whispered, suddenly warm all over.

He stood in the hallway. "Upstairs or down?"

"Up," she said. "No more hiding downstairs."

"I was hoping you'd say that," he said, approval lacing his tone.

Ryder carried her up the stairs and laid her on the bed, coming down with her, his big body a warm shelter above hers. "I know," she whispered before he could kiss her lips. "I know about the mating process. Marisol told me."

He pulled back, turbulence in his eyes a moment before he squeezed them closed. "I didn't want her to tell you."

Her hand touched his face. "Why?" she asked, confused by the emotions in him. "Why would you not want me to know?"

"Because I know your big heart. You will save me because of a sense of destiny and obligation. Because I'm one of the good guys, and you saw those Demons. You know what is out there, what I face, what I could become." His voice turned raspy, intense. "I don't want obligation. I want you. You, Alexis. A woman who *chooses* me as her mate."

Her heart tightened, warmed. Any fear of speaking her mind was gone. It hurt her to know she'd created such doubt in him. That her need to protect herself had obviously caused him such torment. "I love you, Ryder. *I love you*. I should have told you what I felt. I should have said, no, no, it's not okay that you leave. Not now. Not ever. *I love you*. I'm not saving you. You saved me. You were what I was missing."

"I want to believe that. I want to—"

She kissed him. Pressed her mouth to his and tried to tell him she loved him in yet another way. "Make me yours forever," she whispered against his lips. "Save me. Let me save you."

He pulled back, searched her face. "You're sure?"

She nodded. "Absolutely." She smiled a bit nervously, thinking about the mating process Marisol had described as erotic. "You have to bite me, right? On the shoulder?"

"Yes," he said. "While we make love."

Alexis wrapped her arms around his neck. "What are you waiting for?" she asked, teasing him. "I don't have all day."

He didn't wait any longer, his mouth claiming hers. Passion-filled kisses followed, gentle caresses, tender stares. Soon they were naked, intimately entwined. Ryder sat with his back against the headboard, Alexis on top of him. They were kissing, swaying together in a slow, erotic rhythm. Desire began to change from smoldering heat to overwhelming demand. Alexis could feel the need in Ryder, in herself. Feel the moment approaching when life would change forever.

He pulled back, looked at her, his eyes dark, swirling with a yellowish hue of Beast and man. "You're sure?" he whispered.

"Absolutely," she said, wanting this, wanting him more than she'd ever wanted anything in her life.

Ryder buried his face in her neck, and she felt his teeth sink into her shoulder. Alexis stiffened with shock a moment before pleasure soared through her limbs. Everything inside her warmed, filled, felt complete. She smiled to herself, filled with happiness, and the promise of an eternity of tomorrows to come.

* * * * *

# MORTAL ENEMY, IMMORTAL LOVER

*Olivia Gates*

To two wonderful ladies. My incredible editor, Natashya Wilson, for always encouraging me to spread my wings. And Silhouette Nocturne's Senior Executive Editor, Tara Gavin, for opening this new door for me. Thanks, ladies, it's been a blast writing this story.

***OLIVIA GATES***

has always pursued creative passions, but only one of her passions grew gratifying enough, consuming enough, to become an ongoing career—writing. When she's not writing, she is a doctor, a wife to her own alpha male and a mother to one brilliant girl and one demanding angora cat. Visit Olivia at www.oliviagates.com.

Dear Reader,

The paranormal has always been my first love. I've always built worlds where my imagination reigns supreme. In these worlds, I create universes populated by beings who are at once human and far more than human, beings who lead lives complicated by dangers and dilemmas, sacrifices and triumphs in direct proportion to the powers that bless and blight their existence.

But somehow, it took me a long time to publish my first paranormal. "Mortal Enemy, Immortal Lover" was my twentieth contracted work. I certainly hope it will be the first of many, many more.

It felt like coming home as I wrote the dark and intense love story of Javed and Desirée. The backdrop of the complex urban fantasy setting provided the perfect catalyst to ignite the sensuality—and the high stakes—surrounding them. And I can't wait to write more about their universe, and hopefully, more of their story.

I hope you enjoy your "bite" of my paranormal writing. And I hope you will come back for more when I publish my next works in the Eradicators' universe and in the paranormal genre that knows no limits.

I'd love to hear from you, so please visit my Web site www.oliviagates.com and contact me with your opinions.

Here's hoping you enjoy your every reading adventure.

Olivia Gates

# *Chapter 1*

Desirée was extracting his soul.

With each glide and pull of her lips, Javed felt her dislodging more of its newly anchored tethers. He didn't mind. He wanted her to have it. She'd sown it inside him, anyway. Maybe if she succeeded, their situation would stop tearing him apart.

He surrendered himself to her fever, let its flames rage out of control, his and Desi's presence in the packed nightclub the only thing stopping him from taking what she was begging him to take. Only in his tortured imagination would he fling her to the ground, shred that bloodred, madness-inducing device of a dress and bury himself inside her, pound her to satisfaction and drench her with his own.

Desirée sundered the fusion of their mouths only to deal him another blow, latching her lips onto his ear, a bolt of stimulation skewering his brain and lodging in his erection.

"Stop tormenting me…both of us…"

Her whimper felt as if it were generated inside his head, torn from his body. He bucked, nearly entering her soaking heat through the barriers of their clothing.

*Why?* everything within him bellowed. Why was he stopping?

Her next sob told him why. "Take me home with you tonight. I can't wait anymore, please… I'll die if I'm not with you tonight…."

*She'd die.* That was why he always stopped. Because she *would* die, one day. Because she was human. Because he was…what he was.

That had stopped him from claiming her that first night five months ago. And every night since. But it hadn't stopped him from surrendering to the compulsion and torment of seeing her every possible minute of these months.

But he'd surpassed the limits of endurance. The force of her craving had corroded any pretense at control. Everything writhed inside him as she writhed in his arms, forcing his decision.

*Take her before your mind gives, before that heart racing inside her stops. Celebrate her life now, until you…until she…*

He froze with a dread he hadn't considered before.

Could he ever get enough? Could he move on if *she* did? What if…?

He unhooked the fingers convulsing in his flesh. "I can't…"

Thorns seemed to expand in his throat, cutting off the words. And it wasn't from the hurt in her eyes. It was from the panic he suddenly felt, then saw in other eyes. Many eyes. Across the nightclub. *Vamps.*

Dammit…*no.* This was a humans-only establishment.

Not anymore. Not tonight. There they were. Eight of them. Fledglings, still clinging to their human habits and haunts. But they'd recognized him. Their instinctive horror and loathing had wrenched him out of his fugue as soon as they'd seen him through the crush. Seen him with Desi.

The illusion of safety crashed around him. He'd been deluding himself that he wasn't risking embroiling her in his hideous existence, that his enemies—his prey—would never know what she was to him.

He'd been too weak. Too damn selfish. His precautions hadn't been enough. They never would be. He'd turn her life into a hell she couldn't imagine, one that would end horrifically. Or worse.

This had to end now. This second. The vamps had run out, and he had to perform damage control.

He ripped himself out of her arms, spilled her onto the couch. "Desi…I told you from the start that I'm not…a man you should get mixed up with. Now my reasons for not seeing you again have become irreversible. It's over. It should never have started."

Tears had filled her eyes when he'd pulled back, as they always did. Now they gushed, a flood that seemed to drain her very life force. They shriveled the heart he hadn't known he possessed.

He exploded to his feet before he lost whatever was left of his mind. Succumbed. Destroyed her.

She clung to him. Everything inside him roared, *Don't look back. Or you'll come back. You can't… Never again…*

He looked back. Damn him. Far more than he'd already been damned. But if he couldn't stop himself, he had to stop her.

He tore her hands off him. He had to hurt her enough that she'd forget about him.

She winced but lunged back, clung again, harder. "I can't let you just leave my life, Javed. I will never feel like this again. And I know you feel the same." She let go of him, fumbled inside her purse, dragged his hand, pressed a folded paper in it. "Damn whatever you're hiding, and damn not sharing personal info… I live here, and I *love* you. I'll take anything I can have with you, for any length of time, at any price."

He'd had stakes hammered into his palms. He'd had his hands dipped in molten lead. That piece of paper hurt far more.

Her address. The very information he'd refused to seek out, as if ignorance would stop him from obsessing over her when he had to walk away. He made the mistake of looking at it. It became engraved in his mind.

"I can't…afford for anyone to see me coming to you."

She closed his hand tight around the scrap. "My place is far, isolated. Just come through the forest and no one will see you. I'll wait for you tonight."

Then she streaked away, giving him no chance to refuse. Leaving him no choice.

He had to go to her. To end it.

But he had to end the threat to her life first.

# Chapter 2

In the thousand years he'd lived, Javed had killed multitudes of vamps and demons.

He didn't keep count. But with as many as ten kills per day—far more on some of his more...*enthusiastic* episodes—simple math said he'd wiped out millions. All breeds of vampires and demons were in danger of extinction at his hands.

He'd long thought it poetic justice. He was the spawn, after all, of the supernatural breeds' war for supremacy over one another as they all strove to conquer a mostly oblivious, if still dominant, humanity.

They'd brought him into existence at the cost of putting aside their abhorrence of each other and of hybrids, in the first controlled experiment of its kind. They'd hoped to create a progeny with every breed's strengths and no weaknesses. After countless failed monstrosities, they'd gotten *him.* If Javed had weaknesses, they were yet to be discovered. But his creators had failed to fathom the source of his invulnerability to replicate it in themselves, had instead unleashed their collective nightmare.

After a century-long childhood and adolescence with no awareness of the outside world or that his "elders" were actually his jailers and that life was more than their endless and agonizing experiments, he'd learned of his mother's even more horrific ordeals.

A hybrid herself, bred for this experiment, she'd been constantly raped and impregnated by every supernatural creature there was, in hopes of producing more offspring like him, but more amenable to probing and exploitation.

When he'd learned about her by chance, he'd cut down most of his captors and escaped to save her. He'd been too late. She'd finally managed to kill herself to escape their abuse.

He'd made a vow that day. Every breed in his gene pool, everyone who'd had a hand in his existence, would pay with theirs.

His vow had ceased to sound like the bravado of a disgruntled youth centuries ago. Every breed now believed that, given long enough, he'd make good on his word. And being immortal, he had forever.

He didn't have forever now.

Those vamps who'd seen Desi with him had about ten minutes' head start. He couldn't give them ten more.

And there they were, in the clearing of a junkyard. Too far to scent him, though he'd scented them fine. His vampiric senses were levels beyond even a major vampire's, let alone a fledgling's. They were hooting and high-fiving and kissing in the abandon of those celebrating a narrow escape. They sounded, hell, *felt* like college kids out on a group date....

He stopped. What if they weren't termination-worthy?

He had criteria for that now. After a centuries-long rampage, he'd realized that not every demon and vampire deserved to die. Some were just hustlers, some tried to co-exist, some were even "good," whatever the latest definition of that was. Hell, some were victims. While those weren't the norm, he now made sure he didn't kill the wrong creatures. He had enough blood of the innocent—or at least the non-death-worthy—on his hands.

For a while, his hunt had slowed down due to his new rules of discrimination. Then, the emergence of an even bigger threat to the vulnerable among the non-predatory humans, fey and witches had brought him almost to a standstill. An epidemic of murders that went beyond anything in his experience in methodical viciousness had made him set aside his hunt to investigate them. Evidence said the culprits were daylighters, who passed for human but possessed strength beyond even that of a nether demon. This all pointed to a mysterious breed rumored to be energy absorbers.

He'd never cared to track down that breed before, since there had seemed to be few of them and many vigilante activities had been attributed to them throughout the ages. He'd assumed they were sort of on his side when it came to demons and vamps. But with all the new evidence painting a clear picture of a ritualistic collection of life forces, probably to feed their powers, it seemed that their reputation had been a smoke screen to hide the true depths of their depravity. As for why they'd suddenly changed their M.O., he could only assume they'd grown so powerful they weren't bothering to disguise their intentions anymore.

He thought he'd been close to capturing one when he'd followed an irresistible pull to that nightclub, seen Desi, and realized it had been *her* vibe that had drawn him there. And one thousand years of solitude had ended.

His mission forgotten, he'd sought her out, told her within minutes that he would have her. She'd scoffed at his presumption, embroiled him in the exhilaration of wrestling with his match. But she'd made it clear she'd felt just as drawn to him.

Instead of coming to his senses and walking away, he'd come back, every day and night. Soon she'd told him she loved him. And he'd repaid her love by exposing her to mortal danger. Possibly immortal damnation.

He was done doing that. After dealing with this situation, he'd disappear from her life, and she'd be safe.

But how *would* he deal with this situation?

He stood there, watching the fledglings, torn over how to proceed. He couldn't just kill them as a precaution.

And he wouldn't. If they were counting their blessings, intending to do the wise, self-preserving thing, to never mention seeing him with Desi, he'd leave them be.

He tuned his supernatural hearing to eavesdrop on them.

"...I was sure that Javed guy was some urban legend to keep us young, rebellious vamps in line."

"He's real. My every cell screamed in recognition the moment we walked into Cisco's. I thought that the response all vamps and demons are supposed to feel at his presence was another myth."

"Myth shmyth. I almost dropped to my knees just feeling him there."

"Yeah, me, too. And he didn't even make a move."

"I wouldn't have made one to go after enemies, either, if I was busy feeling up that human babe."

"Babe? Not only am I still here, you jackass, but we were this close to being dusted. And you had the nerve *and* the testosterone to ogle her?"

"Hey, I'm undead, not dead. A babe of that magnitude I can draw from memory after a single glance."

"Wait till we tell everyone we saw our so-called scourge schmoozing it with that blond bombshell."

"We'll be celebrities. The vamps who stumbled onto Javed and walked away to tell the tale."

"Make that *ran like hell away.*"

"So we ran. But we also discovered he has a taste for human babes."

"At least for a certain one. I bet the bartender can tell us who she is. I bet it'll come in handy to keep Javed from killing more vamps."

"Yeah, and if her taste in dates is that extreme, maybe she'll date me, too."

Javed shut his eyes. They'd just signed their death warrants. They *would* leak info about Desi, might even seek her out. He couldn't let them do either. He could threaten them, but they were too young and cocky. Stupid. Intimidation wouldn't keep them silent. It was their lives against hers. No contest.

He could afford them only one mercy. He'd make it painless. He needed a weapon for that.

He plunged his fingers into the hood of a car—like a mortal would through paper—and ripped, then pressed the strip of metal into a makeshift sword. He shape-shifted his face from the human one he usually wore to that of the unique hybrid that his whole was. Then, from a standing start, he bounded, landing inside their circle.

Their shock and fear smelled and tasted partially human still. It made him gag. They didn't try to fight, only to run. It was better this way. They didn't see the killing blows coming.

In two minutes, eight bodies were scattered around him. And eight heads. They'd been turned so recently that they weren't disintegrating into ashes. He felt he'd just decapitated eight young humans.

Bile rose. He went down on his knees among his massacre.

*It was you or her. You forced me to choose. If you didn't deserve to die otherwise, forgive me....*

Granting forgiveness was for their souls. And his.

He'd thought he had no soul. He'd believed he'd been born unequipped to feel, let alone experience the transfiguring emotions Desi inspired in him. But what he felt for her was far more than this "love" that seemed to be the source of all races' motivations and turmoil. It was something so pure and total, it had ignited a soul within *him.*

Not that it made any difference. He'd been insane to think he could claim her under false pretenses. He'd already damaged her enough by letting her get so emotionally involved with him when she had no idea who—or what—she was getting involved with.

He'd go to her now. Not only to end it, but to tell her why he was ending it. He owed her the truth. Even if it sent her running away screaming. As it would. Only then would she be free of him. While he…

He didn't matter.

Within an hour he was following her instructions, cutting through the denseness of a forest in which even nocturnal creatures would be blind.

Then he saw it. A glimmer among the trees in the distance. Desi's home. He was glad, now, that he knew where it was. He'd watch over her for as long as she lived. He couldn't imagine a time when she wouldn't, but her life filled him now, enveloped him.

Something tore through him, back to front.

Pit demons had charged him at a hundred miles per hour. Bazooka rockets had hit him. Nothing had ever impacted him as hard as this perforation. It felt way beyond physical.

He stumbled forward. His senses converged on the damage taking place inside his body, his mental faculties documenting it with the detachment of disbelief.

A spear. Wood-silver-titanium-gold. Each component screamed at each gene belonging to the breed vulnerable to it, even as his whole self recognized only the kinetic devastation of the inch-thick, diamond-hard projectile. Propelled by enough strength to be faster than a bullet, it had torn through skin ten times tougher than a rhino's and muscles as solid as compact rubber, shattered a scapula harder than concrete, and corkscrewed its way into his chest cavity, shredding structures that had stopped shrapnel, ripping through his pericardium and missing his cardiac muscle by millimeters. He felt it splinter his sternum, watched it burst through his chest, spewing muscle and skin, forming an exit wound half the size of his fist. He blinked at the triangular head jutting obscenely between his exposed ribs.

This wouldn't kill him. It couldn't, not even if it had ripped a bull's-eye through his heart. But it hurt. Worse, it was loaded with a neurotoxin designed to incapacitate with pain. It did.

It felt as if a comet hurtled through him, its head a pinpoint of destruction, its tail a flare of agony that radiated to engulf his whole body.

He roared. Agonized. Enraged. Confused.

This couldn't be happening. No one *ever* crept up on him. He hadn't even sensed an attacker.

*He still didn't.*

He dipped his fingers into his wound, pinched the tip of the spear and, roaring again, ripped it out. Healthy tissue sprouted from the walls of the tunnel of damage. The wildfire of healing seemed to pour gasoline on the sensations ripping through him. He swung around, disoriented by too many stimuli.

Someone slammed into him, took him down. Someone as strong as him. Faster. And he *still* didn't sense his attacker.

How…?

Suddenly the pain vanished. Something burst into the vacuum it left, something unknown, overwhelming. Helplessness.

Desirée. *She* was his attacker.

She straddled him, all moonbeam hair, lithe cream limbs and killer-red dress, eyes no longer the violet he adored but a glowing crimson. She raised her supple arm, her lovely hand fisted. He didn't see it descend.

The blow exploded against the side of his head with the impact of a cannonball, synergizing with the wholesale synaptic disruption, then…

Nothing.

# *Chapter 3*

Nothing that hurt like this should be survivable.

Times like this, he hated being indestructible. Times like this, he wished he'd discover he wasn't.

There'd never been a time like this. He could have never imagined there would be.

He'd come to, about four minutes ago. During the first minute, he'd processed just who and what the hell he was. The second, he'd scanned his surroundings, with sight and other senses. A dank cellar, rank with the stench of snuffed lives, reverberating with echoes of violence. The third, he'd remembered. Desirée—his soul made flesh—mercilessly, methodically hunting him. He'd realized she had bound him on his back like a sacrifice. With high-voltage cables.

He'd heaved with shock and rejection then. And the fourth minute had come.

It now stretched into infinity as enough electricity to power a factory razed through him, charring his pain receptors, coagulating his blood, bursting his cells, fusing his insides.

Suddenly, it was over and regeneration tore through him.

"Hope you're done thinking you can escape." Desirée. Coming forward, those eyes, the memory of which he'd thought would sustain him in his endless existence, turned to slits of fire, the voice he'd thought would echo inside him forever, an ugly scrape. "If not, there's plenty more juice where that came from. I'll black out the city to convince you."

His instincts had been dead right that first night. He *had* been on the trail of one of the energy-absorbing breed he'd been hunting. Her. Then the sight of her, her influence over him, had derailed him, blinded him, messed with his sanity.

He slumped, everything dissipating. There was nothing left. Not even rage at her for conning him so completely. Only a suffocating desolation remained.

The woman he worshipped didn't exist.

In her place was a monster who lived to lure victims into her trap, only to mutilate them to death so she could feed off them.

He didn't want to live with the knowledge.

"Kill me." Despair bled from him. "And a word of advice—find some other way to do it. You can black out the entire state and I'll still recover. Kill me now, while you have the chance. These bonds won't hold me long."

He wanted her to kill him. He didn't know if anything she did would be enough. He might even survive if she cut off his head, like one of the demon breeds whose genes made him up. But he wanted her to try to kill him until she succeeded. He needed it to be over, needed to see her mutilate him and revel in his agony. He needed to see the face of the monster he'd been hunting, to erase the face of the woman he'd given himself to, heart and soul.

"Oh, I will." Her coldness gouged more fault lines into his psyche. "But first, I want to see your real face."

"And first, I want to see you screw yourself, Desirée." He slashed back, wanting to smash through her icy demeanor, make her just *do* it. "*I* won't do it, no matter how much you beg. And if you don't kill me now, make no mistake, I *will* make you beg—"

The slap that landed on his face would have torn a mortal's head off. After the gamut of hurt she'd exposed him to, he barely felt it, but the act agonized him so much that his hybrid monster surfaced to roar its disillusion and heartache.

Desirée had known what he was since she'd seen him kill those four couples. And it had still been part unreal.

He made it real now, changed from the man she'd been willing to die for to the monster she'd found out he was.

It was only because she'd loved him beyond reason that she had discovered his secret. She'd been scared he wouldn't come to her, would disappear and she'd never find him again. She'd run back minutes after she'd left him at the club, prepared to do whatever it took to keep him in her life.

But she hadn't run to him the second he'd emerged. The look on his face, his vibe, had frozen her. They'd both been…scary.

Until that moment, she hadn't even known she could feel fear.

She hadn't been afraid of him for a second but, gripped by a terror she couldn't handle or rationalize, she'd followed him as if mesmerized.

And she'd seen it all. The man she loved, stalking those four couples, landing among them in a single, two-hundred-foot leap and proceeding to decapitate them in total efficiency and silence.

She'd fallen to her knees in shock, just as he had in that forgiveness-seeking ritual that had made it all more horrifyingly macabre.

She'd run, tears blinding her, until she found herself back home, heaving her guts out.

Then she'd felt him. Approaching. From the forest, as she'd stupidly instructed him to do. She'd decided to show him he'd picked the wrong victim this time.

But damn her, even after realizing what he was, she hadn't speared him through the heart. She'd been lucky the injury had incapacitated him long enough for her to capture him. When she shouldn't have captured him—she should have finished him.

She still couldn't finish him. Even now, as ever more hideous realizations twisted the knife that she felt was embedded in her chest.

He wasn't a vampire, since she'd seen him during the day. He wasn't a were-creature, since she had seen him during a full moon. And now that she'd seen his real face, she knew he didn't belong to any breed of demon, vamp or hybrid she'd ever seen. That meant one thing.

He was the unique monster that she and her fellow eradicators had been hunting. The one who'd made them put aside their crusade against all other monsters, his crimes atrocious enough to make finding and eradicating him their priority.

But why the charade of the past few months? A monster who hunted down the most defenseless humans and non-predatory supernaturals—from babies to the elderly to the disabled—mutilating them first for no apparent reason but pleasure, couldn't have become smitten with her, as he'd pretended.

She had only one explanation. He must have recognized what she was that first night. *His hunter.* One of the breed who were every monster's hereditary enemy. He must have been amused when she didn't recognize him for what he was. It must have been the ultimate thrill: manipulating her until she was so desperate for him she revealed where he could find her, *begged* him to take her. He was probably coming tonight to take her, all right. Take her life.

Destroyed, crazed with grief, she leaped onto the platform. He lay still, his fangs gritted, his whole body stiff, his face averted. She threw herself over him, straddling him, madness spiking as her senses surged and her insides clenched with need at feeling the power and perfection of him between her thighs. She *still* wanted to tear off his clothes and bury him inside her, all the way to her heart.

She clawed her fingers into the luxury of his hair, grabbed him by his silver temples and wrenched his head to face her, looked into the marrow-liquefying, all-black stare of the fiend that he was.

"Just for laughs," she said, seething. "What kind of torture and gruesome death did you have in store for me? I bet raping me wasn't part of the fun you had planned. Bet you didn't *screw* me all this time because you can't. And this is how you compensate, right? Boy, are you light-years more perverted than any monster I've had the pleasure of eradicating. I'll take far more satisfaction in taking you apart."

His laugh lashed out and hooked into her rawness like a barbed wire. "Me? A perverted monster? When you've been preying on defenseless creatures of every breed in such macabre ways as to make the most vicious predator look humane? You, with the face of an angel, a body that is your name incarnate and the soul of a lower fiend? The one who's been so cunning you fooled even me?"

She stared into his eyes as they changed from liquid obsidian to blinding white to bloodred. His words, the pain radiating from him, buffeted her.... What did it mean? Could he...?

*The bastard is trying to confuse you.*

And he was succeeding, even now...

She raised a hand to strike him with all the rage and agony that threatened to make her head explode if she held them back.

And she pitched forward like a pin to a magnet, ended up with her whole body welded to his.

Her mind took seconds to catch up, to realize what he'd done.

He'd thrown the switch, closed the circuit, caught her in the electrocuting current. Not with magic. She would have felt it.

Telekinesis. No vampire, demon or hybrid that she knew of had that power. He did.

She couldn't break free. He'd turned her weapon against her. And she'd been so stupid, so emotional, that she'd again opened herself wide to him. It was as if something deep within her wanted him to finish her rather than live with the knowledge that she'd been so wrong about him, that she'd lost so much. Too much.

And she was getting her subconscious wish. Her cells absorbed the electricity—at first in delight, boosting her power. But it wasn't long before horror set in as the stream of unrelenting energy started to feel like molten lead rippling under her skin, shooting along her nerves, corroding them. Her heart started to buzz emptily, pumping nothing as her blood began steaming in her arteries until she felt them ballooning, about to burst. Her very marrow felt like it was curdling, her brain moments from combusting. While he…

He'd told the truth. He was in a league of his own, far superior to any breed she'd ever encountered or even heard of.

She'd realized the extent of his recuperative powers when she'd found his wound almost healed in the minutes it had taken her to bring him here. And now she had to face it—this was what had made her electrocute him. Fool that she was, she wouldn't have done it if she'd feared she'd cause him irreversible damage.

As it was, electricity would only cause him pain and temporary incapacitation. She was the one who would char to a cinder. He'd walk out over her smoking corpse.

His scent filled her lungs even over the stench of her own burning flesh. She tried to make believe she was clinging to the man she loved, not locked in the death grip of her murderer.

Something told her that was it. The final moments. She struggled to raise her head, to look down into his eyes.

They were again the eyes of the man she loved.

Soul-deep agony and regret overwhelmed her.

*I loved you so* was the last thought that trembled in her mind before everything receded.

# Chapter 4

Shards of agony shredded the vacuum. Nausea seeped in through the jagged gashes like cold, viscous blood.

Was death supposed to feel this bad?

Suddenly everything heaved, bringing awareness crashing back on her.

This wasn't death. This was something she'd felt a hundred times before. Every time her system had been depleted or damaged, the energy absorption that ignited her powers recharged her or healed her injuries. The agony was a hundred times greater in magnitude now, as it equalized the energy overload, re-sequenced every fractured gene, reformed every congealed cell.

She was still alive. But how?

She'd been slipping away. In one more minute, the damage would have been beyond her regenerative powers. In a few more, she would have blown apart like some miniature star going supernova.

Suddenly, memory lodged in her brain like an ax.

Javed. He'd convulsed, broken the current's hold on her, thrown her off himself and sent her crashing to the ground.

Why had he convulsed? How? The current had locked their muscles into a continuous contraction, paralyzing them. There hadn't been a spike in power, or she would have convulsed, too. She hadn't. It had been only him. It should have been impossible for him to move, let alone that explosively.

Suspicion mushroomed. She lurched around, raw eyes seeking him. He was still arched off the platform, eyes and fangs clenched, a prisoner to the lethal flow. The flow that he could terminate. Or was it scrambling his brain so much he could no longer access his powers?

Horror at the doubts, at the burnt-flesh scent that filled the cellar, at the fear she might have been out too long and the damage would be beyond restoration, forced her up like a broken puppet.

But she couldn't cut the current. Her eye-hand coordination was shot. She tried to hit the switch, kept missing. She was weeping by the time her hand finally, *finally* smacked it.

She shook with the thud he made landing back on the platform, quaked with the reprieve as pain unclamped his body, breathed as air once more rattled into his lungs, leaned her head against the wall and let silent sobs rack her body.

Had he thrown her off himself to save her?

She stumbled toward him. She had to have answers.

He watched as she neared him, his bone-deep burns receding before her eyes. She was nearly a foot away when he growled, "Finish me, Desirée. Just do it, damn you. I want to kill myself for letting you go when *I* should have finished *you.* But if you laugh over how under your spell I still am, all bets are off."

He *had* chosen not to kill her. And…under her spell?

Could it be? He hadn't been entertaining himself with her, his next prey? Could she be wrong about it all?

But how could she be? She'd seen him kill those eight people....

She reached out to his face, as if she'd know the truth if she touched him, connected with him. And he roared.

She froze in shock as he rammed his head back, splintering the six-inch solid oak platform, simultaneously expanding his chest to snap the two-inch cables even as they gouged furrows into his flesh. Then, in a blur that she registered only with her accelerated senses, he slammed into her, a hurtling train of ferocity pinning her to the ground.

For a suspended time, he just lay over her, the heat of his blood singeing her chest through her charred clothes, before the flow stopped as his healing kicked in, his eyes human again now, silvery-hot probes boring into hers, bombarding her with too many emotions to process. Then he swooped down.

Instead of fighting, she went limp. And instead of crushing her, he buried his face in her neck, opened his mouth over her pulse before grazing up and down its long arch with his fangs.

"How are you still doing it?" Fury permeated every word that vibrated against her flesh as he nibbled and suckled her until she felt something vital within her overloading again, with the need to open her legs for him and beg him for everything. "How can I still want to take you, even knowing you'll want only to take my life while I lose myself inside you? Why do I think my life a fair price to pay for the pleasure of having you, if only once, when everything between us has been a lie? But lie or no lie, my feelings for you were so real, they ignited whatever was inside me into a soul. A soul that I compromised, maybe forfeited, by killing eight young vampires tonight."

She lurched under the avalanche of memories his words set off. Her breathing nearly stopped as they replayed in her mind. The nuances recorded by her eradicator's senses allowed her to bypass Javed at center stage in her recollections and focus on the background. On his victims. Victims who *hadn't* gushed blood under pressure when he'd slashed off their heads. She zoomed in on the silence—the *psychic* silence, a sure sign of inhuman presence. She hadn't felt their dying throes because they were already dead.

They *had* been vampires.

He nuzzled her harder, yanked her arms above her head, locked her hands in one of his. "I killed them because they saw you with me, because I heard them saying they'd find out who you are, would tell others of their kind about you…the innocent, vulnerable human I thought you to be. And now I know that you're something that gives them worse nightmares than I do. But you know what's pathetic? I don't care. That's how deep you have me in your power. So I take it back. Laugh, Desirée. Whatever you want to do, I'll let you do it. Just not yet." He unclamped his thighs from around hers, pushed between them, cupping her buttocks, tilting her for the thrust of his arousal. "I must have you first. Whatever your agenda, you want me, too. Let's just have this once. You can kill me afterward. I'll even help you."

She closed her eyes and melted into the grip that was rough only with the urgency of passion, feeling buried. Under the enormity of realizations, of the misunderstandings that had driven her to nearly kill the only man she could ever love.

She wanted to explain, weep, rewind time, take it all back, open herself and give all that she was.

He'd assume it was a maneuver because he had her overpowered.

She owed him conclusive proof. She tensed, averted her face.

"You don't want me?" He thought her tension was aversion. From the anguish in his voice, it seemed as if that hurt him even more than believing she wanted to kill him. He raised his head, and his pain hit her worse than the current had. "How did you fake your arousal, Desirée? How are you still lying to my senses now? I can *feel* you melting inside for me."

She choked on the confession that she was. She had to prove she wasn't at his mercy when she made it. She'd throw him off and—

He took the chance away. With the rumble of a mortally wounded lion he slid off her and got to his feet. Then, giving her his back, leaving himself open to the attack that he believed would come, he walked away.

She zoomed after him and rammed him into the wall, her chest to his back. He was almost twice her weight and had about ten inches on her five-foot-ten, but she'd been battling demons double his mass and size for half of her twenty-eight years. In seconds she had him in an inescapable hold.

She expected him to fight her off. He stood still instead. She applied more pressure, climbed his back higher, put her lips to his ear to urge him to give her a chance to prove her sincerity.

He shuddered in her hold, twisted his face around to hers, rubbed his open lips across hers in a heart-piercing gesture of longing and heartache before wrenching away. His touch and taste, the feel of him filling all her limbs, his upheaval—everything he was—made her press herself harder against him, her heart struggling to sever its tethers.

She poured all her need to heal the injuries she'd inflicted on him into her words. "I'm not who you think I am, Javed. I'm what's called an eradicator. We're human anomalies who can absorb the energies of nature, channel them into physical and sensory superpowers—regenerative, too. We're stronger than all supernatural breeds, as we need to be to eradicate them. You're probably the only creature on earth as strong as us."

Vitriol crackled from his depths. "Interesting. Very. And now that you've told me, you have to kill me? Oh, wait, you're going to kill me anyway. Get rid of the competition."

"No, Jav, no. This was all a horrible mistake. I'm just trying to show you we're evenly matched, that I'm not afraid you can overpower me, that the only reason I'm saying this is because I want to. Because it's the truth. Because I trust you."

His laugh was bitterness made audible. "Of course you do. I've swallowed your lies as you laughed your head off at my stupidity. I just offered to help you kill me in return for a—"

She pressed harder on his neck, making him groan, stopping the crudeness from exiting his lips. "I *trust* you, Javed. Until just hours ago, I trusted you with my life, and I trust you again now—"

He suddenly jolted so hard that he almost broke her grip.

She drew on reserves she hadn't known she had, clung to him as if to life. As she was.

She couldn't live if she lost him this way.

At last he stopped, stood so still and tense that she felt he'd turned into a stone statue. She wrapped herself around him harder, not in a wrestling grip anymore, but in a tight hug, desperate to make him give her a chance to explain.

He suddenly went lax in her frantic embrace.

*Yes.* He was going to listen to her.

Suddenly he pitched forward, rammed his head into the wall.

Half of it exploded outward into the adjoining underground chamber as if hit by a wrecking ball. The rest collapsed.

He followed.

# *Chapter 5*

The rubble of the three-hundred-year-old wall settled.

Desirée lay trembling over Javed's inert body, shock waves still expanding inside hers.

She'd heard his skull crack, felt him go limp as she went down with him, saw his blood pooling beneath his head inches from her eyes. She dry heaved over the metallic richness of its scent, felt its viscosity permeating her skin, curdling her soul.

He wasn't breathing. She wasn't either, waiting for him to heal. He didn't.

What if he couldn't? Smashing a wooden platform was one thing, ramming through a four-foot stone wall was another.

Dread constricted her insides, choked her. Screams rang in her mind. *Come back to me…please—*

Suddenly a sensation sank talons into her. It was as if she felt his life force being sucked back into his body.

She froze, every cell bristling for confirmation. "Javed?"

He didn't move. Didn't breathe. He only hissed, "Get off me."

She fell off him like a dead limpet, feeling boneless with relief. He dragged himself up and away, propped his back against a three-foot pillar, the remains of the wall.

She struggled up. "Javed, please, let me ex—"

He slammed down his fist on a boulder. It detonated as if a bomb had hit it. "Stop. We both know it doesn't matter if you're as strong as I am. You're not as invulnerable, and I can snap you in two if I want to. And you've figured out that you can't kill me. You've also realized that I won't retaliate now, so you're buying insurance for the future. You're afraid your spell will wear off and I'll end up hating you as much as I loved you, and then you'll meet with a far worse fate than that of the prey I simply terminate. But don't worry. My condition isn't temporary. Even though you're a brand of monster I never thought existed, I'll never be able to bring myself to harm you. Happy? Now *stop acting.*"

The darkness, the defeat in his voice almost broke her heart. "I beg you, Javed, just listen. It was all a *mistake.* I thought *you* were the monster. I came back to the club to beg you to stay in my life, was so scared you'd just disappear. And then I saw you leave, and you had that…look on your face. Now, I know you were in hunting mode. But then, it scared me so much, coming from the man I loved. I followed you and saw you kill those vamps—I didn't realize they weren't human. I was so shocked by your actions, by discovering *you* were not human. And when they didn't turn to ashes, that threw me, too. It all made me miss the evidence that should have been obvious to my senses—that you were killing the monsters I, too, live to eradicate."

The distrust in his gaze wavered. She swooped in on the chink in his rejection, scrambled to him on all fours, touched his face. He wrenched away. She followed, cupped it, begged him without words to let her know this side of him. When he finally looked at her, the pain and reproach still muddying his gaze had tears welling again in her eyes. She squeezed her lids shut, attempting to stop their escape. That just gave touch free rein.

Her palms filled with the essence of toughness, her fingers absorbed the pattern of uniqueness. She followed feel with sight, opened her eyes and feasted on every line and ridge and slash and hollow. Even through the distortion of blood and resolving wounds, this manifestation of him was…was…beyond words. And to her, as beautiful and already as beloved as his human face.

Her breath rushed out in a hot tremolo of wonder and yearning. "God…you're breathtaking."

His lips twitched, something far more heartbreaking than hurt or distrust flooding his eyes. Vulnerability. Hope. She'd injured him in the only place he could be wounded, as only she could. His emotions.

She threw herself at him, hugged him with a strength that had crushed demons. "I'm sorry… Oh, God, I'm so sorry, Javed. I jumped to all the wrong conclusions, not only because of what I saw, but because I've been hunting a monster that's neither vampire nor demon nor known hybrid, and you seemed to fit the bill perfectly. I thought you found out I was hunting you and decided to play me—"

He tore out of her arms. She lunged after him, cried out, "Please, believe me, don't pull away again. It's not self-preservation, I'll do *anything* to prove it isn't…"

He held up a hand, his expression a mask of watchfulness. "It's not that. Tell me about this monster. Why are you hunting it, and how do you know it's none of the breeds you mentioned?"

It took her a moment to adjust to this detour, to access the information to answer him. Then she did.

As he listened, his face shifted back to the one that had occupied her every thought since she'd first seen him. She could almost feel his thoughts streaking, processing what she'd told him. The richness of his psychic aura and her ability to detect it was one more thing that was unique about him, yet it had never made her suspect he wasn't human. She detected predators by the void they emanated.

Maybe she detected his aura and thoughts only because she loved him. Because he let her.

He inhaled. "Tell me more about your kind, those eradicators."

She surged forward again, hugged him. This time he let her. She pressed her face against the blood-crusted scar where she'd speared him, quaking with guilt and anxiety. "Do you…do you…?"

Hands that could mangle steel lifted her with heartbreaking gentleness. He took the hand that had replaced her face on his scar and buried his face in it. Then he exhaled, as if letting go of a burden that had been crushing him. "I believe you."

And the dam broke. She sobbed until she felt she'd shatter.

She sobbed harder when he cradled her, warded off her anguish, murmured things literally to die for.

When the impetus slowed down, he leaned back, still smoothing soothing hands over her hair and tear-swollen face. "You had reason to think the worst. Now stop tormenting yourself with what-ifs. You didn't kill me. It's over. Forget it. I have. Now tell me."

She nodded gratitude for his understanding, hope that he was at peace with it so fierce they were indistinguishable from pain.

"We don't have a definite history...." Her voice quaked out of control. She stopped, breathed firmness into it, went on. "Nothing that dates back more than one hundred and fifty years, anyway. But it's said we came into existence with the first predators, to keep the balance. Seems we didn't do a good job of it, for what must have been millennia. It's been only recently that we've started to cut a real swathe through their ranks."

He bent as if compelled, bit into her lower lip's tremor. "Why is that?"

She clung, but he only pulled back. She grudgingly answered. "Because the world wasn't always a big village. Eradicators could be born anywhere, and the odds of being found by our attendants— those said to be born in advance to nurture and train us—were slim. From the number of eradicators recorded throughout history compared to the numbers we've found recently, it seems many went undiscovered. We can only guess at the tormented lives they led, hiding their powers or abusing them or God only knows what else. In the last century and a half, the attendants finally got connected, found more eradicators, but they still had the wrong idea about how to make use of us. They never put us in touch, so we never became a force to be reckoned with. Then enter the Internet and the communications revolution. We've since found out exactly how many of us are there and struck out on our own. We've gotten networked and organized and we now search for budding eradicators and train them ourselves."

He stroked away a tear that still trembled from her chin. "So you've become as dangerous as I am to all predatory breeds."

"Yeah, we've become pretty much unstoppable in the last couple of years, and since we cut our ties to the attendants, untraceable, too, and…*hey!*" She sat up, clutched his arms, curiosity suddenly blazing. "Why are you so dangerous to them? What *are* you exactly? Tell me everything!"

"So you can strap me with explosives this time?"

"God, Javed, I swear I—" She stopped, stared at him.

He was teasing her. In that exhilarating, laughing-with-and-never-at-her way of his. And she did what she'd thought she'd never do again. She burst out laughing.

"I need to go that far to make you talk?" she spluttered.

His eyes grew heavy as he watched her, sensuality radiating from him, until laughter choked into a moan of need.

His thumb caressed the lips that now trembled for his touch, his possession. "Considering I offered to help you kill me when I thought you didn't love me, I bet a pout would make me do just about anything else."

She'd never pouted. She gave it a try. His lips replaced his thumb, crushed hers as he groaned against them. "Thinking you were human, I was coming to tell you part of the truth tonight, that I was *in*human, and leave it at that. But you want everything, and though I'm afraid that might still be too much for you, you'll insist and I can't refuse you. So save your pouts of mass destruction. I give in. I'll tell you."

Then he did. She listened in mounting wonder and awe. Almost intimidation. He was right. It was too much.

The man she loved wasn't only the strongest, most indestructible creature she'd ever seen or heard about, he'd lived dozens of her lifetimes. Might well live forever.

The web of implications tangled inside her. But there was one thing that remained the same. Her love for him.

Then a new realization hit her. Hard. The full picture.

He seemed to sense her epiphany. "You see it, too, don't you? The rhyme and reason behind the apparent madness."

She nodded, dazed. "It's all been our enemies' doing. We were crushing them like bugs between us, and they came up with a plan to pit us against each other instead."

He drew up to his knees, towered over her. "There's no other explanation. I'm a common enemy they all want to destroy even more than they want to destroy each other, and they hadn't been able to do it for a millennium. But when your team gained momentum and entered the equation so strongly, you gave them a weapon strong enough to do it for them. If used right."

She let out a whistling exhalation. "And boy, did they use it right. I just wonder how they committed all those murders in a way that pointed you to us and us to you."

"Now that I know they did, I have many theories. But what matters is that their plan almost succeeded. If I hadn't met you first, I would have eventually found one eradicator after another and would have eliminated you all with the same efficiency I do them."

She shuddered at another thought. "Or we might have ganged up on you and managed to kill you."

His laugh was grim. "It must have felt like poetic justice, manipulating us into getting rid of each other for them—or at least having one eliminate the other, leaving them only one threat to deal with."

She frowned. "One thing I don't get. We've developed mental barriers that make us invisible to the most potent psychics. That's why they haven't been able to find us to retaliate. Why did they think you'd be any better at finding us?"

As he considered her question, she fully believed that he was the bane of the predators' existence. He looked fall-to-your-knees daunting.

At last, he drawled, "With my tracking ability transcending any of theirs, they must have counted on my finding you. And as they rarely found me and always regretted it when they did, they must have counted on your tracking powers to locate me, gambled that I wouldn't feel your approach, since you're not part of my gene pool or anything I've tackled before. They pointed us in each other's direction and hoped we'd find one other. As we did. At least, I did. I found you."

She shook her head. "You didn't. Not the eradicator in me, or you would have found the others, too. You found *me.* As I found *you.* I felt your presence, but I couldn't have dreamed what it was. I thought my power was pointing me to my quarry. That night at that club, I entered figuring the monster would find it a great place to pick victims. Then I saw you and realized I'd been following your vibe, the man I'm destined to love. And tonight I could have killed you. If I'd forced myself to aim for the heart…"

Silver light flashed from his eyes. "You didn't miss?"

She stared at the beauty of the glimmers twinkling in the aftermath of that burst, hiccupped. "I don't miss."

He digested that for a long moment. When he spoke, his voice was thickened with emotion. "You wouldn't have killed me if you *had* aimed for my heart."

She assimilated that in turn, numbness spreading, twisting her tongue when she answered. "But I could have kept trying until I did. Or you could have killed me. We just love each other so much that we held back. But if this had happened earlier, before we were this involved, or if we'd lost control, we…we…"

She stopped, started shaking. A rumble rose from his depths.

They stared at each other, panting, as it all hit bottom.

He reached for her just as she hurled herself at him.

# Chapter 6

The leash on his inner beast snapped.

This was his woman. Nothing, starting with him, would ever harm her again. He was taking her, hiding her inside him.

She met his ferocity halfway, the same horror driving her, the same need to protect, to claim. She sank her teeth into his lips, thrust her tongue inside him, occupying him, draining him. He twisted his fingers in the silver-gold silk of her hair, imprisoning her for his invasion. She fought him for dominance until the stimulation of their mouths mating became distress.

When they tore apart, she stared back at him, body heaving, eyes storming through the spectrum of fire before slamming back into him, an impact that would have shattered the minds of most creatures.

He still held back. He'd never unleashed his full power other than to destroy. Feeling his reticence, she bit into his deltoid, broke his skin, her fingers sinking into his flanks as she crushed him to her. He growled the pain of his pleasure, tentatively raised her five. She raised him a hundred.

Something unyielding and bleak shattered inside him. Isolation. Loneliness. He was no longer alone.

It was true. Her strength and resilience rivaled his. Her unbridled power pulsed in his arms, dueled with his, almost equal. And the freedom of letting go, going all out with another, was unprecedented. Undreamed of.

When they'd met, it had eaten through him, craving her so much yet believing her a breakable human. He'd leashed his impulses until he'd bloodied them. He'd thought that, even if he ended up taking her, he'd give her pleasure but never attain true release himself. And all along she'd been suffering from the same misconception. Now this. Reward beyond measure.

"Bed… Desi…where's your bed?"

"No…here… I need you inside me…*now.*"

Her keening sent his beast howling. It wanted to mount her, invade her, defuse their overwhelming need here and now.

He held it back. She might be able to heal quickly, but with all the jagged edges and splinters of rock and wood around them he'd shred her to pieces by the time he pounded her to the first orgasm.

He threw her over his shoulder. She screeched her protest, sank her teeth into his shoulder blade. He almost stopped to take her against the nearest erect surface. He thundered out of her dungeon instead, seeking somewhere with yielding surfaces, pulverizing one door after another on his quest.

The moment he felt his feet sink into something thick

and soft—a rug—he hurled her down, knowing she'd relish his urgency, that she'd been born and built to take it, that it would fuel hers. As he flung himself at her, she sprang up, met his descent halfway, brought his momentum and passion crashing into hers.

Then she was all over him, tearing at his clothes, possessing his lips, sinking into him, all hunger and teeth and nails.

Response rocketed through him as he answered in kind, his fingers filling with tatters of the bloodred creation she'd worn to meet him tonight intent on overloading his reason. And how she had. Madness expanded now as she rewarded each rip with a fiercer cry, a more violent tug on his hair, a harder grind of her core into his erection, a more blatant offering of herself.

He rolled her beneath him only for her to reverse their positions. The struggle to get closer, take first, give more, raged, over and over, buffeting them in a frenzied tangle of straining flesh. He heard crashes, felt things splintering around them until the refuge of the rug-covered floor became as dangerous as her war-zone dungeon. Then an obstacle broke their momentum. He blinked, found them intertwined at the foot of a huge couch.

He exploded to his feet, hauled her up with him, thrust her back down. She bounced onto the couch, riding the movement, undulating her voluptuous body in carnal offering.

He'd feast on every inch later. Now…now…

He descended on top of her, crashed his lips onto hers, rumbling incoherencies, grasping at thighs that only wrenched wider and engulfed him, meeting his assault with hers. He didn't need to make sure she was ready. Her arousal scorched his senses, slashed away the man's skin and left only the beast in the grip of mating frenzy.

He tore inside her, swallowed her scream, let it rip inside him as her flesh yielded to his shaft, sucking him into an inferno of sensation. The carnality, the reality, the *meaning* of being inside her was too much to process.

He'd been waiting a millennium. Hadn't known he'd been waiting. For this. For them. For her. He'd lived endlessly, yet he hadn't lived at all. Not until her.

The one. Made to need him, to take him. All of him. He needed to cede his all to her, to pierce her essence and consume hers.

The need broke through his daze. He withdrew, his shaft gliding in the molten heat of her clinging folds, then pummeled back.

And doubt registered. Why had penetration taken such force? Why was her body a bow of tension? Her scream hadn't sounded of excess pleasure but of…pain? He'd hurt her?

"Javed…you're my first…my only." Her confession burned his ear, traveled up his nervous pathways, lodged into his brain with the force of a bullet. Her first. Her only.

The knowledge savaged him. Possessiveness seethed with exultation. His. In more ways than he'd thought. In every way.

He hadn't known. He should have. He'd never known a capacity for passion like hers, but it had felt inborn, untried.

Selfish, callous, *blind* beast. Instead of initiating her with every cherishing care, he'd hurt her. It didn't matter that she was built to take pain and heal any injury. What mattered was that he'd torn into her with a force that would have turned a vampire to ashes, had crushed her couch flat. Her core was throbbing around his invasion, her torn flesh weeping from the injury he'd inflicted, bathing his shaft in the red-hotness of her blood-mixed arousal, seeming to singe his flesh. And damn him, arousing him beyond insanity.

He tried to withdraw, give her respite, take himself the hell away before he rammed back into her. But her quaking legs held him prisoner. Then she pumped her hips up, impaling herself further on his erection. Sensation blanked out his mind.

He struggled not to thrust back, to groan, "I hurt you."

"Still are..." He heaved up in horror. She clenched him, inside and out, her eyes flaring bluish then crimson purple, as if fluctuating between pain and pleasure. "I needed you to, this first time, to brand me. That's why I didn't tell you, so you wouldn't go slow and gentle. All these months, I fantasized about how mind-blowing it would be. And that's when I had no idea you were my match. If I'd known you could do this to me, I would have forced you to take me ages ago."

"Desi...let me pleasure you some other way this time."

She thrashed her head, her chin-length hair a fan of light framing her flushed face. "No. I was made for you, built to take you. Hold nothing back, Javed, nothing..."

He gave in, rose between her splayed knees, cupped her hips in his hands, tilted her. "Then watch me take you, Desi. Watch."

She scrambled up to her elbows, eyes wild, swollen lips open on pants. He thrust halfway in. She bucked up to take more of him, her high cry harmonizing with his bass groan.

Madness riding him again, he drew out, thrust back, more this time, and she collapsed, breathing hot gusts of passion, opening wider for each thrust, an amalgam of agony and ecstasy slashing across her face and rippling through her body.

He bent, drank of her lips, infused her with his wonder. "Did you see how you capture me? How I invade you? How beautiful it is?"

She writhed beneath him, her hair a splash of sunlight in the dimness, her breath coming in gasps. "Yes, yes...I love it... I love everything you are, the feel of you, the idea of your flesh in mine... More, Javed...all..."

Her words, her need, rode him. And he rode her until her cries rang out again, shattering him with spikes of stimulation. She was a raging inferno beneath him, around him, more destructive than every threat he'd ever faced combined. She was the one thing that made him live, that could annihilate him, that could consume him.

Pleasure soared, the barrenness of his eternity of existence dissipating it its blaze, an accumulation of so much energy its release might be the one thing that could permanently damage them both.

He bellowed, forging deeper into her sheath, soaring higher on the scent and sounds of her intensifying pleasure. She augmented his force, drove her heels and shoulders into her support, crushed herself against him as if to merge their bodies, catapulting him into a frenzy. He pounded into her now, knowing that only his full power would unleash her pent-up needs, wring her magnificent body of every spark of pleasure it could yield.

The heat, the friction escalated until he sensed she couldn't take any more, needed release before she burst from the buildup.

He sank his girth inside her to the root. She lurched like a flailing marionette, shrieked. He adjusted his position, thrust again, the deepest plunge yet, and she bucked so hard, she lifted them both clear into the air before they crashed, plunging him even deeper inside her.

The convulsions that swept through her would have broken a mortal's spine. The gush of her pleasure around his thickness razed him, the force of her orgasm squeezing his shaft until he felt she'd engulf him whole. Her seizure triggered his own.

He detonated from his loins outward, unleashed himself into her. Surge after surge of scorching pleasure shot through his length and gushed deep into her as if trying to put out the flames before they consumed them.

His groans echoed her sobs as pleasure hit an almost agonizing plateau, left them straining against each other again, like they had in the closed circuit of destruction.

He could be right. They might not survive this.

He didn't mind.

# Chapter 7

Desirée had died. And gone to heaven.

Okay, so she hadn't died. But she'd gone to heaven anyway.

She was draped all over it. Her own six-foot-eight hunk of indestructible virility, of heaven. Javed.

His daunting size and power cushioned her, filled her. Where their bodies joined, he hadn't subsided, not a fraction. She'd bet he hadn't even while she'd been unconscious.

"So…along with super strength and speed—" she moaned into his chest "—you have super sexual prowess, too?"

His laugh rumbled beneath her ear. "Seems we both do and never knew it. I've been rock-hard ever since I first saw you. But it stands to reason. Sexual hunger is triggered in the mind. And no one but you has ever unlocked my mind's every door to release all my cravings."

She rose, looked down at him.

Everything. That was what he was.

She bent and opened her lips over the chiseled beauty of his chest, the tremors in her core gaining momentum.

Suddenly her gliding worship ended on a disfiguration among the perfection. Her breath fractured, her heart compressed.

He'd been lying there, head thrown back, eyes closed, letting her savor him. He moved when he felt her agitation, clasped her head with such tenderness, raised her face off his chest, his voice breaking over her, a bass sweep of comfort. "Don't."

"Your scar. It didn't disappear," she choked.

He looked down, his eyes flaring with surprise, before becoming neutral, careful. "It will."

"You don't have another mark on you anywhere. And I'm sure you've had your share of horrific injuries. Why is this one not healing completely? What if this means you didn't heal inside, too?"

"I did." His eyes flashed that silver light she could watch forever, his expression becoming wicked as he pushed deeper inside her. "Don't tell me you didn't notice how… in top condition I am."

Her muscles fluttered around him, massaging him in delight, her body pouring more molten welcome. She dug her fingers into his thighs, stopping him before he overpowered her reason. "You're not going to distract me. You know why you're not healing."

"I know only that I'm inside you, and I want to make you faint with pleasure again." He teased her with shallow, languid strokes.

She clenched her muscles around him, trying to stem the tide of mindlessness. "Do I have to pout?"

He exhaled. "Dammit. I knew I shouldn't have given

you that final weapon. All right, but I'm only theorizing here, since nothing like this—as you noticed from my body's pristine condition—has ever happened to me. I think I haven't healed completely because the injury was not just physical, but emotional, too."

She gasped, pain blossoming behind her eyes.

"Stop feeling guilty, Desi. It wasn't your fault. And those whose fault it is will pay a higher price than usual for the pain they caused you. I won't allow them to cause you one more second of grief." He surged beneath her, ramming the head of his erection against that trigger inside her. She went limp with the blow of sensation. "Not one more second."

She gave in, lurched up until she sat straddling him, then she slid down, her folds sucking him deeper, moaned, "You feel like fire, all the way inside me, stretching me to bursting..."

He eased back. "I'm too big, it was too rough. You're sore."

She crashed down on him, cried out. "You're too... everything, and I can't get enough of how sore you make me. I'm only sorry I heal so fast. You'll have to make me sore often. Do it again *now.*"

He surrendered to her demand, gave to her, invaded her to the hilt, his hands palming her breasts, kneading them, playing with her nipples until she felt they'd burst if he didn't...didn't...

He did, raised himself up, engulfed one nipple after the other, softly suckling and grazing their engorged sensitivity to the rhythm of his thrusts, pulling harder as his plunges grew rougher, faster. Too soon she started to ripple around him, to buck over him. He was everywhere, seemingly invading her to the heart, wrapping around her last nerve ending, burying her under layers of sensation.

When she could no longer get her lungs to work, he pressed her breasts together, buried his face between them, crooned against her flesh. "Come for me, Desi. Take your pleasure of me, drench me, finish me with your orgasm."

And she splintered, ecstasy pulsing from the deepest point inside her to radiate in one shock wave after another to the last surface cell on her skin, overloading her more than any energy ever had.

It broke his dam. He roared, let go, his seed jetting into her womb. The force, the sight and sound and knowledge of his release shot her into an even more powerful paroxysm.

It was a long time before ecstasy loosened its grip, let her melt against him, quaking with aftershocks. It was far longer before she could get her speech faculties to function.

She sighed in marrow-deep satiation. "So this is what they mean when they say someone almost died of pleasure."

His rumble revved deep in his chest beneath her ear. "It's an exaggeration in anybody else's case."

"Not in ours." She stretched in the luxury of his embrace, cracked open an eye, sighed again. "We trashed the place."

His eyes swept around, taking in the havoc. He grimaced. "I'll fix it. No, I'll buy you a new place. Somewhere a demon or a vampire won't feel right at home."

"But I want to keep the mayhem as is, a memorial to your making a woman out of me. As for moving, forget it. I don't stay here much anyway, with the way I'm always on the hunt or at Eradicators Central, but this place was my great-uncle's. He's the only family I knew, and I spent my early childhood here, so I'm never parting with it."

"You don't have to. But I'll buy you another place as your base, any place you want in the world." He rose on his elbow, turned her on her side, ran a hand heavy with possession and appreciation over her, everywhere he paused becoming an erogenous zone. "A place worthy of all this uniqueness and beauty."

She arched into his palm, giving him license to own. "Ooh, big spender. You never told me you were rich."

"You never asked. One more thing I love about you. But I'm a few levels beyond rich. You don't get to be a thousand without having your assets…multiply in value."

She gaped at him. "I can't even begin to guess how much thousand-year-old possessions are worth."

His smile grew crooked. "Net worth? A few dozen billion."

She collapsed on her back. "Ack!"

"Yeah, I've squandered a lot."

She poked him, then charged him, plastered herself all over him. "I won't hold your obscene wealth against you if you make love to me again. I'll even agree to use my bed this time."

He was on his feet and she was in his arms in one of those blurs. "We'll pulverize it."

She giggled, clung around his neck. "I'm counting on it."

They didn't pulverize her bed.

Javed proved he could make her faint with pleasure, over and over, without wrecking one more thing in her house. And the things he did to her, the ways he took her… She burned and throbbed just remembering his lips and tongue and teeth and fingers and every other part of his body exploiting every fiber of hers, arousing her to fever pitch before sending her hurtling into oblivion.

In twenty-eight hours he'd made up for twenty-eight years of celibacy. And then some.

Then he'd let her own him, all that magnificence, had even loved her in his demonic guise.

*That* pleasure they almost hadn't come back from.

She sat up in bed now, eating cheese and crackers, the last food in the house, watching him approach with the tea he'd gone to make her, prowling in his tattered pants like the ultimate predator he was, muscles rippling, painfully male and beautiful. And his face, all noble planes and harsh slashes and…grimness?

Her heart jumped into her throat.

She struggled up as he put the mug on her bedside table, sat beside her, reached out to smooth the hair off her face. His eyes said so much. She just knew she couldn't bear to hear any of it.

When he spoke, his voice held such melancholy that her tears surged again. "Desi, what I feel for you is way beyond anything I thought I could feel, beyond anything you feel for me…."

Was that it? She pitched forward, grabbed his face in her palms. "Don't you dare tell me how I feel. If you think because you lived longer, you can love more—"

He shook his head, the bleakness deepening. "It's not that. I have lived longer than you can imagine, but for me decades passed like weeks did to you. My existence revolved around the accumulation of knowledge and money and kills. Emotionally, I came alive only when I met you."

Relief rushed through her. "See? Even in that we're even."

He still shook his head. "There is so much you don't know. So much I have to explain so you'll understand. But no matter how we both feel, it won't change a thing. I still have to leave you."

She opened her mouth. Nothing came out. She dropped back against the pillows as if he'd severed her spine.

His gaze grew beseeching. "I told you I was coming to confess my nature last night before begging your forgiveness for leading you on when I can never give you what you need or deserve. I won't apologize for what happened. It was beyond both of us not to have this time together. But I can't let it go on. Even though you're not the frail human I feared you were, you're still human. A woman. And you'll come to want what I can never give you. A family, children. So before I do more damage, I have to disappear from your life."

Desperation burst out of her. "*No,* Javed. I can't... I *won't* let you leave me." He started to pull back and she wrapped herself around him. She had to convince him. Her life depended on it. "Javed, for God's sake, I'm an eradicator. I don't know of any of us who ever had children. It never crossed my mind to have any. As for a family, you're all the family I want. I have no idea what other sort there is. We had to leave our families as children to become eradicators. Stayed away from all humans for their protection, made no friends and formed no connections. After I left him when I was six, I barely stole visits to my great-uncle. I have only my fellow eradicators for company, and as you discovered, I never sought physical relief with any of them. We all forget day by day that we're human in any way. And you want to leave me so I can have a *normal human life?* When I don't know what that is and I don't want it anyway?"

She could feel him wavering. Just as she began to breathe, he unlocked her hands from around his neck, the regret in his eyes, the considerate power in his grip far worse than if he'd punched her. "That's what you think now. Desi. But you're still young, and five years from now, ten, twenty, you'll change your mind and I…"

*She was losing him.*

She exploded from the bed, stood on it glaring down on him. "And you don't have to worry about that, since I only have two years max to live."

# *Chapter 8*

Desirée stared down at Javed, frozen by the sight of his eyes turning solid black again.

He dragged her down to him, his heart-snatching eyes storming over her as if scanning her on a cellular level. "Are you sick?"

She shook her head, then just shook. "N-no…"

"You were being melodramatic? Advocating living in the moment as if we'll die tomorrow? Now I think of it, you must be like other superhuman breeds, with the potential to live far longer than humans, barring fatal injuries or incurable diseases."

And she had to confess. "Actually I'm a step below normal humans."

His grip tightened on her arms, crimson seeping into his eyes. "What the hell do you mean by that?"

"We all die young. I don't know of any eradicator who

lived past thirty. It's our powers. They burn too hot, consume us too fast. Or they desert us at crucial times, and our enemies finish us."

He stared at her, his face inanimate. Then his eyes became black holes, sucking light, energy, from everything…from her.

He squeezed them shut, launched himself to his feet, his hands shaking as they pressed against his head, as if to stop it from exploding.

"This is worse than anything I could have imagined."

The desolation in his voice made her stumble up after him, grab at him as if to stop him from vanishing. "So I have an expiration date. That's even more reason to live every second I have left as if it's the last."

He staggered away. "Have mercy, Desi. I thought the horror I'd live with was to watch you age until you crumbled and died. Now, instead of decades of watching over you as you live a full life, you want me to love you for a few months, stand by as your power consumes you, accumulate thousands of memories and hundreds of nights of love only to…to…"

He felt silent. And she saw them. His tears. A black, viscous trickle, flowing from his eyes, literally scorching his flesh.

They scorched her, too. With the realization of the depth of the injury she'd inflict on him if she clung to him.

He'd stay with her, if she did. And she, who'd long ago made peace with her timed existence, would wallow in his love for the rest of her finite life, then leave him to suffer torment for what might be an eternity.

She was the one who should beg his forgiveness for involving him with her when she had no life to offer him to share.

All she could do now was curtail the damage she'd caused him. She had to let him go.

She started to say the words that would set him free and end her world. "Javed, I—"

And the world around them detonated.

Javed stirred beneath the rubble.

An explosion. A rocket, launched through Desi's window.

He'd been blind with grief, his senses locked on Desirée and their turmoil. As hers had been. Their enemies hadn't just tracked them; they'd managed to sneak up on them.

He sensed them now. But they didn't matter. Only Desirée did.

After the last crashes faded, he heard her heartbeat. Fast but strong. He hurled off debris, rose just as she did, covered in pulverized stone.

"We let down our barriers. They found us." He nodded at her steady summation. The distraught woman was gone, the lethal warrior back in the driver's seat. "I'm sensing five breeds of demons and two of vampires." She raised her face, sniffed. "Can't be sure how many. Seventy. Maybe eighty."

"Ninety-four." His ability to identify his prey's nature and number was much keener than hers. He rummaged through the rubble where her decimated wardrobe was, threw her the first piece of clothes he pulled out. "Put this on and leave. I'll take care of this."

She jumped into the paint-covered coverall. "Only ninety-four, huh? Should we be insulted? And are you for real? What am I? The damsel in distress? I owe those bastards as much pain as you do. And it's my calling, eradicating them. To you, it's a hobby."

Before he could protest, their enemies poured in from

every side. From the demolished ceiling, walls, even the floor.

Without a word, Desi plastered her back to his.

And it started. It was as if they'd been fighting together all their lives, knowing what the other was thinking, what their next split-second move would be. He roared in vicious triumph as he used a pit demon's horns to decapitate vampires, as she ripped off a saw demon's serrated arm and hacked his allies with it.

They soon made a dent in their attackers' ranks. Beckoning to her, he had her following him through the hole in the floor to her cellar. They could end this without weapons, but if they reached her arsenal they'd raise the odds of ending it with no injuries on their side. On hers. He never wanted to test her regenerative powers again.

She threw him an ax and a sword, took two swords herself and again, back to back, they hacked and smashed and slaughtered, until he could feel the last seven monsters trying to retreat, and another four outside…

Outside? What were they…?

Before the suspicion became conviction, a rocket bombardment began, rocking the whole house.

Suddenly Desirée flew at him, kicking both feet into his midriff, sending him hurtling across the cellar through the wall he'd blasted through yesterday.

He crashed into the adjoining chamber's far side, helpless for the second it took Desirée to disappear under the collapsing ceiling.

"Desi!"

The butchered bellow ripped out of him as he tore through the wreckage.

The entire house had collapsed. On top of her. He wasn't

buried only because she'd kicked him into the one place that had no support structures to pulverize. She'd saved him.

And he ranted. "I don't need saving, you fool. I can't die. I don't matter. Only you do. Where are you? *Desi.*"

He found only their last seven enemies. He finished them off, couldn't give the four outside, or possible reinforcements any thought. He had to find her. Get her out. Whatever her injuries, her regenerative powers would take care of them. They had to.

He had to beg her forgiveness. Had to tell her he'd been a stupid, self-pitying ass. It didn't matter if he had only today with her. He would take anything he could have of her, welcome eternal torment as a small price for the privilege and the pleasure of having her at all.

One of the boulders that he heaved away weighed more than three tons.

She was beneath it. Mangled beyond recognition.

He crashed to his knees.

She opened her eyes. *Alive.* But not for long. He felt her energies struggling to seal the breaches, failing. She was dying.

With so many bones crushed, so much flesh mashed and no doubt many internal organs ruptured, any other creature would have been dead already. She hung on. Seemed determined to say goodbye.

Then she smiled. He wept, acid tears charring his eyes and soul.

"I...hope...this reincarnation deal...is real," she rasped. "If it is...I sure am...coming...for you...again...and again...."

He howled his agony. "I can't let you go. I *won't,* Desi."

He turned into the beast, fell on her, blindly going for her neck.

She lurched. She understood. With her last breath, she wheezed, "Kill me…if…I turn…evil."

He snapped his gaze up. "You won't," he pledged. "Evil isn't a curse or a nature, it's a choice."

The look in her eyes before they fluttered shut, maybe forever, was of disbelief. She'd lived in a black-and-white world. Didn't know how many grays there were.

But he'd never turned anyone, didn't know if he even could.

Maybe he could do even more. Give her his life.

He sank his fangs into her carotid, drained her ebbing blood and power. He quaked as her ruptured heart finally stopped trembling, as her body cooled. Then he punched through his own chest and pierced his heart.

He fell over her, chest to chest, letting his torn heart pour their combined blood into hers.

# *Chapter 9*

He'd failed.

He hadn't been able to give Desirée his life.

Back in her cellar, he'd lain on top of her, drained, useless, feeling the wildfire of healing reproducing his blood and reforming his tissues. His damn life force had clung to him.

Then he'd felt her tissues catching the fire.

He'd staggered up, pulseless, and watched her.

There'd been no transformation like he'd seen in other turnings, only healing spreading through her like an accelerated graphics effect. She'd looked and felt intact in less than five minutes. That beat even his record.

That had been five days ago. She still hadn't woken up.

He *couldn't* wake her.

He tried again, bent, kissed her half-open lips.

She clung to his lips, arched her breasts into his chest, pressed her knee into his groin. And still slept.

He'd stopped driving himself crazy about this three days after he'd brought her here, his nearest home. Her body had been destroyed and then reformed. It needed the recharging power of sleep.

He'd since moved on to making himself nuts, wondering what she'd be if she did wake up.

"I'm hungry."

The thick purr startled him. Afraid to hope, to believe his own ears, he bent to her again.

After a moment, her eyes opened. And they were red. Not the beautiful glowing crimson of her irises when they blazed, but his hybrid's solid bloodiness.

His heart thudded. "What do you want, love?"

"Blood." He started. "Yours. Anyone else's will do, too."

He gaped at her, his mind racing, alarm descending.

She lunged at him. He let her flatten him to the bed.

Then she was on top of him, raining bites and kisses and giggles all over him. Giggles…?

She raised her eyes, and they were…the incredible violet they usually were. And full of mischief.

"God, sorry, darling." She chuckled. "You were looking at me with that 'Uh-oh. This time she *is* a monster' look and I couldn't resist pulling your leg." He growled, flopped her onto her back, pinned her arms beside her head, his eyes devouring her in the wisp of a white satin negligee he'd dressed her in. Every ripe curve screamed with femininity and vitality. Her power, now so kindred to his, reached out and rubbed against his, entwined, nuzzled, opened wet, hot lips and suckled. Then she did the same, taking his tongue, feeding him hers as she dragged him between her legs, pressing herself into him, scorching him with her moist heat even through his thick denim jeans.

"But I *am* unbearably hungry. For you." She giggled again. "And for beef flambé. With flames still blazing. What a dilemma this must be for you, craving fire with one part of you and dreading it with others. Seems I now share your problems."

Jubilation had a taste. It tasted of her kiss, her hunger, her love. Desirée. She'd come back to him. Whole. His.

He gulped down all he could, of it and of her, until he felt drunk. "Then you have none. I enjoy all the quirks of all my genetic relations without sharing their frailties."

She broke away, raised her eyebrows. "Are you sure about that? *No* weaknesses?"

"None that I know of. It's why they called me Javed. It means eternal. Maybe my regenerative powers aren't infinite, but I've never found their limit, and I'm not putting it to the test. Especially not now. But I do have one fatal weakness. You."

He could almost feel the blast of her love, and mortification. He soothed her. "You're also my greatest strength." Her cry sent his heart thundering as she drew him into another soul-extracting kiss before he went on. "As for you, you're now more of a hybrid than I am. With my blood and your eradicator genes, there's no telling what kind of powers you now possess. But from your miraculous healing, it seems your regenerative powers now rival mine. And while I'm not sure if this makes you a true potential immortal like me, if you share even a measure of my longevity now I've sort of turned you, a year can now become a hundred. Maybe far more."

Her eyes grew wider as the import of his words hit her. Then her smile spread with wonder and delight. "So if I eat my veggies, exercise and avoid collapsing ancestral homes, I might get to spend two hundred years with you instead of two? I can live with that." She stormed up, switched their positions, rained hunger all over him. "And I intend to. Just let anyone, starting with you, try to stop me."

He spread himself for her to take of him what she would. "Me? When I would have taken two days, two *hours* with you? I'll do *anything* so you can have me." He hated to continue. But he had to. He stopped her sweet, suckling torture down his body, pulled her up. "But there's no telling what else besides our location our enemies saw in our minds while our barriers were down. I'm even afraid that now, with our senses being so open to each other, those barriers will never be what they were. We have to assume more secrets are now in their possession. And that means that you and the other eradicators are in jeopardy, that we've won only a battle in a war that's just beginning."

Her eyes darkened as he spoke, the plausibility of his words, the implication that everything was going to catapult to new, unimaginable levels, eclipsing the buoyancy of moments ago.

Then she took his face between her hands, kissed him hard before pulling back, her face solemn, her words ragged with the passion of a pledge. "I'm ready for anything, as long as I have you, be it war or the end of the world. Whatever it is, we'll stop it, together."

He looked up at her. Powerful, unequaled. But still so…young.

And he couldn't douse her fervor, couldn't prophesize the trials and losses that loomed, all of which might test even their bond. It wasn't right to burden her with the insight that his far longer existence had blighted him with. She had so long to live now, to learn at her own pace. He'd be there for her, buffering the disappointments, diluting the punches the fates would deal.

"You have me, Desi. You have my life, my all," he pledged to her. "I'm yours. Your lover, your ally, unquestioningly, forever."

And he knew. She was right about one thing. Even if they were entering a war that might end the world as they knew it, even if they couldn't stop it, or even win it, all that mattered was having her with him through it all.

He told her that as they drowned again in their intensifying passion, their deepening union.

Whatever the future holds, bring it on…

* * * * *

# CLAWS OF THE LYNX

*Linda O. Johnston*

To B.D., a heart-captivating feline,
and to her owner, my wonderful mother-in-law,
Evelyn Johnston, with thanks for everything—
including Fred!

***LINDA O. JOHNSTON'S***

first published fiction appeared in *Ellery Queen Mystery Magazine* and won a Robert L. Fish Memorial Award for "Best First Mystery Short Story of the Year." Now, several published short stories and many novels later, Linda is recognized for her outstanding work in the romance genre. She lives near Universal Studios, Hollywood, with her husband and two Cavalier King Charles spaniels.

Dear Reader,

I love writing about the Alpha Force! My very special ops unit of shape-shifters is composed of dedicated, hardworking and unusual members of the military. And since most of them are werewolves, the heroine of "Claws of the Lynx" is one of the most unusual of all.

I hope you enjoy reading about Lt. Nella Reyes and how she deals with her first solo Alpha Force mission…not to mention meeting up again with her lost love Alec Landerson. They'd once shared a sizzling romance that begs to be rekindled!

Please come visit me at my Web site, www.LindaOJohnston.com, and at my blog, www.KillerHobbies.blogspot.com. And watch for the next Alpha Force story!

Linda O. Johnston

# *Chapter 1*

This was it! Lt. Nella Reyes was about to receive orders for her first solo mission for Alpha Force, the covert military unit to which she was assigned. She leaned forward eagerly, her camouflage fatigues easing the discomfort of the wooden chair.

"This is an especially delicate situation," said the unit's commanding officer, General Greg Yarrow. Gray-haired and especially impressive in his dress uniform, he had called Nella and told her to appear this morning at nine hundred hours at his office in the Pentagon.

The room was ordinary compared with the general's office at Fort Lukman on Maryland's Eastern Shore, where Alpha Force was headquartered. There, he had a whole collection of first edition books on wall shelves behind his mahogany desk. Here, his desk was worn and well used, and the only decoration in the office was the American flag.

"I can handle it, sir," Nella said confidently. The general

had selected her for this assignment. She would do it, whatever it was. "Just give me the particulars."

General Yarrow's smile bisected his long face and lifted the wrinkles at the corners of his eyes and mouth. "I'm sure you can," he agreed, then grew somber. "But the assignment's not without danger, including the potential for the worst kind of exposure. You're a medical doctor with plenty of important things to do for Alpha Force. I'll understand if you want to opt out once you hear what it is."

"That won't happen."

He studied her for a long moment with the piercing stare that could make the most self-assured officer wilt. Nella didn't flinch, although she felt like it. She tried to maintain a confident expression on her face, ignoring the urge to touch her hair, make certain that no strand had escaped the tight bun at the back of her head.

"Okay, then." The general leaned back in his chair. "Here's the brief explanation. A journalist, Sherman Jonash, has stolen a computer thumb drive from Congressman Crandall Crowther. It contains highly sensitive information about Alpha Force. Fortunately it's password protected, and Jonash is unlikely to have been able to get into it. It also has a GPS chip inside, so we know where it is. We need someone with your special abilities to sneak in and get it back. Fast."

Nella translated silently. She knew who Sherman Jonash was. Who didn't? He was a sleazy tabloid type who loved to create controversy in the reports he gave on network TV news.

The media giant he worked for, Omnibus International Communications, had been sued more than once for shenanigans Jonash had allegedly pulled. She didn't know the results of the lawsuits, though. OIC had settled out of court, and one of the conditions had supposedly been absolute confidentiality.

But all that was irrelevant now. What was important was that, apparently, wherever the thumb drive was now hidden, a normal person couldn't just slip in and retrieve it. But Nella could. Stealthily, in the dead of night. Scaling walls if necessary. Hidden by who and what she was.

"Yes, sir," she said.

A knock sounded on the office door. "Come in," the general called, then turned back to Nella. "Glad you agree, since here's the congressman now. Oh, and instead of one of our usual Alpha Force handlers for backup, you'll be assisted by the congressman's chief aide. He's particularly aware of the location and details about the building, and he knows the sensitivity of the mission."

Even a solo operative of Alpha Force always had backup, but Nella had never heard of it being someone outside the unit. Yet she was used to following orders, and she had confidence in the general.

As two men entered the office, she turned—and froze.

She recognized them both. Congressman Crandall Crowther was in the news all the time. He was the head of the House of Representatives' Armed Services Committee, known for his outspoken position on keeping things in the military solid and efficient—with funding of even the most covert ops under strict oversight of appropriate government personnel with highest security clearance. Despite that, he secretly supported Alpha Force and everything it stood for. That meant no official oversight, since government scrutiny would be contradictory to its very special mission.

His grip was firm as he greeted Nella after the general's

introduction. She wasn't sure what she said in response as she tried to keep her eyes politely on the congressman.

And then she attempted to be cordial and unemotional as she was introduced to the congressman's aide. The man who was assigned to be *her* aide as she performed her mission.

The man she had known and loved in college, with whom she had engaged in the hottest and most unforgettable sex ever. She had even dreamed of sharing a future with him.

Until he had seen who she really was and couldn't handle it.

"Hello, Alec," she said.

Good thing Alec Landerson had taught himself long ago to control his emotions—at least outwardly. It was the only thing good that had come from years of hell as a kid.

There'd been that lapse when he had first left home and been on his own at college, of course. That was when he had met Nella Reyes. His drinking and carousing had felt like a welcome relief from life with his demanding abusive father. But it had blown any chance of a future with the woman he now faced for the first time in nine years.

Losing her had hardened him. Changed how he directed his life. Made certain *he* was always in control, even as he chose to follow instructions…his way.

"Hi, Nella." He approached casually and shook her hand as if this was the first time they had met.

He almost grinned at the wryness in her memorable golden eyes. He still recalled, in his rare vulnerable moments, how they had heated in passion when they had kissed and touched and…

Hell, this wasn't the time to think about that.

But she remained one good-looking woman, even in that sexless light green camouflage uniform and with her soft brown hair pulled back from her face. Her perfect features were a little older but youthful, free of makeup except for the pink shimmer on those still-kissable full lips.

"You two know each other?" Crandall asked. Alec's boss, the congressman, was nothing if not observant.

"Back in college." Nella shrugged slender shoulders. "We didn't know each other well. Different majors. Different interests. Good to see you again, Alec."

Half of that was a lie. They'd known each other very well…for a short time. Different majors? Yeah. Different interests, too. But Alec was sure, from the studiedly indifferent expression she assumed, that it was anything but good to see him again.

"Have a seat." General Yarrow pointed to chairs across from his desk. The guy's face looked as if he'd been around for a while. He sat, too, and looked at Crandall. "Have you explained to Alec what's going on?"

"Part of it." His boss looked toward him, eyebrows raised above narrow glasses. U.S. Congressman Crandall Crowther was a good guy, one who took his responsibilities as a representative of his Wisconsin constituency, and his country, very seriously. But Crandall was also all about appearances. Of course. He was a politician.

Alec had worked for Crandall for six years now, right out of law school and passing the bar. Respected him. Liked him. Was trusted by him. Crandall assigned him all the jobs he didn't want to even describe to other aides. Ones where the person executing the orders could soil his hands. Ones that could get the asses of both the congressman and his aide kicked out of the House and into prison if things went wrong.

Some job for a lawyer.

Alec loved it. Excelled at it.

He had gotten to know, from experience, when Crandall

kept something to himself. As he'd been doing ever since telling Alec of a special secret assignment that would be a huge favor to Crandall, and to the entire country.

That could mean he was really in trouble if Alec screwed up.

Something was wrong, and Alec was about to learn what it was.

"All I know—" Alec looked at the general while feeling Nella's and Crandall's gazes on him "—is that something sensitive was stolen, and I'm to help get it back."

"Exactly." The general's smile crinkled his face even more.

"Crandall, explain to Alec and Lt. Reyes what it is. I've given Nella some background, but you give the rest. Then I'll tell them our plan for them to recover it."

Sitting in the closest chair to the window, Nella couldn't help cringing inside. Nor could she resist watching Alec's face as the congressman, who sat between them, began to speak.

Alec hadn't believed his own eyes before. Would he believe his boss? As if he'd have a choice.

Would he blame that on her? And why, after all this time, should she care?

"I'm very glad to meet you, Nella," the congressman said. "And I'm especially pleased about your unusual skills. You can help us all out of a very touchy situation."

"I'll try, sir."

"I also want to tell you how proud I am about the progress Alpha Force has made since its inception, Greg," the congressman said. The two older men, who obviously knew each other well, engaged in conversation. Nella listened without concentrating—her mind, and gaze, on Alec.

The years had only increased the strong masculine appearance of the man who'd once stolen her heart. His features were angular, his piercing brown eyes unreadable beneath straight heavy brows. He wore his deep-brown hair a lot longer than the military types she worked with.

Under his suit jacket, the breadth of his shoulders was apparent. She wondered if he was as buff as he'd been back when.

*Attention, soldier.* She made herself tune in again to Congressman Crowther. The man was shorter than his imposing presence in the media suggested. He wore a button-down white shirt that emphasized the darkest shades in his salt-and-pepper hair, and a striped tie, but no jacket.

"As you know," he was saying to General Yarrow, "I've been attempting to obtain additional funding for your *pet* project—ha, ha—Alpha Force."

That brought a brief smile to the general's face, but a look of puzzlement to Alec's. Obviously he hadn't heard about Alpha Force. And wouldn't have believed it, anyway, considering how he'd acted with her so long ago.

"For those with the highest clearance, I'd loaded a lot of information I'd collected about Alpha onto a memory stick with lots of capacity. Didn't want to leave it on the computer at my office, since even with all our security, I was concerned about hackers. And here that fool tabloid reporter Sherman Jonash. Ah, yes, I can tell from your expression, Nella, that you know who he is." His grin was wry. "I've got some bills up for consideration for appropriating funds to the military, including Alpha Force. Sometimes it spurs other representatives to act if the media start pushing, so I agreed to let him interview me. It was the off-the-wall stuff I anticipated, and I handled it fine. Only…well, he'd come to my office. I didn't realize until after he'd left that the thumb drive wasn't where I'd put it, in a drawer under my computer keyboard. I'd been called out for a quick question by an aide—a minute, two tops. Most other stuff the bastard could have grabbed would have been harmless, but… Anyway, he could expose the existence of Alpha Force if he finds a way to get through the passwords and other safeguards on that stick. Bad for you, and bad for me, too, since in public I support strict supervision over military forces and operations, even covert ops. And we all know that's not how Alpha Force works. We need that memory stick back, Nella. That's where you come in. And because this is so sensitive for me, I want my most trusted aide, Alec, to work with you. You okay with that?"

All eyes in the room were suddenly on her. She inhaled slowly. *Was* she okay with it?

She knew she could do the job, but all regular Alpha Force members were to fulfill their missions only with someone else watching their backs.

Congressman Crowther trusted Alec. General Yarrow was going along with it.

She stood and approached Alec. "I'm fine with it," she said, "if Alec is. We did know each other years ago, General, Congressman. Our brief acquaintance did not end well." She looked down. Alec's gaze was emotionless—except for his eyes. They shot fire at her, both anger and…well, she could be imagining it, but a hint of the old attraction seemed to lurk there, too.

She would turn it off immediately with her next words. "I can handle your assisting me, Alec, if you can. I gather that the congressman hasn't confided in you yet the nature of Alpha Force."

"Doesn't matter." He rose. His turn to look down on her. He apparently still needed to feel in charge. Well, if they worked together now, she'd teach him that wasn't always possible. "I'm in."

"Fine," she said. "Then you can accept that Alpha Force is a covert Special Forces military unit primarily comprising shape-shifters. And that what you saw in the woods all those years ago was true, and not a result of your being drunk. I do, in fact, shift into a lynx, Alec." She turned away from him. "And, Congressman, I accept your assignment. I can enter any premises while in lynx form and steal back your memory stick."

# *Chapter 2*

"So I could have believed my eyes that night?" Alec's tone was as neutral as his expression had remained over the past hour. If not for their previous relationship, Nella might have thought he accepted everything without question.

Might have figured that bringing him here, to the hotel room she had booked while on this mission, was a neutral thing, too. She'd needed to come here to pick up items necessary for her part in their operation. He was supposed to accompany her as her backup. They would go after the thumb drive that night.

So here they were. Sitting momentarily on the uncomfortable sofa in a generic hotel room that smelled of cleaning solution. Pretending to be strangers.

Well, hell, they *were* strangers now. Sure, she used to know him well, or so she'd believed. Now she didn't know him at all…and that brought back all kinds of old hurt.

Even as the king-size bed across the room brought back memories of another kind…

"*Could* have believed your eyes?" she responded as offhandedly as she could. "Sure. *Would* have? Well, I knew you wouldn't. And didn't. So that was that."

"So *that* became your reason to dump me."

Nella closed her eyes briefly, then opened them to glare into Alec's indifferent brown ones. Lord, how she wanted to goad him. Make him drop his ironclad control. Bring back the best of their hot memories.

Grab him, tear off the rest of his clothes—he had already removed his jacket and tie—and make love with him for the rest of the night, instead of carrying out their mission.

*As if.*

"I didn't dump you," she said with a shrug of one shoulder. "Not really." She picked up the large leather bag from the floor beside her, unzipped it and pulled out a couple of items, including the bottle of very special Alpha Force elixir that she had brought from Fort Lukman. "You made a huge fuss out there in the woods, then ran off." Not that she'd dared run after him, not when her change had already occurred. "Next day when we got together, you tried to pretend nothing had happened, only you looked at me like some kind of freak. Which, to you, I was. You rationalized it all. You'd hallucinated after getting drunk—again. After promising you'd stop. *Really* drank too much that time, you kept saying. At least I felt relatively sure you wouldn't give me away. Not when you didn't believe it yourself. Even so, I couldn't live with your attitude and figured you couldn't accept the truth. So that was that."

A pat description of the end of a relationship that Nella had thought, for a little while, would go on forever. She had imagined she would find a way to bring up the subject of shape-shifters in a straightforward manner, get Alec to accept the possibility and then let him in on what she was.

Instead, she had kept it to herself.

"That *wasn't* that." The words were spoken so low that Nella almost thought she imagined them. She turned to look at him.

Ah, finally. He was no longer in complete control. He glared at her with fury. And something else. Something that turned her to hot flowing lava everywhere inside.

He wanted her. Still. And did she want him? Hell, yes. But that couldn't be. Not with what had passed between them.

"If you'd bothered to talk to me after that," he said, his tone ominously intense, "you'd have found out how angry I was with myself. Yeah, I'd been drinking. Again." He raised one large hand as if to stave off whatever she was about to say. His eyes glinted, and his handsome features seemed to turn even sharper with anger. "You knew I was always drinking then. It was college. My first time away from hell—I mean, home."

She knew the slip was intentional. That had been one of the things that had drawn her to him in the first place. Admiration. And caring. Because he had grown up in such a hellish household as a child and had risen beyond it.

"But, yeah, I'd also promised you I'd stop. And meant it. But that night I slipped. Know why?"

She sat utterly still, the memories of that night washing over her. In premed she had majored in wildlife ecology, an unusual choice, and it had been such a great excuse to tell him each month that she had to go on a camping trip to observe a nocturnal bird that only appeared during the full moon.

"To see the Wisconsin lunar owl?" That was the type of

bird she had claimed to be watching—very rare. So rare as to be nearly extinct.

So rare as to be nonexistent.

She looked away from those piercing eyes again, pretending to concentrate on the bag on her lap.

"I was majoring in poli-sci before law school," he said. "Didn't give a damn about birds, even pretend ones." She looked up in surprise. "Yeah, I knew it was a ruse. I'd done my homework, knew that kind of owl existed only in your imagination. Or something. I suspected you had a guy on the side you slept with every month. Worked myself up to punch him out and dump you that night. That was why I was drunk. Real drunk. Then when I caught up with you, saw you look up at the full moon and turn into a cat, I figured I was having the d.t.'s." He stood, fists clenched at his sides as if he again considered punching someone. He closed his eyes, apparently trying to get control. When he opened them again he said, "Since then, I haven't had another drink. Oh, a beer now and then, but only on special occasions. I remain in control. Period. But you…you avoided me later when I tried to get the truth. Apologize. Whatever. You stopped talking to me for good."

Tears rose into Nella's eyes, and she kept her face averted. "I… My family… It's important that what we are stays secret, especially then, when we weren't in contact with others like us. I was so afraid you'd tell other people, that word would get out. It was so much easier just to be angry. To agree you were made crazy by the alcohol and hallucinated. Then not to take the chance you'd see me change again. Especially when you made it clear you despised anything you couldn't understand."

"But it turns out I wasn't hallucinating." He grimaced, obviously not fully accepting it even now. "Hell, I'd no idea woo-woo stuff like werewolves and shape-shifting lynxes could exist. And now I learn that my boss, a guy I really respect, has been secretly making sure that funds are appropriated for your classified military group where everyone supposedly shape-shifts." He shook his head as if trying to clear it.

She rose. One way or another, she had to make him understand. Of course Congressman Crowther and General Yarrow had pledged Alec to secrecy—and trusted him to comply. He had top-secret security clearance, and this was absolutely confidential.

Plus, they had discussed Alec's qualifications before leaving the general's office. Sort of. Without revealing any details. But Nella had understood that nothing would stop Alec from doing his assignment for the congressman. *Nothing.*

And she? Well, she certainly hoped he could be trusted. And she needed to do all she could to encourage it.

"Not everyone in Alpha Force shape-shifts," she said softly. "Those who don't are animal trainers and other backup who help us in exercises and in the field. Each of us has the kind of animal we shift into as a pet, to help with our cover. We're a last resort, able to sneak into situations that military troops, with their kind of strength, can't handle."

For the first time, he smiled. She loved that smile. It lit up his whole face, reminding her of the way he used to smile at her. And his eyes softened. As if he gave a damn about her once more. Still.

Which nearly made her melt—even if she was reading too much into his expression.

"I can see you with a pet cat," he said softly. "Right from the first, without knowing or even imagining that you were...well, kind of feline yourself, I thought of you as resembling a cat, in the best of ways. Soft and sleek and self-contained, yet lovely. Aloof when you wanted to be, but a sex kitten in bed. With those observant, teasing eyes. Your hair was—is—the sexiest mane I'd ever seen. And…"

Nella wasn't sure which of them moved first. More likely it was simultaneous. But quite suddenly she found herself in Alec's strong embrace, held tightly against his chest. Oh, yes, it was still firm. Buff. Sexy as hell, or so it seemed through his clothes. She wanted to pull his shirt off.

But before she could act, his mouth was on hers, kissing her, familiarly yet differently. Hotter. Even sexier than ever, if that was possible. His tongue slipped into her mouth, exploring. Tasting. And she sparred back with her own.

"Nella," he whispered raggedly against her. "I've never forgotten you." His hands ranged down her body to grip her buttocks. Hold her even closer.

As she pressed into him she felt the evidence that he was as aroused as she was. She gasped his name.

She tore at his clothes, not like a kitten or even a lynx, but a lioness readying her prey to eat. At the same time, he undressed her, fast, as if he couldn't wait, either, to bare what was beneath.

In no time they wound up on that bed Nella had tried so hard to ignore. She indulged herself and stared at Alec's naked body. It was harder, tougher than when he had been a youthful college student. Why was this lawyer, political aide, so well toned? So gorgeous? So sexy?

She didn't have more time to study him. Not when his lips regained hers, his tongue sliding into her mouth and teasing hers with thrusts and parries as his body rolled on top of hers, also taunting. His hands were between them, cupping her breasts, thumbing her nipples, then lower, lower, until his fingers dipped into her wetness. "Alec," she moaned, even as she, too, let her hands explore him.

For barely a moment he moved away, only to return with a condom package in his hand. Good move. She ripped it from him, tore it open, then tormented him by insisting on unfurling it around his large, enticing erection. Having so little experience, she moved slowly, carefully, smiling as he groaned.

And then he was inside her, thrusting. This time she screamed his name while meeting his every stroke. Faster. Harder—and then over the top into ecstasy, even as he, too, climaxed.

## *Chapter 3*

As he donned his clothes, Alec couldn't help watching while Nella, standing at the far side of the bed, did the same. Her pale body was slender, sleek and sexy as hell as she pulled on jeans and buttoned on a black shirt. No bra to cover those tempting breasts…

"Here, make yourself useful," she said. Her camouflage uniform was slung over a chair. She yanked the top sheet off the bed from beneath the coverlet. "Fold this up. We need to take it along."

He was curious but didn't ask why. Instead, he did as she requested. She joined him in a minute, and together they finished folding.

Her gaze met his as she took possession of the sheet. For a moment she looked vulnerable. He wanted to pull her back into his arms. But then her golden eyes turned steely. "I guess we needed to get that out of our system before we could work together." Her tone sounded indifferent, and she turned away and crammed the sheet into the larger of the two bags she'd said they needed to take along.

What the hell was she talking about? The fact they'd had sex? "I'd say it's anything but out of our system," he contradicted irritably. "If anything, it's just whetted my appetite for more."

"Get over it," she said. "You're about to lose interest real fast."

Sitting in Alec's high-end sedan as he drove to their destination, Nella didn't feel even an iota of the nonchalance she showed. But glibness hid her sense of longing for what could never be. Sure, they'd just made love—again, after all these years—and it was even more phenomenal than back then.

But his interest in her as a person, let alone a sexual partner, was about to evaporate.

To accomplish their goal, she was about to shift. She knew how he reacted to that. Knew that, even with his boss's assertions, he couldn't quite accept it.

Well, he would. Soon.

And what if something went wrong? She could hardly inform him that she was about to drink a shape-shifting elixir that was an earlier formulation than the one currently approved for use by Alpha Force. The newer formulation had made her ill recently, when combined with her human female hormones at the wrong time of the month. That wouldn't be a factor today, but even so, she didn't consider the later formulation the best for her. The earlier version, while imperfect, was preferable for now.

The elixir gave Alpha Force members the ability to shift

at will. Otherwise, they would only change during the full moon, with no control over it—the way it had been when she was in school. The elixir also enhanced their ability to retain human awareness while changed.

"Tell me anything else you know about the location of the thumb drive," she said, mostly to make conversation.

"You've seen the best information I could get. We have a general fix on Jonash's office, thanks to the GPS chip. But its layout and furnishings…well, that you'll have to play by ear."

Before leaving the hotel room, Alec had booted up his laptop computer and shown her their destination—the headquarters of Jonash's employer, Omnibus International Communications. Alec had scoped it out as soon as the congressman discovered that the thumb drive was missing, and they'd tracked its location. He had obviously leaped in, taking on his mission even before realizing what it really was about, something Nella had seen in him before. And admired.

Because the target building was a historic landmark built in the late nineteenth century, it was featured online on sites devoted to Washington, D.C., architecture. Plus, there were other Internet resources such as Google Earth that allowed people to look at any location from cameras on satellites and even zoom in on structures from multiple angles.

Fortunately it looked like the kind of building Nella should be able to access with ease. Only a few stories high, it had architectural details that made it a lot easier than a sleek modern structure for her to get into. And Alec had already scoped it out in person, too, and seen that windows were often left open on the upper floors. Maybe the old building's air-conditioning system needed an upgrade. All the better for her to fulfill her mission.

"Then tell me everything else you know about Jonash and OIC," she said.

Alec glanced at her with another unreadable expression, which changed to irritation. Even so, he complied. He talked about Omnibus, telling Nella mostly things she already knew but that showed he had done his homework here, too—left nothing to chance. For example, OIC, one of the world's largest media conglomerates, had a mega-structure that included everything from cable-television networks to tabloid magazines and newspapers.

Nella shuddered to think what would happen if Alpha Force was revealed in any of them, let alone in all of them. It could no longer function as the ultimate covert military unit.

That couldn't happen.

They arrived at the OIC headquarters building quickly. Nella couldn't help feeling nervous. She shook it off. She would succeed.

She had become a medical doctor because she had wanted to learn everything about physiology and the scientific possibilities surrounding beings like her.

She'd joined the very specialized Alpha Force to associate with other shape-shifters and to use her special talents for the good of her country. And of course, to obtain the benefits of its wonderful elixir and participate in studies to improve it.

She might never have another assignment as critical—especially if she failed now.

"It's your game." Alec's growl suggested he wasn't pleased with that idea. "Where would you like me to park?"

"I saw an alley on the east side when we looked at the layout on the computer, between our target and the office building next door. See if you can pull in there—but watch out for security cameras."

Fortunately they saw none. The alley was remote and dark and seemed perfect to Nella, especially since it had an area for trash containers beneath an overhang that was currently empty, a good shelter for her to work in. "Let me out here," she said. "Then go find somewhere to wait."

"No way." He glared at her, then pulled the car into the shadows beneath the overhang. "It wasn't my goal to become your assistant, but since that's my job now, I'll stay with you as long as possible. Watch your back. You got any problem with that?"

She did…and she didn't. "Have it your way," she said with an indifference she didn't feel. She grabbed her two bags from the backseat of the car, then got out.

At the front of the car, she pulled the vial of liquid crucial to her operation out of the bigger bag, followed by the other important piece of equipment: the battery-operated light that, when turned on, was close enough to moonlight to allow her to change.

Without another word to Alec, she set up the light right in front of the car, turned it on and, bracing herself for all that was to come, she drank the elixir.

Alec stood between his car and the building, his back against the wall in the darkest gloom of the alley. Watching. Waiting. Preparing himself to scoff at how gullible he'd been to think he was going to see some woo-woo transformation right in front of his eyes.

The same transformation he had seen all those years ago and hadn't believed because he was drunk—and didn't want to believe.

Well, he was cold sober now. And he still didn't want to believe…did he?

The light Nella turned on was focused into a small conic

area, but very bright. She had unscrewed the lid from a glass jar and drunk the contents. And then…

She glanced at him as she yanked the sheet they had folded out of the larger of the bags she had brought along, shook it open and held it up as if planning to hide behind it. But then, glaring at him defiantly, she instead shoved it back into the bag. And started peeling off her clothes.

His body reacted as he stared at her lovely form once more, quickly nude. He reacted, subduing an urge to grab her. Make love to her again.

But he realized what she was doing: getting ready to morph into a lynx.

Wasn't she? Was it real? Did he want it to be real?

Hell, yes. It would mean that he hadn't been crazy or hallucinating then. That his boss, Congressman Crowther, was a crafty SOB who spouted platitudes about the transparency and openness of the U.S. military to the government employees with sufficient security clearances to supervise its ops, while ensuring that it had the finances to use the most bizarre and potentially useful kinds of really covert resources imaginable. Or unimaginable.

And that he, Alec, had made love with one of the world's most unique women.

That should bother him, shouldn't it?

Hell…

He tensed. Nella's pale body shivered, even as she hunched over. Grew smaller. Smaller?

She had freed her long, light brown hair from its knot behind her head. It appeared to grow shorter—even as fur of the same color appeared on her shrinking body.

In moments Nella was no longer there. In her place stood a feline creature, with dark tufts of fur on its—her—pointed ears. She stood still for an instant as if orienting herself to her surroundings, then turned and ducked so that the strap of the smaller bag Nella had brought draped over her head.

Then she turned and stared straight at Alec with intense golden eyes. Nella's intense golden eyes, clearly aware of him. Challenging him.

Alec stared back—and to his surprise felt no revulsion, but interest. Attraction of a kind he didn't understand. Didn't need to understand. Not now.

For suddenly the lynx bolted from their cover beneath the overhang and into the darkness of the alley.

# Chapter 4

*First step of the mission: accomplished.*

*She was aware of the changes to her body: smaller. More agile. More lithe, elastic. More alert, senses heightened.*

*All lynx.*

*She spared a sidelong glance for Alec, her handler and more. Much more, but that did not matter now. Had he accepted what he saw?*

*She left him far behind as she loped toward the building.*

*The older-formulation elixir had worked well this time, at least so far. Now she was fully changed, felt fine, was fully cognizant of her surroundings and who and what she was—more so than when, before joining Alpha Force, she changed at the full moon each month and became a cat without as much human awareness.*

*The cover of darkness was useful. There were street lamps and a small bit of illumination flowed through the building's windows, where lights were left on inside. She needed neither, not with her keen sense of sight in minimal light.*

*She reached a rear entry to the low, pale stone building, a closed door. No matter. Despite the empty pouch attached around her neck by a loose strap, she leaped effortlessly from the ground onto the ledge that extended below the windows of the second floor. The architectural detailing on this classic structure was her friend.*

*In lynx form, she was small enough that a person could mistake her for a large domestic cat. That would help with her cover. Not that people would expect to see a cat scale a commercial building.*

*Slowly, crouched as she moved, she continued along the ledge around occasional fluted columns, scouting each window. In this form, she could not test to see if any was unlocked. She had to trust that, once again, some careless human had left a window somewhere in this building cracked open enough for her to slither inside.*

*Not on this floor. Just as well, perhaps, since the office that was her goal was on the top floor of this ornate structure—the third. Reaching a suitable part of this ledge, she leaped onto the floor above.*

*And soon found the entry she wanted. What human would worry about the lapse in security by leaving an office window open here, on the third floor? Not the occupant of this office. The opening was narrow, but she compacted herself into as small a form as possible, stared into the darkness to make certain that nothing, no one moved in the room. Listened for any noise that heralded the arrival of an intruding human. Hearing none, she slunk inside.*

*This wasn't the office she sought, but it wasn't far away.*

*She meandered around a short while to find doors that weren't closed. Soon she was in the empty, dark hall.*

*Carefully, using her enhanced senses to confirm she remained alone on this deserted floor, she traversed the hall. This was the home of a media conglomerate, but no television filming or radio broadcasting emanated from here. This was merely an office building. One that, at this hour, was largely empty.*

*A minute later she was in Sherman Jonash's office.*

Still standing in the shadows by his car, Alec got his mind back under control. He had seen what he had expected to see.

Nella Reyes, the hot sexy woman to whom he was damned attracted, with whom he had made love, was, in fact, a shape-shifter.

And as he watched, she had made what had appeared to be a leap of supernatural height, from the ground onto the decorative projection framing the building. He hadn't been able to see her easily in the near darkness. And he had soon lost track of her.

He was supposed to wait here, be ready to take off in the car with her as soon as she reappeared with the thumb drive in the bag around her neck. Twiddle his thumbs. Yeah. Sure.

Alec wasn't a military guy, used to taking orders as Nella was. Sure, as a political aide with aspirations to hold office someday himself, he did as Congressman Crowther directed.

Including using his own ingenuity to take care of things in a way that wouldn't harm the congressman. *That* was his real job, why the congressman had hired him. Relied on him. After all, with his background as a lawyer, he knew that directions were always subject to interpretation.

He examined the alleyway around him. Then he started walking in the direction from which he had driven here.

* * *

*One benefit of being a shape-shifted lynx: she had accessed this office so much more easily than if she'd been human. Even if no one was around on this floor, she knew, from Alec's reconnaissance, that the building's entry was subject to security.*

*A benefit of being a shape-shifting human: if she had been solely a lynx, she would have had no idea where to look for the stolen thumb drive. But, with particular thanks to the elixir, she retained her human awareness and intelligence.*

*Another benefit of being a shape-shifted lynx: no need to turn on lights to see her surroundings and its contents in near darkness. With an easy jump Nella was on the desk.*

*Only...a drawback of shape-shifting: in this body, with paws instead of fingers, searching through piles of paper on the desk, boxes of pencils, pens and clips, through desk drawers and behind files, was not easy.*

*It was, however, possible.*

*So was quickly scanning documents she pawed through. Some seemed quite interesting. She maneuvered her body around to shove them into the bag around her neck. But she had to focus on her real mission: finding the memory stick.*

*One obvious place to look: the desktop computer that dominated one side of Jonash's messy desk. Was it attached there?*

*Most people generally removed extra memory or backup accessories from their computers. Jonash was apparently one of them.*

*Plus, he was unlikely to want to call attention to his possession of this particular item, since he had stolen it.*

*No, more likely he had hidden it. But where?*

*In plain sight? Nella walked along the desk, feeling her way with all four paws. But all she found in a similar shape to a thumb drive, beneath newspapers and notepads and other things cluttering the surface, were pencil stubs and small staplers.*

*She had to get into drawers. Not easy with small, cunning paws.*

*Maybe she should have found a way to sneak Alec inside to help. He was supposed to be her aide, after all.*

*And the idea of his being here, watching her back—*

*What was happening here? She had shifted. Her human thoughts were not supposed to be emotions. And definitely not sexual.*

*Head toward the floor, she leaned over the side of the desk, wedged her paw into a drawer handle and pushed outward.*

Good thing Alec had done his homework—as always. While standing in the shadows across the street from the Omnibus International Communications headquarters, he saw a bright red sports car turn into the driveway of the building's underground parking. The make and model Sherman Jonash drove. Alec was too far away to see the driver, but he had no doubt.

Jonash would soon head to his office.

Damn! Alec slipped from concealment and crossed the street. Under ordinary circumstances, first thing he'd do was whip out his cell phone and call the person searching that office, warn them to get out. Fast.

Only, Nella wasn't a *person* searching that office. And she certainly hadn't hidden her cell phone on her sleek feline body. Not in the bag she carried, either. No way could she answer it if she had.

Watching Nella's back was Alec's reason for being here. Even if it hadn't been, he wasn't about to allow that amazing sexy creature to be caught by scheming media thief Jonash.

Alec thought fast. Sneaking in around building security wasn't an option. If it had been, Congressman Crowther wouldn't have enlisted anyone from Alpha Force in the first place. That was one of the first things Alec researched for the congressman.

Physically stopping Jonash wasn't an option, either, despite Alec's initial inclination to simply render the man incapable of heading for his office. But such an action had too many hitches, and some might reflect badly on Alec's boss.

He had to use his brain. And his lawyerly and other negotiating skills. Fast.

Before the metal security gate closed behind Jonash's car, Alec slipped inside and followed the car down the ramp toward the parking area.

*The drawer was locked. For good reason.*

*She had a way to deal with it. During maneuvers at Alpha Force, she had honed this skill along with the others that made her, in feline form, unique among her fellows in the unit.*

*She unsheathed her claws. Still leaning over from above, she inserted the longest claw into the hole in the desk drawer where a key should go. Felt around. Pushed carefully at the protrusions within the mechanism till she felt something release.*

*She opened the drawer. Looked inside.*

*There! A memory stick with a key-chain loop attached. On it was a charm depicting a mace with an eagle on top, the symbol of the United States House of Representatives, along with the initials CC: Crandall Crowther. The same as the photo she was shown.*

*She had to separate it from the bulldog clips and memo sheets covered with handwritten notes. Get it into her bag.*

*A few words on some of the sheets caught her attention. She curved her paw into a scoop and thrust them out. The thumb drive, too. Fortunately there was a rug below to cushion it and prevent it from making much noise as it landed on the floor.*

*She pushed the drawer closed, then dropped effortlessly onto the floor, again carefully scooping all she needed into the bag around her neck.*

*Suddenly a pain shot through her, one so intense that she emitted a shrill feline moan. Oh, no, not now! She felt the pain yet again.*

*Just as she heard voices outside the office door.*

# *Chapter 5*

"Look, Jonash, I'm not hearing what I want to." Alec raised his voice as if in anger. What he really wanted, standing here in the now well-lit hallway with the sleazy reporter, was to make sure Nella heard him and got out—since choking the guy unconscious still wasn't an option. Alec had had to sign in with security, too. "Do we have a deal?"

"It's a definite maybe." Jonash gave Alec a smile as broad as the Capitol rotunda. That was part of why the guy was so successful. He looked so damned trustworthy. Short dark hair. Big blue eyes that oozed sympathy and reliability. A face as youthful as a choirboy's.

No wonder people, especially women, all over the country seemed to believe every word he said, despite the ridiculous lies he often told.

But those lies were, in fact, interspersed with truth that

he had excavated from politicians and film stars and even ordinary folks by using his charm, sincerity and all the lowest, filthiest contrivances imaginable. Thievery was one of the nicest tricks he engaged in.

"You know how it goes, Alec," Jonash continued affably. "You've been in politics long enough to know that everything you tell me has to be substantiated before I can use it."

Yeah, sure he substantiated everything. Like meeting aliens from outer space face-to-whatever passed for a face.

But all Alec said was, "I understand. But that computer memory stick that you…well, that's now in your possession. Doesn't it substantiate everything?" What Alec really wanted to know was whether Jonash had already gotten beyond the password and into the meat of what was on the drive—such as the existence of Alpha Force. And its shape-shifting members.

"It helps," said Jonash. "But anything else you can add would be great."

That sounded vague enough to let Alec hope the contents remained unaccessed.

"Of course." Alec tried to sound convincingly eager.

"So, to repeat what you said on our way up here, Congressman Crowther somehow blames you for allowing me to…borrow that memory stick, and he fired you. You're pissed and willing to do what it takes to blow the whistle on the congressman and the military unit that's his favorite project."

"You got it." Alec watched as Jonash reached for the door to his office. Was Nella there, or had she left? Had she found the thumb drive, retrieved it?

Before the door opened, Jonash pivoted to look at Alec. His youthful appearance was supported by his slight physique. He was shorter than Alec. Thin. But strong, or so it had appeared on the news segments he had filmed where he participated in everything from triathlons to benefit offbeat charities, to martial arts, to faked wrestling matches.

"We could make a really good team here, Alec," he said, "if you're not pulling my leg. You might even be able to work for me. Act as my political adviser. Help me dig up stuff on the people who run this country so we can make sure the American public isn't kept in the dark. But if you're lying..."

"I'm sure we can work together." It killed Alec to try to sound frantic, as if he really needed to convince this guy.

"We'll see." Jonash turned his back and pushed open his office door, flicking on the lights.

At first Alec felt relieved. No indication of a cat anywhere on the desk or furniture. The desktop appeared a mess, though. Had Nella done that, or was Jonash a slob?

But then...he saw a pair of feminine legs on the floor beyond the desk. "What the hell?" Alec shouted.

At the same time Jonash yelled, "Hey!"

Alec pushed by him. Nella, in human form, lay on the floor. Naked. Barely conscious, although her eyes opened slightly.

She looked hazily toward Alec. "What happened?" she asked softly.

And then she looked over Alec's shoulder, toward where Jonash stood—and screamed.

It was the best she could think of to do under the circumstances. She had the feeling, thanks to what she had found here in Jonash's office, that this impulse would save her. And Alec's reputation.

And, most of all, Alpha Force.

She quickly curled herself into a ball. She hated being nude, knowing that these men stared at her. Jonash, especially. She knew what he was, and his eyes on her made her shudder.

"What are you doing here?" the reporter demanded.

"I… I'm sorry. I just woke up. The drugs… I know I promised I'd leave before, but what you gave me…"

"What the hell is she talking about?" Jonash demanded. He was looking at Alec as if he had all the answers.

Alec probably didn't know what she was up to, but bless him, he'd removed his shirt and quickly draped it over her. He clasped her shoulders briefly in support before standing again and glaring angrily at Sherman Jonash.

"What drugs?" he asked in a calm but furious voice. He was a damned good actor. Or maybe it was his fear that they'd been found out, that his boss, the congressman, could be blamed, that made him so tautly emotional.

"I have no idea what she's talking about." Jonash crossed his arms. In anger—or to protect himself?

"Do you have a cell phone?" Nella asked Alec calmly, although her voice shook. She couldn't believe what she was going to ask him to do, but she did it, anyway, when Alec nodded. "Take some photos here. Of Mr. Jonash, and his office…and me. This way. Although I want to keep your shirt on, if I may."

"Sure," Alec said, and quickly started doing as she said.

"Hey. No!" Jonash lunged at Alec and tried to grab his phone, but Alec shot a picture of that, too, and kept the cell away from his attacker.

"No more stealing," Alec said with a smile as feral as any Nella had seen on her fellow Alpha Force members. He turned to Nella. "Would you like for me to call the police, miss?"

Good. He wasn't acknowledging that he knew her, at least for now. That might work better in the long run.

"Not yet." Nella made sure the shirt covered her as well as possible as she stood. "Although it might make sense to call building security. Make sure they let the OIC executives know exactly what happened here."

She caught the momentary glance of fury on Jonash's face as he pushed himself off his desk and toward her, hands outstretched as if in attack.

Calling on her military training, she prepared to utilize her most effective self-defense techniques—but Alec, thrusting his cell phone into his pocket, interposed himself between Jonash and her. Hell, he was a lawyer, a politician, nonmilitary. Even so, he maneuvered around till he was behind Jonash, his arm tightly around the journalist's throat as the man ineffectually tried to beat at Alec with his fists—until Alec tightened his grip.

She couldn't have done it better herself. She grinned at Alec but saved her questions for later. But damn, his smug smile over Jonash's shoulder was sexy.

Nella walked around the desk and took a seat in the chair behind it, intending to appear in charge. "Okay, Sherman," she said, "as you know, I am a member of Alpha Force, and I was sent here to retrieve the computer memory stick you stole."

"I know no such thing," he retorted stonily. She'd always thought he looked like such an innocent young man on news broadcasts. Now he looked older. Angrier. Devilish.

"Then you chose to sexually assault a total stranger for the fun of it?"

"I never—" He started to struggle, but Alec's grip around his neck tightened even more.

"But you did steal the thumb drive, didn't you?" she asked calmly.

"I…borrowed it. Congressman Crowther wasn't answering all my questions, and the public has the right to know about the boondoggles he's trying to get funded."

"And what did you learn from it?"

"Not a damned thing!" he exploded. "I put it into my computer and the message that came up on the screen said it would not only self-destruct but destroy the computer if the right password wasn't given. I was going to get one of the company's best techs involved but haven't had time. When Alec, here, approached me, I figured he could help. But I take it that you haven't been fired by Crowther, after all."

He tried to turn toward Alec, who didn't let him. "Nope. The congressman and I are on the best of terms."

He glared next at Nella. "And you found the thumb drive?"

She raised her brows and shrugged. "Could be. One more thing. What did you think you'd find on the drive?"

"I didn't know. Crowther claimed that his favorite military project, Alpha Force, was just developing some top-secret new technology to combat terrorism. But I'd heard rumors of…well, shape-shifting."

Nella burst out laughing and was glad when Alec again followed her lead. "Like I told you before, Sherman. I'm a member of Alpha Force. Do I look like some kind of wolfwoman to you?"

"No," he replied gruffly.

"Good answer." She stood and walked to the side of the desk, retrieving the sack she had brought to the office from the floor. "In case you're wondering, I did manage to find some of the paperwork on and in your desk from your employer, warning you not to get into any more trouble or you'd be on your own. Fired. Out of here on your ass. You've got those pictures on your cell, Alec?" she asked. No problem now acknowledging that they knew each other.

"Sure do."

"So Alec and I are leaving with the thumb drive and photos. If we ever hear of your bothering Congressman Crowther or making claims about his pet projects—especially Alpha Force—the classified report I'm about to make about what you did to me, including photos, will become unclassified and sent directly to the OIC powers that be. Is that clear?"

"Crystal," he said angrily.

"Then I think you can let him go now, Alec."

Alec complied, although he clenched his fists as if eager to use them on the journalist if he made any further threatening gestures. But all Jonash did was gingerly rub his neck.

"See you, Sherman," Nella said, and headed toward the door.

"Wait," Jonash said as Nella and Alec were poised to step into the hallway. "One question."

"Which is?" Nella asked.

"How did you get around building security? How did you get in here?"

"You're the one who drugged me and brought me in," Nella said sweetly. "You tell me."

"Besides, that's two questions, Jonash," Alec said, and led Nella out the door.

# Chapter 6

"Excellent job. Both of you."

Alec watched, smiling as Congressman Crandall Crowther accepted the thumb drive from Nella, then shook her hand.

"My sentiments exactly," said General Yarrow. "Alpha Force owes you."

"Just fulfilling our mission, sir," Nella said. Her modesty made Alec want to shout out how well she had done under pressure. But he figured the congressman and general already knew.

It was the next morning. They had rallied once more at the general's office in the Pentagon—after Nella and Alec had spent the rest of the night in her hotel room, celebrating by engaging in the most phenomenal sex of his life. And that was saying something, considering all the love-making he and Nella had already done.

The congressman held out his hand to Alec. "I knew I could count on you," he said. "With your special ingenuity, you're going to go far in service to our country. Maybe run for office yourself one of these days—as long as you don't oppose me."

"Don't worry about that, sir."

"Enough chitchat." General Yarrow waved them toward the seats facing his desk. "I want to hear all about how you pulled this off."

"Yes, sir!" Nella saluted, even as she pulled the papers she had taken from Jonash's office out of the small bag. As she sat down, she looked at Alec and smiled so warmly that he wanted to grab her right there. Kiss her again, the way they had so often last night. "It was a great joint effort between Alpha Force and the best of the staff of the U.S. Congress."

After Nella told her part of what had happened, she knew what the general would say. "You changed back into human form that quickly?" he demanded.

"Yes, sir. I used an older formulation of the shape-shifting elixir since I'd had an even worse reaction to the more current one. It's geared more to those who shift into canine form than feline. I'll be using my medical background to experiment more with this, along with the others at Alpha Force who are most into the tonics."

"Like Lt. Drew Connell," said the general.

"Exactly. Also, we're planning to enlist those who shift into other kinds of beings, so this should help in that, too."

"Good. Best of luck with it." The general stood, clearly a dismissal. "I want to do a little brainstorming with you, Crandall, about how to avoid this kind of situation in the future. We'll talk to you two further later on."

Alec rose at the same time as Nella, and they both headed for the door. Before they left the office, though, Alec said, "General, I want to visit Fort Lukman and get a better sense of all that Alpha Force is about."

As Congressman Crowther watched with obvious amusement, the general grinned, his gaze shifting from Alec to Nella and back again. "I have a feeling there's more to your visit than that, but we'll be glad to have you there."

"So…I'll just drop you back at your hotel," Alec said when they were again in his car.

Nella looked at him. He was watching the road, and she studied his sexy, masculine, beloved profile, absorbing it, wondering if she would ever see it or him again.

She had dared to hope so, with his last comment in the general's office. But if he was just going to dump her out now…

"Sure," she said casually. "That'll be fine. It's been fun, Alec. And I really appreciated how you handled yourself in Jonash's office. You acted as if you were almost reading my mind, you were so great about following my lead. And the way you physically took control of Jonash—how did you do that?"

"I study martial arts to stay in shape, and just for the fun of it." His sideways glance suggested there was more to it than that. Maybe it was just his attitude, and maybe something more. She'd get it out of him later…she hoped.

"Excellent job," she said. "And I think the congressman's right. You'll make a good politician. And?"

"Hush," he said. And then he leaned over, grabbed her gently by the back of her head and kissed her soundly. Sexily. With his tongue playing excruciatingly, tantalizingly hot games inside her mouth.

Good thing they had stopped at a red light.

A honk sounded behind them. Alec broke away with a laugh. "Time to go," he said. "Oh, and by the way, I'm dropping you at your hotel while I go grab a bag of my stuff. You can check out, and then the two of us can take a well-deserved vacation for a couple of days, wherever you say."

"Oh. I thought you—"

"Were running away from you? No way. And isn't the night after tomorrow a full moon?"

She drew in her breath. "Yes. And that means—"

"You'll change whether you want to or not. I got that. And I'll be there, watching your back. Again. That okay with you?"

He hazarded a grin toward her, then turned back to the road.

"So this time you won't be drunk. I won't be able to claim you're hallucinating."

"You won't be able to dump me," he asserted with a nod. "So we're clear on that? We're going to see where this relationship goes, lynx-lady?"

"Fine by me," she said, and wearing a huge smile, settled into her seat.

* * * * *

# WILDERNESS

*Barbara J. Hancock*

For my mother…
the strongest woman I'll ever know.

***BARBARA HANCOCK,***

when she's not in the middle of creating fiery conflict between passionate lovers, is enjoying living in the foothills of the Blue Ridge Mountains with her own real-life Survivor Man and three awesome sons. You can visit her at www.barbarajhancock.com.

Dear Reader,

*Knowing what has to be done and actually doing it are two very different things.*

"Wilderness" is a story about a woman embracing her psychic powers for the first time. It's also the story of a man who inspires even as he represents the biggest challenge of all! Colin Masterson is powerful, dangerous and wild. He's a werewolf. He's been captured. And it's up to Tess to save him.

Can you imagine that moment? Would you be brave enough to free a sexy werewolf from his chains?

I've always enjoyed stories that leave me exhilirated and inspired. Paranormal romances are my greatest love because they have an intensity that no other genre seems to match. When the stakes are high, passions natually run higher still and I so enjoy that rush! I hope "Wilderness" leaves you feeling brave and bold…and just a little bit in love with a wolf.

Barbara Hancock

# *Chapter 1*

He was chained.

Tess Haverty examined the silver bindings that twined once, twice and again around his bare, muscular torso. Considering her plans, it was lame to mentally go down the list of how well he was bound…arms to chest (*check*)…wrist to wrist (*check*)…ankles to floorboard (*check*). She chalked it up to nerves mixed with a hearty dose of survival instinct. She had known this would be dangerous, but somehow knowing and seeing were two very different things.

His dark eyes followed her movements. Only those eyes reacted to her sudden presence when she came out from her hiding place behind a lopsided stack of crates. Beneath her feet, the cargo truck rumbled and shook. Her steps were unsteady at best, awkward, stumbling and not the least bit heroic at worst.

She braced her feet apart in a wide stance and tried to ignore everything about him but the chains. It wasn't easy. The chains, however daunting and relevant to her mission, suddenly seemed insignificant.

Colin Masterson. Six feet two inches. Two hundred and twenty pounds. Those facts on paper hadn't translated to a real, solid man in her imagination.

He *was* real. *Too real.*

She stood at five feet six inches and one hundred twenty pounds (after a pizza binge), and even the muscular physique she'd managed to build up with a few months of intense preparation and training didn't seem anywhere near adequate for her task.

His eyes burned with anger, curiosity and interest. She didn't know which was the most threatening.

Tess reached for the compact bolt cutters she'd stowed in one of her pockets, all the while unable to look away from those all-too-attentive eyes.

He lifted his eyebrows when he saw what she held and for the first time his whole body reacted by stiffening. She saw the tightening of his fists and the resultant bulge of muscle in his arms. She noted how the chains bit into his straining flesh. Even in the gloom, she could see the angry red welts caused by his skin's severe reaction to the pure silver links.

With a deep breath, she dropped to one knee. This was the do-or-die moment. Tess knew the truck was only about fifteen minutes from its destination. It was time to act. She just wished she didn't have a sudden twist in her gut that redefined the moment as do *and* die.

"I'm with H.A.E.S. I'm here to help you."

Humans Against the Exploitation of Supernaturals. Tess had never been a thrill seeker. Unfortunately, in the past six months the thrills had sought her out and changed her life forever. Funny how you couldn't turn a blind eye toward government labs capturing and studying supernatural creatures when your twin sister was one. H.A.E.S. had saved Lily from the clutches of scientists, but she'd committed suicide before Tess had gotten a chance to see her, before Tess could try to help her. Ha. Tess helping Lily. That would have been…unusual. Tess had always been the mouse, the timid one, content to let Lily shine while she preferred the anonymity of shadows. After all, her occasional dreams were nothing compared to Lily's dazzling visions.

Colin Masterson was on his way to the same lab that Lily had been sent to. Once there, hidden in the foothills of the Blue Ridge Mountains less than fifty miles from Washington, D.C., he would be poked and prodded and traumatized with exploratory surgeries.

Of course, Lily hadn't been a werewolf.

It was crazy and dangerous to get anywhere near Masterson, but Tess was here. She had been too late to help her sister, but she was here, now.

She swallowed and repositioned the tool in her fist so she could get to work.

"Wait," he ordered. Amazingly, the low growl of his voice sounded unbound, as if he was in command of the situation.

Tess stopped. In fact, she froze. Survival instinct again. It told every nerve ending in her body that his voice must be obeyed.

His voice was human even while it was low and urgent. The only growl in it came from the masculine quality of its tones. It was a whisky-kissed burr of syllables, but, far from monstrous, he had the kind of voice perfect for pillow talk, deep and seductive.

Her heartbeat kicked up a notch and she felt her eyes

widen. She knew the involuntary physical reaction that displayed her fear was a mistake. She just didn't know how to stop it.

*Don't be prey. Don't be prey.*

The mantra didn't come to her rescue. Her pause extended as he held her motionless with a look that had taken on a predatory gleam.

She knew that her training had been rushed. She knew the people banded together to form H.A.E.S. weren't experts. Through trial and error, they had learned that Masterson's kind didn't change into bushy-tailed canines with soulful howls nor did they become the silly wolf-man from old Hollywood movies. She'd heard the morph described as more subtle and terrifying than either of those myths.

When provoked or when they chose…the jury was out on that one…they simply changed into something that wasn't quite human.

Tess watched Masterson for any signs of change as he held her in place with the force of his will. His face was angular and well balanced. In spite of the five-o'clock shadow, or maybe because of it, he looked like he could carry off an ad for expensive cologne. He was rugged, but in an attractive, exotic way. Definitely not pretty, but handsome wasn't a stretch. Of course, his body was perfect. In this instance, under these circumstances, *scarily* so.

Six-pack abs. Serious arms and pectorals. And much of it on display because silver worked best on bare skin. He wore jeans and nothing else. Not even shoes. Rather than make him seem helpless, he looked less-than-civilized, *wild.* His hair fell to his shoulders in a dark mass of unkempt waves.

But in the dim light, Tess saw no elongated canines

marring his firm, perfect lips. His hands had unfisted and she saw no claws.

"If you do this, men will die."

She hoped he meant "men" as in the two evil thugs currently driving him to hell and not "men" as in mankind. Anyone willing to transport innocent people like her sister to labs little better than concentration camps deserved what they got.

"I understand," she whispered through lips gone cold with the realization of what she said. The bolt cutters in her numb fingers may as well be the pen signing their death warrants.

So. Be. It.

She wasn't a mouse. Not anymore.

Suddenly, she was free to move. Her eyes flew to his as she swayed forward. She had to brace herself with her free hand against his chest or fall right in his lap. One of his brows quirked higher than the other, and she thought she saw a corner of his mouth tilt slightly. It did *definitely* tilt when she jerked her hand away from his warm, firm skin.

"Steady," he said.

She didn't know if his amusement was enough of a promise for her safety, but she positioned the snipping head of the cutters over a link of chain anyway.

"For Lily," Tess whispered as she used both hands to bring the tool's handles together.

The chains rattled slightly and she looked up at him once more. He didn't speak again, only waited. She could feel his tension, his preparedness. Tess shivered. Then she cut another link and then another.

Finally, the chains slipped to the floorboard in a gleaming puddle around his feet. Tess looked at the shining pool and braced herself. She held her breath and thought about moonlight and swing sets and chasing fireflies in the dark. Deep in her mind her most treasured memories echoed with Lily's childhood laughter.

She drew in a quick breath when a warm hand touched her face, but she didn't flinch. She didn't try to pull away when his calloused fingers cupped under her chin.

Loosened from his bonds, he had come away from the wall slightly to sit on his heels. She knelt between his knees with the bolt cutters in her hands, evidence of her bravery or her stupidity, only the next few seconds would tell.

Tess let her head fall back to look up at his face. He still cupped her chin, but lightly. His fingers brushed her skin as soft as a caress. She struggled to remember what she was supposed to do now. In this moment, confronted by the powerful man she had been sent to save, Tess wondered if she had fooled herself. Was she really up for this?

He leaned to bring his face closer to hers. She breathed lightly, trying not to panic.

*Don't be prey. Don't be prey.*

He smiled as he took in her reactions. It was a grim, barely there curve of his sculpted lips, but it was a smile nonetheless. His fingers tightened, but only slightly, holding her in place as if she wasn't too scared to move.

"My savior," he breathed, and it was a sigh even while it was a tease.

He saw her fear, was amused by it, and he was still grateful. The appreciation shone in his eyes. His chocolate-colored eyes, she noted, now that he had tilted forward, slightly away from the shadowed wall.

"May you never live to regret it."

Tess's heart leapt with those words, or maybe in reaction to his movement, because the last was murmured right against her lips before he jumped away quicker than her eyes could follow.

One minute, she felt the heated brush of his lips on hers, the next, he was at the rear of the truck ripping open the sliding door.

It was over quickly, but that didn't make the blood less red or the screams any less gut-wrenching.

Tess was thrown against the wall of the truck's interior when it lurched sideways and surged into the ditch. The blow to her head left her dizzy, but it didn't knock her out.

More's the pity.

She crawled out the steel door Masterson had torn apart with his hands and she fell to the ground.

It was weak to lie there in the tall grass by the side of the road, but she allowed herself to do it for several long moments. She could have told herself it was to catch her breath and regain her equilibrium. She could have lain there even longer as spots swam before her eyes.

Tess didn't.

She knew why she didn't want to get up on shaky legs and walk around to the cab of the truck. Knew why a tight knot of dread had settled in the pit of her stomach.

In the aftermath of cutting the chains, surviving the crash and hearing the screams, it seemed surreal that birds sang in nearby trees and the verdant odor of crushed grass should fill her nostrils. It would have been easy to pretend she didn't have to move, but Tess had learned life wasn't easy a long time ago.

She pushed herself up from the ground and forced herself to look around.

He was gone.

And the two men who had captured him would never turn over another innocent for torture.

Tess vomited in the bushes.

Again, knowing something had to be done and witnessing it…two very different things.

She was bruised and battered. She was pretty sure her nightmares (and possibly even her dreams) were refueled for the next six months, and Lily was still gone too soon.

Tess limped her way to the rendezvous point haunted by Masterson's dark eyes and his even darker words.

## *Chapter 2*

Colin ran and his blood coursed through his veins like liquid joy. He had been less-than-alive for a week. First in a holding pen that smelled of despair and unwashed flesh, then in the back of a truck that reeked of gasoline and loss.

Except, of course, for the vanilla cappuccino.

He'd known she was there the whole time, even as his captors were oblivious. The scent of creamy sweet coffee hadn't come from the cretins who threw his silver-weakened body into the back of the truck. Neither had the teasing scent of lavender shampoo.

He had waited patiently for her to show herself, but he had still been surprised. By her beauty, by her fear, by her intentions in spite of her fear.

As each link fell away, severed by her purposeful but shaking hands, he'd been caught in another trap altogether.

Her vulnerability paired as it was with her obvious determination snared him as surely as wicked silver. He shouldn't have touched her, but the heady rush of freedom's call had overwhelmed his good sense. Now, he ran *because of her.* He lived again, *because of her.*

She had given him a second chance to save his people.

His father hadn't been so lucky.

Jack Masterson had led their pack for twenty years, and he had kept them safe and prosperous. But he had led them during years of a population explosion when it was easy to survive happily on the fringes of society without being noticed.

Now, their pack was down to fifteen, including himself. They were his now to guide and protect. At twenty-eight, he didn't even have his first gray hair, but he was Alpha.

Colin felt joy as he ran in the night, but he also ached. For years, he'd had the luxury of scoffing at ancient tradition. He hadn't felt like a prince and hadn't intended to be one. His father had talked of persecutions so old he couldn't even imagine the time when they'd occurred. In the age of cell phones and civil rights that kind of wolf hunt just hadn't seemed real.

Then an influenza pandemic changed the world. Suddenly, people with unusually strong immunity stood out. Werewolves and countless others who were different.

All of them were lumped under the term *Supernaturals*.

After the pandemic, his people and the other Supernaturals had no rights. They could be hunted, caged and killed, or worse-than-killed, all in the name of science. Scientists struggled to map and isolate the genes responsible for immunity, but he suspected that much of their time was spent trying to unlock the secrets to power.

Supernaturals held secrets in their blood and the government wanted those secrets.

His father had been one of the first to die. He'd actually gone willingly into the hands of authorities, hoping to shield his pack with his sacrifice.

No one spoke out against the experiments. Survival justified any measures the government cared to take. No one cared except for H.A.E.S. and naive little heroines with vanilla-flavored kisses.

Colin ran on.

Tess sipped a fresh, steaming cup of coffee. The whipped cream that floated on top wasn't frivolous. It was medicinal. She needed the caffeine and the calories and the comfort. Her nerves were so shot she could almost hear them crying out for her favorite indulgence, but the brew didn't prove itself as soothing as usual.

For one thing, the steam floating off the top of her foam cup teased across her lips like a moist reminder. Tess shivered and licked cream off her upper lip.

She was twenty-four years old. She'd shared a few kisses, but none had left her trembling hours later. Her lips still tingled from the werewolf's kiss. The *Super's* kiss. She corrected herself and looked around guiltily in case any of her fellow H.A.E.S. had detected her less-than-PC thoughts.

Supernatural was the appropriate name for any human with special abilities. Like Colin. Like Lily. Even like herself. Though, in her case, *special* might be too strong a term to describe her dreams. She had escaped being put on the government's wanted list because she'd almost died from the flu. She'd been ill for weeks. Lily hadn't had so much as a sniffle.

Logically, Tess knew she'd been weakened by her long bout with depression following her parents' death. Her will to live had been shaken. Her hope for the future almost lost. Then, she *had* lost her sister and suddenly she'd found new depths of resolve. Logically, she knew that she and Lily shared the same genes and similar psychic abilities. Still, in her heart of hearts, Tess didn't consider herself a Supernatural. She wasn't super in any way. No cape. No tights. And she'd never heard of anyone shouting, "Dogged determination to the rescue!"

Tess took another sip. Colin Masterson's kiss had been slight, soft and fleeting. It shouldn't have left her lips tender. She shouldn't feel marked by his touch. The hot coffee didn't burn away the memory. Just like the scratchy wool blanket around her shoulders didn't stop the occasional shiver that racked her body.

The team's medic said it was just a delayed reaction to adrenaline and stress. He was a dental assistant, but Tess decided to trust his diagnosis. Even though her lips wanted to call it "desire."

Later, after the sun had set and the moon had risen, Tess walked through the park behind her apartment complex in Chesterfield, Virginia, with a steady stride, refusing to be cowed.

She had expected nightmares.

Instead, vivid, sensual dreams had driven her from her bed.

She paced along the path because Colin Masterson had been in her dreams and she hoped the cool air of early spring would clear her head. Unfortunately, the dim, shadowy night reminded her of the shadows that had enveloped her and Colin in the cargo truck. The exhaust fumes, the roar from the engine, the fear…none of it had managed to detract from the intimacy of kneeling between his powerful thighs. Nothing had taken away from the way his touch had affected her pulse rate.

Tess rubbed her arms to fight the chill. Had she imagined the interest in his eyes and the promise in his parting words?

"You know monsters are real, but you walk in the night without a weapon. That's a curious contrast."

She stopped midstep. The garden hadn't morphed into a jungle. The path still seemed perfectly groomed, but suddenly she knew she'd wandered into the wilderness. Slowly, she brought her feet together and turned to face him.

Colin Masterson had found her.

Faraway lights in the parking lot gleamed, but, here, only moonlight prevailed. It outlined his tall form, but kept his face in shadow.

"Should I be afraid?" she asked, though her mouth hadn't asked for permission to speak. Her pulse throbbed, her respiration quickened. She took in a sudden gulp of air when he stepped toward her as he replied.

"Yes. I'd be a liar if I said you shouldn't."

"Why?" She held her body in check. It wanted to run, but she wouldn't give in to its demands.

"Because I'm not easy to know."

It sounded regretful, as if he wished he was a nerdy accountant in a nondescript cubicle somewhere rather than a powerful Supernatural wandering the night.

Nothing about him seemed "easy."

He was closer now and she could detect the tension in his shoulders. Though his movements were careful and casual, though each step slid into the next with liquid grace, she sensed his tension. Suddenly, she was reminded of a virgin trying to lure a unicorn from the forest. It was his untamed intensity that made her want to know him. Had she taken a walk to escape her dreams or had she been out trying to find them?

She heard the warning in his voice. Of all the Supers, werewolves were the most feared. Hunted. Trapped. Hated. Wasn't she shaking in her sneakers even as she found him almost painfully alluring?

"I'm tougher than I look," Tess replied and then she wished she could reach out and grab the words and swallow them back. Her hands actually twitched.

Her throat grew hot and the heat of a flush spread up to her face. Thank God for shadows. There was no way he would see the blush that clarified the invitation her words only hinted at.

Shadows or not, he drew in a breath and paused. Her words had surprised him. She knew, shadows or not, he sensed the heat on her skin.

"And more vulnerable than you know," he cautioned.

He resumed his movement in her direction. Tess caught a hint of pine, fresh and sweet. She realized the free scent came from his skin and hair. She didn't stop the urge to breathe it in. He had brought the wilderness with him into her safe, manicured garden. It was suddenly darker, more mysterious and magical than before.

# *Chapter 3*

Tess held herself very, very still as he approached. If he was a unicorn, he was a stallion, unpredictable and fierce. If she ran now, he would catch her before she could even cry for help. Part of her, the part that her old instincts directed, wanted to run and hide. Part of her, the newer, braver Tess, waited…for what, she wasn't sure.

He came into her personal space and then he came closer still. It was a challenge, but it was also a temptation. He didn't stop until she had to tilt her chin so her nose wouldn't touch his chest. The warmth of his pine-kissed skin washed over her. The natural response to his closeness would have been to step back or twine her arms around his neck. She did neither. She wanted to do both and couldn't decide.

"More vulnerable than you know," he murmured, softer this time. His breath came warm against her forehead.

Tess didn't cringe or faint or run. She figured that was enough to reiterate her own words without actually speaking, which was good because she didn't think she could. Her lungs functioned, but she was breathless. Her heart beat, but every cell of her body was paused, waiting for his touch.

She was shocked and she knew if it weren't for the blessed cover of moonlight her face would be glowing. It was one thing to decide not to hide anymore. It was another thing entirely to meet danger with anticipation.

"There aren't any chains for you to cut. You can walk away. I won't stop you."

His arms stayed at his sides, matching her stillness. His chest brushed against her breasts with each quiet rise and fall. His thighs, heated from running, warmed hers. His mouth was so close her skin felt his words, but he didn't touch her. He tempted. He dared. He seduced with his nearness. But he didn't touch.

Could she walk away? Did she even want to?

Her body answered by swaying toward him. As soon as her body fully touched his, she knew it wasn't fear making her knees weak. It was desire.

Though his hands still didn't move, hers did. She caught herself with the best available prop, and his shoulders proved steady and strong beneath her hands. They also proved warm and smooth and firm. The heat and the silky steel of his skin made her gasp.

"Steady," he spoke into her hair and, amazingly, laughter bubbled up and burst out of her lips against his neck.

Finally, he wrapped his arms around her.

He took the laughter, the fear, the desire and her pain and somehow made it partly his. Tess stiffened. She hadn't had anyone to lean on since Lily, and she had always leaned on Lily too much. Their parents had died when they were only sixteen. Her sister had taken charge and Tess had let her. Lily of the confident visions had easily encouraged her sister with the amorphous dreams to follow wherever she lead.

Lily had used her abilities to put on a show. Tess had feared her own talents, hiding from them and avoiding the dilemma of how to act upon them after the tragedy of her parents' accident.

Until the government had claimed Lily's freedom. Until the military scientists had stolen her soul.

Tess held Colin. Gradually, her muscles relaxed. He was dangerous, but she held him. Coming out of hiding could be frightening, but it could be exhilarating as well.

His kiss shouldn't have been a surprise, but it was. Cool, at first, the lips that touched hers were chilled from the night and the forest air he brought with him. Tess warmed them quickly with hers, responding as if they weren't strangers, as if this wasn't crazy and dangerous, and maybe a little with the thrill that it was.

Unlike the brush of a kiss they'd shared earlier, his lips lingered. He tasted. He caressed. He coaxed an ever more heated response from her lips. Tess held the lean length of his body with steady, sure hands and soon the night's chill faded.

Earlier, she had seen his intensity. She had sensed it. It had filled her dreams with power and heat and a magnetic call she didn't refuse. Now, she shared it. Deep inside she knew when a dormant spark she'd never allowed to burn began to flame up in response to the fiery man she held in her arms.

It wasn't safe.

It wasn't mousy.

It was bold and daring and…

Later, Tess would wonder if anything short of Armageddon would have interrupted them. The roar of approaching helicopters and a convoy of huge, black SUVs screeching into the parking lot forced them apart. She took a couple of automatic steps toward her apartment building before Colin grabbed her hand.

"Looks like it's my turn to play savior."

Pulled and coaxed by her sister, Tess had once ridden an especially fast and swooping roller coaster. Colin was faster. Before she had time to protest or grant permission, he had lifted her into his arms.

He avoided moonbeams and clearings. From shadow to shadow, he flew. Twisting, turning, jumping, sliding, until Tess had to close her eyes against the bite of the wind and sting of branches. As if sensing her discomfort, even as he ran for both their lives, Colin reached to press her face against the sheltered hollow of his neck.

In no time, the commotion was far behind them. Colin slowed to a brisk walk.

"I have to warn the others," Tess gasped. If the military had discovered her, surely other members of H.A.E.S. were at risk.

"We'll send word as soon as we can, but it's probably too late," Colin warned.

"Most of them haven't done anything illegal."

"And I have? Or my father or Elizabeth or Charles or Warren? Jacob is only fifteen. They took him just before they took me. *Fifteen.* His biggest crime was…*is* a poor taste in music, for God's sake."

He held her tightly as if he could prevent the government from taking her with his two strong hands. Tess touched the side of his face to remind him that she was breakable. His hold eased immediately.

"My sister's name was Lily."

For some reason, it felt like a confession.

"I didn't save her," she continued around a sudden lump in her throat.

Tess had complained of nightmares for a week before Lily was taken, but none of them had been clear enough. Lily had laughed them off because her own visions showed no sign of danger.

"You saved me," Colin reminded her.

"H.A.E.S. saved you," Tess corrected.

He squeezed her again, tight to his chest like something precious he wouldn't allow to fall.

"I remember who cut the chains."

Although Colin's people lived in RVs instead of colorful wagons, they were a lot like gypsies. They welcomed her with barbeque and campfires and old Southern rock music. It soothed her nerves and made her tense all at the same time because they had so obviously carved out a place for themselves in a world where they didn't fit in. Now that they were actually being hunted, what would they do?

"None of that Supers mumbo-jumbo 'round here, mind ya'. We're wolves plain and simple." An elderly "uncle" spat into the fire as he spoke. The reflection of flames danced in his eyes. "Just different. Born different. Live different. Die different."

"But why?" Tess wondered.

"Why's a daffodil different from a tomato? Genes. Fate. You be the judge. There's good and bad wolves. Good and bad psychics. Good and bad shifters. There's good and bad humans. There's good and bad in us all."

Tess ate with the old man as Colin spoke quietly with some of the others. A few shot her furtive glances. One or two glared at her as if she had brought trouble down on their heads. She felt like a Carrier must have felt back during the Outbreak.

Several young children chased fireflies between campsites. Their laughter made her eyes burn.

She knew Colin was telling the others to leave without him. She knew he was telling them what to do if he didn't come back. It bothered her that she knew his plans. She wasn't Lily. Her dreams weren't reliable. Still, she couldn't shake the certainty.

Colin was going to try to save the latest member of his pack to be taken. He'd mentioned Jacob, and when he had, she'd seen his young face in her mind and she'd recognized it from past dreams.

One older woman approached "Uncle" with a bottle of beer in her hand. She nodded at Tess with quiet dignity, but there were tears pooled in her dark eyes. She twisted the cap off the bottle and handed it to the grizzled man. As he drank, she smoothed gray hair from his forehead.

"He's the last of the Masterson line. He has to survive. We've lost too much. We can't lose him, too."

Tess knew she was talking about Colin. Goose bumps rose up on her arms and the fire heated the skin of her face. She wanted to go back home and pull her sheets over her head.

A young boy came up to Tess with a steaming cup of fragrant coffee. Tess shivered again, this time in appreciation as vanilla sweetness hit her tongue. She looked across the fire, over the jumping flames and saw Colin watching her drink.

She knew the coffee was a gift from the Alpha wolf. She

cupped both hands around the hot mug and sipped again, accepting the warmth of the gesture. And the dangerous attraction implicit behind the seemingly innocent offering.

She was not going to hide anymore. She was going to help Masterson save Jacob. And she was going to make sure he made it back.

Tess thought back to a night eight years ago when she'd known her parents were in danger. She'd woken from the worst nightmare of her entire life only to begin living it immediately in horrible detail. Her dream had come too late for her to prevent her parents from getting into the wrong taxi at the wrong time. Frantic calls to their cell phones had been sent to voice mail again and again. Lily had fainted, overwhelmed with a sudden vision, even as Tess continued to try to punch in their parents' numbers.

It didn't console Tess that Lily's vision hadn't come soon enough either. She only knew she had totally failed to save her parents because her dreams were unreliable.

For eight years, she'd ignored her abilities. She'd been almost glad when she caught the flu because it practically proved her dreams were worthless. She welcomed the long-running fever and the body-racking aches as justifiable suffering.

Then, she'd lost Lily.

Her dreams still weren't dependable, but she had to try. The wolves needed her. Colin needed her. And she needed to do something, *anything,* even if she risked failing again.

Tess finished her last swallow of coffee and placed the empty cup on a nearby tree stump. The stump was already graced with a forgotten wineglass and a pretty vase that held a bouquet of daisies, as if someone had decided to proclaim this nature's bistro. Such determined good cheer made her smile in spite of what lay ahead.

Suddenly, the children flowed around her in laughing waves of reaching hands and skipping feet. Fireflies winked off and on, always flitting above the children's heads just as their fingers tried to grasp. They didn't care. It wasn't the catching that was important. It was the joy they found in the effort. Their energy and enthusiasm spilled over into Tess and she found herself jumping up to be swept along on the chase.

# *Chapter 4*

It must have been almost dawn when Colin came to her.

Tess knew the others would be heading in a loose convoy to another camp, pulling out one by one in increments spaced about thirty minutes apart.

"It isn't safe to go with them and it isn't safe to stay with me."

Colin sounded frustrated as if her lack of safety plagued him.

"I haven't been safe for a long time. I told you I'm tougher than I look."

Tess got up and moved to sit in the loose circle of his arms. With Colin at her back and the dying fire in front of her, she was warm for the first time since he had held her earlier in the night.

"Jacob's alive," he said softly.

It wasn't a question, and her mind hiccupped because

it was so conditioned to hide who and what she was from a world that wanted to hurt her.

"How did you know?"

She wouldn't deny it. She had been building the courage to talk to him about her dreams all night long.

"Your reaction to his name when I mentioned him and the way you drank those cups of coffee tonight. Like each was your last."

His arms tightened around her as if in preparation of protecting her from dangers they had yet to face.

"Cappuccino deserves to be savored," Tess teased lightly even though it was a serious moment.

"You know where he is."

"Yes."

"You know how we'll get him out."

"Yes."

"You're psychic."

Tess couldn't say "yes" again. She wanted to warn him not to count on her. To list her failures.

She didn't.

Colin needed her to be better than that. Jacob needed her, too. She placed her hands on the strong arms wrapped around her waist and vowed to be just as strong herself.

"My dreams haven't saved anyone. Ever."

The words came in spite of her resolve. She had never spoken about how weak her hazy dreams made her feel. How impotent she felt in the face of imperfect visions that pushed her to act.

"Before you cut those chains, I was helpless. *Helpless.* And Jacob was lost. Even unbound I have nothing but teeth and claws and strength. Without you and your dreams, I'm like a weapon without a target."

Tess moved her hands to his, where they had fisted as

he spoke. She understood his frustration, but she was amazed to be able to compare herself to the powerful man at her back. He was so confident and so bold. And yet, *he* needed *her*.

"I've seen Jacob in my dreams. It's almost as if I forget until the memory is triggered. When you said his name, I knew. I remembered," Tess rushed her words in an effort to sooth Colin and to share what she knew before she lost courage. "He's at the same lab where they held Lily, so I know it well. I've been there in nightmares many times."

Colin opened his hands and turned them up to hold on to hers as she spoke.

"If you can guide me, I want to get him out of there before it's too late."

Tess stiffened and her fingers tightened where they were entwined with his. She'd always been too late. Always. Though she knew they still had time, she was plagued with doubts from the past.

"Have I told you how beautiful you looked when you pulled those bolt cutters out of your pocket?" Colin had leaned closer and pressed his face into her hair. His words and his nearness became the perfect distraction.

"I felt like Little Red Riding Hood without a Woodcutter in sight," she replied, trying to remember how to breathe as he nuzzled even closer.

His laughter rumbled his chest against her back and his lips tickled the nape of her neck as he finally found his way beyond the hair that had shielded her skin from his touch.

"I don't bite, Tess. Much."

The thrill she felt at his words turned to a jolt of desire when he illustrated just what he meant with a sudden nip that made her gasp. He chuckled again at her reaction, then teased across the tender spot he'd made on her skin with his tongue.

They were alone. The sky was still dark. The pinkening of dawn wouldn't happen for another hour. The fire glowed warmly in front of their feet, but it had become mere embers so the dark of night wrapped them in more and more privacy as the flames died.

She tilted her head to the side to offer Colin greater access and he took full advantage. All playfulness forgotten, he gave serious attention to her exposed skin with his lips and teeth and tongue.

She had hidden away for eight long years. She had closed herself off from everyone and everything. Now, she opened herself to Colin. She allowed him to fire her blood and awaken the dormant spark of her spirit.

She had cut his chains. She had walked out at midnight to find him. She had gone with him into the forest and into the night. With every step she took, she had left the old scared and frozen Tess farther and farther behind.

Colin stood up and pulled her gently by the hand to the nearby sleeping bags, but it was Tess who placed both hands on his chest and pushed him first onto the big down-filled, makeshift bed. It was Tess who smoothed her hands over him, encouraging him without words to lay back and stretch out beneath her.

He was so strong, from his square-cut jaw all the way to his runner's thighs. Tess played her hands over the evidence of his strength while he obviously fought the urge to pull her into his arms. His muscles were tense and his eyes watched her with the same kind of interest he'd shown when he'd been in chains, as if he wasn't quite sure what she was going to do.

He had thrown on a flannel shirt sometime during the evening, but he hadn't buttoned it up. She'd welcomed every glimpse of his chest that his movements had allowed, but she liked pushing the flannel aside now even more. A slight tilt of his lips showed her he enjoyed it as well, but the dark intensity in his eyes also told her he would only be patient with her for so long.

Tess ran the pads of her fingers over his chest and down to his flat, hard stomach. One of his eyebrows arched higher as he watched, but he fisted handfuls of the sleeping bag in order to stop himself from reaching for her, so she knew he wasn't as controlled as he appeared. When she dipped into the waistband of his low-slung jeans, he sucked in a sudden startled breath.

And he let go of the sleeping bag.

Tess yelped when he pulled her into his arms. She laughed, but only for a second before she was startled into silence by the sudden coolness against the sudden bareness of her skin. Quicker than her eyes could follow, he got rid of her shirt. The cotton T-shirt lay in two separate halves on either side of their entwined bodies. She had seen no evidence of claws. She had barely felt the whisper of shredded cloth as it was whipped away from her skin.

Colin paused as if he was giving her a chance to run away, but she stayed right where she was with her shoulders back as she caught her breath and waited to see where her bold position would take them next.

She didn't wait long.

Very, very slowly, in contrast to his flashing movements of seconds before, he reached to tease the pad of his thumbs over the tops of her breasts where they swelled up over the lace of her bra.

Tess reached to push his hair back from his face. The long brown waves of it were still damp from a quick shower he'd stolen earlier in the night. She combed the length of it back gently with shaking fingers. It didn't tame his appearance. He must have seen it in her eyes because she was suddenly lost in a whirlwind of movement that left her bare and panting on the cool softness of the sleeping bag with him stretched above her.

The rest of her clothes were in tattered bits all around them.

As he kissed her, she lost her breath once more.

He didn't tease or hesitate. His lips came against hers fully and completely, and Tess welcomed them with all the energy that had lain dormant within her for too long. Taste for taste. Slide for slide. Nip for nip. Tongue to tongue. She was just as passionate, just as powerful as the man in her arms.

Tess plunged her hands into his hair and held the back of his head. She wrapped her legs around him and pulled his body close, then closer still.

She didn't pull back or pause or become afraid when her lips and tongue brushed against his teeth. She arched her back and welcomed him into greater contact with the most vulnerable heart of her body instead.

The smooth, heated length of him penetrated easily.

And then, Colin paused. Even though he was strong and dangerous. He paused.

She was slick for him and he filled her without pain. But he paused to give her body time to adjust to his. Tess closed her eyes and took the time he gave her. She shifted her hips and tilted and enjoyed the pure sensation of their joining.

She opened her eyes and her world spun wildly as Colin rolled to bring her on top of him. The movement didn't break their intimacy. In fact, it rocked her against him perfectly and she moaned in protest when the movement stopped.

Another pause?

Tess looked down into his dark chocolate eyes and she knew he was giving her a chance to control what was happening.

At first, as slowly as possible so she could feel every inch of him slide, and then faster and faster to meet and match the upward thrust of his lean hips, Tess reveled and controlled and refused to pause, to run or to hide.

The moment didn't blur so she knew he controlled his power…barely. He was still *almost* too wild, *almost* too strong, *almost* too… But Tess gloried when his body stiffened beneath her and he cried out. She laughed with joy when her own body trembled in a powerful release.

She wasn't a mouse. Not anymore.

He pulled her into the sleeping bag before she fell asleep and Tess realized that he was as wild as she'd ever imagined, but he was also so much more.

# Chapter 5

Colin watched Tess sleep. She tossed and turned and murmured, but he wouldn't allow himself to wake her. He wanted to take her into his arms and soothe the nightmares away. Instead, he fisted his hands and watched. She faced this for him, for Jacob. It made his heart ache and his muscles stiff. Inaction wasn't easy for a wolf. Unable to soothe Tess, he wanted to pace or run or tear something to shreds.

He still couldn't believe how she had responded to his passion. How could anyone who looked so delicate be so strong? From the tip of her head, capped by sleek blond waves, to her pale skin and willowy form, she looked almost fragile. But he'd slid his hands over the hidden muscles beneath her skin and he'd seen the way the vulnerability in her eyes could suddenly flash to forcefulness.

He savored the memory of the way she had laid him back

and explored his body. He was proud of his control even as he marveled that she had actually tried to make him lose it.

He couldn't resist the urge to reach out and lay his hand against her cheek. He had his father's hands. Their life had always been lived mostly in the outdoors. They had chopped wood for campfires and set up tents and trailers night after night for as long as he could remember. His hand was big and rough against her soft, pale cheek. It was a werewolf's hand.

His people had always been nomads with a tough life, but since the Pandemic, the constant movement had been relentless. Colin hadn't realized how lonely this new world had become. There had been little time for the kind of social networking that had kept their species alive for centuries. Before the 'Flu, there had been gatherings disguised as festivals and concerts. Mates were met and married amid the kind of romantic fanfare that humans had left behind in the Middle Ages.

Even though they bore little, if any, relation, the women of his pack were like family.

He watched Tess as her jaw hardened and her body stilled. Even asleep, she seemed to square her shoulders. Gently, with a whisper of a touch, he ran his forefinger along the side of her face. Somehow he knew this new set to her delicate chin was for Jacob. Tess had come into his life when he needed her most. Not just because she was willing to conquer these nightmares to help his people, but because she had held him and loved him and helped him remember that he wasn't alone.

An Alpha led his people, but he did it best when he had a strong mate by his side.

He had felt a surge of new hope and strength when Tess had stepped out from behind those crates. She had restored his will to fight. She had given him back the opportunity to lead his people.

And she needed him, too.

She had been through a lot. More than he might ever know. He saw her haunted past in her eyes, but he also saw the way she performed the most simple act with thoughtful, sure movements, until jumping up to chase fireflies with the children or bringing an old man another beer became a statement, a rejection of fear.

She inspired him because in spite of how hard her life had been she persevered. He knew they faced a lifetime of hardship, but he also knew Tess was the woman he wanted by his side. He only hoped she felt the same way.

Colin pulled his hand away from her cheek and closed his fingers into a fist. He wanted to hold the warmth of her skin there forever.

The low, sprawling building was constructed of cement block with no discernable windows. Its flat roof was coated in black tar for cheap waterproofing, so that the walls gleamed whitely in the moonlight and the roof seemed to disappear.

They looked down on the compound for mere moments before Tess led the way to an easily breached portion of the fencing she'd seen in her dreams.

She'd never felt this certainty, this surety. It made her hands shake as premature adrenaline flooded her body in anticipation of what was to come.

They didn't speak.

Colin had warned her not to fear him no matter what he had to do or what he had to become. Tess hadn't been able to warn him that her dreams were unreliable. But even as she continued to lead the way, her doubt was a tangible companion on their mission.

Tess had dreamed vividly after being intimate with Colin. She had seen every step they now took. She had seen where Jacob was held…but nothing after that.

She had to hope it would be enough.

They easily timed their crossing of the guard's patrol route. Their steps now brought them without incident to a little-used storeroom entrance.

Tess had seen Colin pick the lock to this door in her dream. What she hadn't seen was the way he consciously grew one elongated claw to serve as the pick. The sight sent chills down her spine. Not because it illustrated Colin's unusual nature, but because it illustrated her *not knowing* something about what lay ahead.

She went through first and navigated the darkened, cluttered room easily, even down to sidestepping a misplaced bin full of office supplies in the middle of the room.

Colin followed.

"Through there and left," Tess whispered. She was sure, but she needed to hear it out loud all the same.

"Anyone out there?" Colin asked.

His voice sounded strange, and Tess knew he'd taken the opportunity to morph further in the dark.

"There'll be a patrol just like outside, but we'll just miss them."

She sounded more confident than she felt.

Sure enough, steps echoed on the other side of the door in a fading cadence.

"You're amazing," Colin whispered.

Tess froze, struck by a sudden panic attack. *Lily* was amazing. Tess was only foolhardy. She risked her life and Colin's in the worst possible way. Hadn't she told him her dreams had never saved anyone?

He must have sensed the change in her because he

moved closer to stand by her side. Her hand was on the doorknob, but she couldn't turn it. She couldn't move.

Colin touched her shoulder. His hand was...different. Bigger, heavier. Oddly enough, it was that difference that calmed her.

Tess turned the knob and stepped into the empty hallway. She turned left without hesitation and counted doorways just as she'd counted in her dream. One. Three. Seven.

The seventh door was barred from the outside. Three massive bolts of steel stretched across the top, middle and bottom of the door and locked it into place.

The hallway was lit with red security lighting. It wasn't very bright, but she could see Colin better than before. He used his built-in lock pick again, and this time he had matching claws on every digit. He didn't look at her.

If there had been time, she would have made him stop and meet her gaze. She wanted to know him. She wanted him to recognize that she wasn't afraid of this side of him. Not anymore. The inner clock she followed said there wasn't time. She settled for a brief touch to the side of his still-handsome face and was rewarded with a startled smile before they stepped into the fortified laboratory.

It was a mistake.

Empty cages lined one side of the room. In her dreams, Jacob waited in the first cage.

Tess wanted to scream. Colin would want to know what to do next and she wouldn't have the answer. She was lost. Her dreams had failed again.

Someone whimpered and Tess knew the sound must have come from her own lips. She stood in the center of the room. Its antiseptic smell burned her nose and made her eyes water. Lily hadn't been in this room, but she'd been in one like it. A nightmare array of instruments lined trays on a nearby cart, and in one corner an operating table with straps waited for its next victim.

Tess began to shake as the empty room filled with images she couldn't seem to shut off. Like a waking nightmare, she found herself not bereft of input, but bombarded by more than she could take. Never in her life had she been anywhere steeped in such suffering.

"Tess, we have to get you out of here," Colin spoke urgently near her ear.

She barely heard him. She didn't see him. Her mind's eye was full of uglier sights.

"We've got him, Tess. We can go. We've got to go."

Colin's words penetrated louder this time and she was suddenly able to separate the images of past horrors that had taken place in this room from the present.

His face swam into focus through the tears flooding her eyes. He held Jacob's unconscious form in his arms.

Tess now saw where Colin had torn the cage's door from its hinges. She saw and she understood that her perceptions had been fooled by fear and sensory overload. The room and its horrible aura had brought forth her worst fear and mocked her with it before she'd been totally overwhelmed by its chamber-of-horrors history.

Tess touched Jacob to make sure he was real. His cheeks were stained with tears and discolored with bruises. His fine dark hair was matted and dirty and shaved bald in patches where electrodes had been.

But he was alive and he was here.

His skin was warm and his chest rose and fell with shallow respiration.

Colin wouldn't have to carry her, too.

Tess forced her feet to move and was soon running to

leave the lab behind and catch up to where her inner timetable said they should be.

Huddled deep in a laurel thicket, they just missed the midnight circuit of the guard patrol.

# *Chapter 6*

To celebrate Jacob's return, the werewolf folk turned their stereo system over to the teenagers of the pack. Instead of Southern rock, they all ate barbeque to the sounds of alternative punk. They had chosen to set up camp many miles away from the lab at the far western edge of the Shenandoah National Forest. Isolated and far from danger, the wolves took advantage of the opportunity to forget about scientists and laboratories.

As the lead singer belted out a throaty anti-establishment rant, Tess moved among the laughing, crying, dancing pack. She shook hands and shared hugs. She laughed and cried and danced. She had been alone for a long time. Each hand that touched her back or shoulders or face, each kiss, each embrace affirmed her decision to reach out and join H.A.E.S. This homecoming celebration was for Colin and Jacob, but it was also for her.

Tess thought back to the moment when she'd found the courage to cut Colin's chains and laughter bubbled up once more.

Jacob sat quietly off to the side while the pack celebrated. She'd been about his age when her parents had died. She and Lily had been alone. Jacob was surrounded by friends and family who would help him deal with whatever he had gone through in the last two weeks. She especially liked the way Uncle sat beside the bruised teenager talking quietly and often touching his shoulder or the top of his head.

She missed Lily.

Even as she enjoyed the party, there was a part of her "listening" for her twin, aching for what might have been. Being needed, here and now, by Colin and the pack soothed her pain, but she would always miss her sister.

This post-Pandemic world didn't offer an easy, carefree life. Instead, it offered her plenty of challenges to test her skills and hone her talents. And, for the first time, she wasn't scared. She was ready.

She *was* a psychic. Her dreams weren't something to fear. They would help her and her new family survive.

Suddenly, in the midst of the jubilant mosh pit of werewolves, Colin was by her side. He immediately claimed her full attention and she came to a standstill. The pack celebrated, but he stood, quiet and strong, enveloped by his people, but somehow held apart. He was Alpha. It was an awesome responsibility, but, then again, he was a man who could easily inspire awe.

Tess smiled.

He was larger than life.

He was not-quite-civilized and beautiful.

And he was hers.

She lifted a hand to touch Colin's perfect, smooth jaw. She wondered if there would ever come a time in the future when such a move didn't feel just a little bit daring, just a little bit dangerous.

She thought not.

He was hers, but he would also always be fierce and wild and free.

Tess was proud when her fingers didn't tremble…much.

Colin smiled.

The wicked gleam in his eyes told her he felt the slight tremor of her fingers…and liked it.

He also liked it when she stepped closer instead of moving away. His eyes widened and he drew in a quick breath. Tess felt the sudden intake of air as his chest rose against her breasts.

"Steady," she teased, though she was secretly glad when his arms moved to hold her. The boldness of her move and the sudden feel of his body pressed so close to hers had caused her knees to go weak, but she was up for it.

"Can you feel it?" Colin asked as his lips nuzzled the tender skin of her neck.

"Hmm?" Tess replied, feeling so much—from the smooth, firm muscles she caressed beneath his shirt to the fullness of her heart, once lonely, but not anymore.

"Their joy. Their hope. You didn't just save me and Jacob. You saved the pack, Tess."

He pulled back to look down into her eyes. Firelight danced in his and Tess watched those flames, knowing they reflected an inner fire, a determination to keep the people he loved safe. His people. *Her.*

His warm determination held her as surely as his muscled arms.

"I did, didn't I?" Tess whispered the teasing agreement

against his lips. Even lightly said, they both knew she embraced her power, accepted her strength.

"My savior," Colin whispered back before he deepened the slight contact into a full-on intimate taste.

The crowd had somehow moved away and now they stood alone in the firelight.

Even with both of her hands under his shirt, splayed against the heated skin of his back, even with her body pressed and held, firmly, warmly against his until she felt every rumble of laughter from his chest as he reveled in her bold kisses…it wasn't enough.

Colin stepped back and Tess went with him. They both laughed as her hands refused to slip away. Then, Colin stopped laughing. With serious, measured movements, he reached down and swept her up into his arms. Tess moved her hands from his back to his neck. There were no threatening SUVs in sight. No helicopters to interrupt. The rest of the night stretched ahead of them. Before, when he'd held her this way, they'd been running for their lives. Now, Colin walked ever so slowly, taking them into the forest, away from tactful but curious eyes. This time she watched the moonlight and shadows play across his handsome face. This time she wasn't afraid.

Oh, there was still a thrill zinging through her veins. Her heart still raced in her chest. But it wasn't fear. It was pure anticipation.

His careful, controlled movements said he savored the moment. His dark gaze never left her face, but even though the path was only lit by moonlight and twinkling stars, he never faltered. Step by step, he took them away from the roaring fire and the celebrating pack and deeper into the shadowed embrace of the forest.

Tess expected sleeping bags in a private thicket, but they

came to a clearing instead. A large meadow opened up under the stars like a sudden secret ringed all around by trees. The sky looked vast above them as they came out into the tall grass, but its star-kissed splendor held her attention for only a moment because the meadow had its own star.

A giant oak tree.

Colin carried her toward it and Tess was amazed by the massive spread of its leafy branches into such a grand canopy.

Somehow Tess wasn't surprised when Colin eased her down out of his arms to stand her by the trunk while he quickly scaled it.

His claws were already receding when he reached a hand down to her from the branches above her head. Tess took hold with both of her own hands and he pulled her quickly and easily up beside him. Her stomach fluttered—from the sudden movement, yes, but also because she finally saw the sleeping bags she had expected.

"It's perfect," Tess breathed in appreciation. She couldn't imagine a more fitting spot. Colin wasn't meant for plush sheets and a cushiony bed.

"You don't mind close quarters?" he asked as he fit himself into the hollow.

He went first then pulled her onto his reclining form. Tess settled onto his firm, warm body. There was just enough room to place her knees on either side of his lean hips, just enough room to snuggle her most intimate warmth against his.

"The closer, the better," Tess replied.

Slowly, he slid his forefinger under her shirttail. She felt the fabric pull then give way as he brought his finger slowly, ever so slowly, up toward her chest. The tip of his claw barely tickled across her skin as he used it to slice her shirt open. Tess shivered, then gasped when a flick of his finger parted her bra as well.

She braced herself quickly by holding on to nearby branches when he made their position precarious by sitting up to taste the tip of one exposed breast.

Tess sighed and arched her back. Her grasping hands had brought the small branches closer until leaves surrounded them. Their coolness fluttered against her naked skin in contrast to Colin's hot mouth.

His hands reached to steady her and hold her hips in place as his mouth moved to her other breast. He nuzzled its peak while the night air peaked and teased the nipple he'd left behind.

Tess let go of the branches and plunged her fingers into Colin's hair. He let her pull his mouth away from her breasts so she could catch her breath, but knowing his lips were then free and turned up to hers, Tess leaned down to claim them instead. The need for oxygen simply couldn't compete with the need to taste him.

As she stroked her tongue against his, Tess again felt fabric pull then part. Colin carefully, slowly, *maddeningly* cut her jeans away. Again, she felt the tip of one claw slip down one side of her hip all the way to her knee then another tip of another claw do the same on her other side.

She gasped into his mouth when those same fingers teased around the edges of her panties, tickling and enticing all at the same time. He morphed so smoothly and quickly that one second he could use a claw to part fabric and the next he could use the warm pad of his finger to stroke between her legs with a soft, intimate touch that left her aching for more.

She shifted to allow greater access, and Colin took the opportunity to push away the remnants of her jeans and the wisp of shredded silk that had once been her panties. He continued to use the pad of one finger to touch her so softly and so carefully she was amazed by his tenderness.

This was her wolf, her Alpha, and yet, for all his strength and untamed nature, he held her and touched her with care.

Suddenly, she felt like the wild one. Desperately needing to quicken the pace. Impatient for the feel of his skin on hers.

"I don't have claws," Tess whispered against Colin's lips. It was a reminder and a complaint. She wanted, needed to be closer to him.

"What's mine is yours," Colin replied and the husky tones of his voice indicated he wasn't nearly as patient as his pace suggested.

Tess pulled back and Colin moved to place his forefinger against the neck of his own shirt. Parts of her tightened and warmed as she reached to take his hand. Carefully, she used his claw-tipped finger to slice open his T-shirt. The fabric parted easily to reveal his muscled chest and taut stomach. She was thankful for the bright moonlight and frustrated with it as well. She could see Colin, but not well enough. She had to rely on her other senses. She pushed the fabric back from his shoulders and ran her hands over his exposed skin.

Colin dropped his head back and sighed beneath her touch as her stroking hands came to the waistband of his jeans, but the sigh turned into a quick intake of breath as she moved his hand to threaten the last bit of clothing that stood in her way.

The angle wasn't right for her to proceed.

Colin realized her dilemma and grinned. She saw his teeth flash. She also felt the obvious evidence beneath her that belied his teasing. He was as ready for contact as she was. He tortured both of them with his play, but it was sweet, sweet torture that only served to heighten her anticipation.

With an exaggerated stretch that slid and arched his body, Colin pressed his heat against hers. Tess was going to protest. She was going to beg. She was going to go for his fly like a madwoman. Instead, she moaned in relief as she felt his hands slip down to his jeans. She felt him hook his thumbs into his waistband and, then, he paused.

Tess held her breath.

He could see better in the dark than she could. She was sure he could see the desire for him on her face. She was sure he could see all the emotions filling her…desire, impatience, need…love.

His hands moved up to cup her face. She didn't see them coming. They were suddenly just there, cradling her jaw, caressing her cheeks. Did he see too much? Was it too soon for her to feel this deeply for him?

"I loved you from the minute you stepped out from behind those crates," Colin said, lightly tracing her lips with his thumb.

Tess released the air she'd held in a long, soft sigh. He did see everything she was feeling and it was all right because he felt it, too.

She reached to touch his shadowed face. Her fingers stroked along the strong, square jaw, the firm, kiss-swollen lips.

"I've known forever," she said, and it was only when the words left her mouth that she knew they were true. She had known. Through all those despairing years, through death and loss and sickness and strife, she'd known this love was waiting for her.

"I love you," Tess said.

The quiet confession seemed like a dream come true, a vision realized. Though she had never seen Colin's face before that day when she'd cut his chains, the hope of him had given her strength when she'd thought she was weak. It was that seed of hope that had propelled her ever forward when Lily was captured, when Lily was lost.

Colin was her love, her hope, her wild and wonderful wolf.

Tess shifted against the powerful man between her thighs. She couldn't wait much longer.

Suddenly with one quick, smooth move he shredded the last fabric that kept them apart, finally, *finally* as fast as she would have liked. He was naked beneath her and even the breeze felt sultry on her skin as their bodies finally, *finally* came together. His groan vibrated against her chest. His hips tilted and hers followed, finding the perfect fit.

Tess let out a gasping laugh as the hot length of him filled her. Her body was so eager, so ready. She began to move, but two warm, strong hands stilled her hips. Before she could protest, he began to direct her movements, lifting and lowering, lifting and lowering, and Tess was struck once more by his incredible strength paired with his incredible care.

She would have rushed. She would have hurried. But Colin made each movement long and lazy.

He drew out the moment for her pleasure.

He used his strength to prolong each slide, each stroke.

And Tess thought she would die.

She leaned down and took his kiss again, telling him with the hunger and urgency of her mouth that she didn't want him to be patient anymore. It seemed as if she'd been waiting for this wild release, this moment of perfect joining, *forever*. She showed him with her eager lips and tongue that she was ready, so ready for him to be *less* careful, *less* patient, *less* controlled.

Colin understood.

Suddenly, there was nothing slow about the way they arched together. The leafy branches that surrounded them shook as their joining went from tender and teasing to fierce and passionate.

The power of his hands at her hips helped Tess to extend every stroke, to enjoy every inch of him even as his speed brought her already aching body to its sweet, sweet release faster and hotter than she thought possible.

Colin slowed only when her whole body tensed. He pulled her close as her sudden tightening brought him to release as well. He filled her with heat as he cradled her close, and Tess never imagined she could feel so wild and so safe all in the same moment.

Sheltered in the tree and quiet in each other's arms, Tess listened to the night as she became aware of the outside world once more. In the distance, she could hear the sounds of civilization. The pack had grown quieter, but she could still hear the occasional burst of laughter or a car door slam. She could hear distant music. Someone had switched the angry punk to a country croon. Perhaps Uncle had claimed the stereo.

Tess smiled.

Somehow, she'd managed to find home and family even as she'd braved stepping into a shadowy wilderness filled with werewolves and danger.

"I'm glad you cut those chains," Colin spoke against her hair. She could hear the pride in his voice. Pride and gratitude and wonder.

"So am I," she replied, rubbing her cheek over the muscled expanse of warm chest she'd first seen bound and hurting. *"So am I."*

* * * * *

# HONOR CALLS

*Caridad Piñeiro*

This story is dedicated to my daughter and best friend, Samantha Ann. You rock and I am blessed to have you in my life!

***CARIDAD PIÑEIRO***

is the bestselling author of twenty novels. In 2007, a year marked by six releases from Harlequin and Pocket Books, Caridad was selected as the 2007 Golden Apple Author of the Year by the New York City Romance Writers. For more information on Caridad, please visit www.caridad.com or www.thecallingvampirenovels.com.

Dear Reader,

In "Honor Calls," I've brought back a character who may be familiar to some of you—FBI Assistant Director in Charge Jesus Hernandez. Since *Darkness Calls,* he's been in the periphery of the stories, advising Diana Reyes and her partner during their assignments. Always calm and reserved and functioning by the letter of the law. Honorably discharging his duties until the day he runs into Michaela, a vampire slayer who is now challenging what Jesus knows to be the right thing to do. What will win out—honor or Michaela's need for vengeance against the vampires who killed her mother and forever changed her existence?

It was quite a lot of fun to expand the universe of The Calling by introducing Michaela, and I'm looking forward to writing a full story around these characters in the future.

As some of you may know, The Calling is a series of my heart. I'm truly grateful to my editors for allowing me this opportunity and to you—the fans—for continuing to follow the exploits of the various characters and the vampire underworld.

Again many thanks to all of you for making The Calling series possible. If you wish to reach me, please visit www.caridad.com and www.thecallingvampirenovels.com.

Caridad Piñeiro

# Chapter 1

Michaela had been tracking the vampire since she'd sensed the elder during her scouting mission in Central Park.

He wasn't the one she sought, but the heightened thrum of his power told her he had just killed. Reason enough to pursue him until she could find the right vampire and dispatch him.

Then and only then could she leave New York City for a kinder, gentler place.

She discovered the elder vamp's victim just beyond one of the jogging paths. The kill was fresh, the scent of the elder strong on the female runner who had been tossed into the underbrush like garbage. As Michaela bent to examine the jogger's body in its shredded clothes, she realized the vampire had not just been content to drain the woman of blood. The victim had been sexually assaulted as well and in the most brutal of ways—ripped apart by the vampire sating his lust.

Michaela opened her senses to pick up every last scintilla of the elder's trail, from the metallic taste of the victim's blood on his breath to the unique wake of energy the immortal left behind.

She reached the southern end of the park and something ahead of her spooked one of the horses attached to a hansom cab waiting along Central Park South. The animal reared up, hooves flailing.

She darted behind the cab and caught a glimpse of a blurry figure speeding through Grand Army Plaza. As she raced to the fountain in the center of the square, the pulse of undead power beat at her more strongly, signaling that she was getting closer to the ancient vampire.

Another indistinct flash weaving through the pedestrians on Fifth Avenue confirmed the immortal was within her reach.

She focused on that vague shape, keeping a watchful eye and a respectful distance as she chased after him. She could not engage the vampire elder out in the open where either humans or other vampires might see what was happening. To do so might expose her presence in the city and possibly bring down the wrath of the vampire council.

Despite her caution, the elder must have sensed that he was being followed.

He increased his speed, weaving in and out of the humans on the sidewalks, climbing to the rooftop of a building in lower Midtown Manhattan and leaping from one structure to the next before dropping to the ground. The vampire moved at an almost frantic pace, as if he knew the nature of her mission.

Michaela kept up her determined pursuit, patiently waiting for the moment when the time would be right. She dodged pedestrians and vehicles as the vampire attempted to elude her, well aware that she had to act before the immortal reached the safe haven of the Blood Bank.

If he made it there, she would have to pull back and wait for another night. There were too many undead in that place to risk a confrontation within its doors.

Too many, and she was just one against them.

She drove back the crush of loneliness that nearly choked her, reminding herself that there was no other way. Her life held too much death and destruction; it hindered any kind of personal commitments.

The few people she had allowed to get close had run away when they discovered the truth about her existence.

The truth about her.

Or they'd ended up dead.

In Union Square, the vampire geared down to human speed, using that pace to lose himself amongst the many mortals still present in the park. The beat of the humans' life forces and their scents served to disguise his presence.

Michaela paused at the far edge of the square, examining the walkways, attempting to separate the humans from her undead prey, but she was unable to pin down the immortal. She waited, hopeful that once the elder moved beyond the boundaries of the crowded area, she would be able to pick up his presence once again.

Her wait was futile.

Long minutes passed with no activity that she could discern.

She finally acknowledged that she had been bested by his subterfuge, but that didn't mean the chase was over.

She knew just where the vampire was likely to go.

If she could beat him there, she still might be able to take him out before he reached the safety of the nightclub.

Hustling at breakneck speed, she arrived at the mouth

of the small cobblestoned street that led to the Blood Bank. At the club's door was the ever-present vampire bouncer and crowd of humans waiting to mingle with both wannabe and real vampires. Not to mention the occasional shape-shifter brave enough to cross into bloodsucker territory.

Michaela had never understood the human fascination with the undead, the near veneration for the amoral creatures who had taken so much from her and others.

Vampires weren't meant to be idolized, she thought.

They were meant to be exterminated.

As she felt the presence at her back, she realized she had guessed right about the vampire elder.

She had barely half turned to face him when he lashed out at her, nails as sharp as eagle's talons raking across her jacket. The leather did its job, keeping his nails from tearing into her flesh.

Bending backward, she avoided the deeper thrust of another vicious swipe toward her midsection and then dropped down to sweep the vampire's feet out from under him.

He landed with a thick thud, while she was immediately back on her feet after a quick jerk and launch of her body, a nice sharp wooden stake in her hand.

"Not what you thought, fang boy?" she taunted as she stood, arms akimbo, above the prone body of the stunned elder.

With a swift move of his own, the vampire surged to his feet, fully transformed. His eyes glowed with a piercing teal-blue light. Long deadly fangs erupted from his mouth and ended at a point below his chin. Such a prodigious length of tooth testified to his longevity. The strength of his elder power jabbed at her senses, threatening just by its very existence.

This vamp would not go quickly, she thought as the elder issued a warning growl and lunged at her again, beginning a dance that could end in only one way…

With one of them dead.

Frustration clawed at his gut as he stared at the picture of the latest victim found torn apart in a downtown alley. As he flipped through the status report on the investigation, a familiar name appeared in the FBI case report.

The Blood Bank.

FBI Assistant Director in Charge Jesus Hernandez expected a fair share of crime in a city like New York, but judging from how often the edgy Goth bar appeared in the reports provided to him, the Blood Bank appeared to be crime central.

He supposed the easy way to find out more about the club would be to ask any of the agents in his bureau what to make of the place. But he hadn't gotten to be one of the top agents in the New York City Bureau by taking the easy way. On the contrary. He believed in personally getting involved when it was necessary.

As he picked up the file again and examined the photo of the body parts found a couple of blocks from the bar, he raked his hand through his short-cropped hair and blew out a disgusted breath.

He'd read the witness statements. Tales of creepy happenings and Goth clubgoers who might be a little more than they seemed.

Even his top agent—Diana Reyes—seemed to believe in the possibility of an underworld that was less than human.

It was definitely time for a visit to the Blood Bank to get his own impression.

Memorizing the address, he rose from his desk and

slipped on his suit jacket. For a moment he considered going by his apartment to change, certain he would look out of place in his expensive suit.

But his apartment would be seriously empty. His last lover had moved out nearly a year earlier, complaining about the time he devoted to his job. Considering that the living room still boasted only the recliner and the plasma television he'd bought after she'd left, she had probably been right.

Plus, as he mentally reviewed the contents of his closet, he knew he had nothing suitable to wear to a Goth bar anyway.

Best just to drive by the place, scope it out and decide what to do next, he told himself. For good measure, he checked to make sure his gun was loaded and tucked snugly into the holster at his side.

The one thing he knew about the Blood Bank: it wasn't the kind of place you went without protection.

# Chapter 2

Shit. The small street on which the Blood Bank was located was not wide enough for the passage of a car. His intent to just drive by wouldn't be possible.

As Jesus rounded the block for the third time, he scoped out a free parking spot a short distance away and then headed on foot toward the club.

He hadn't gone more than a few feet before the heat and humidity of the August Manhattan night had him sweating beneath the weight of his suit jacket. Since he was armed, removing the jacket wasn't possible. He was starting to regret that he hadn't gone by his apartment to at least change into a T-shirt and jeans.

Swiping at a line of perspiration along his brow, he paused at the mouth of one of the older streets in the city. It looked more like an alley, which seemed appropriate for the place he was about to visit.

Ahead of him and about four small blocks down was a line of people at a nondescript building—the Blood Bank, he assumed. The line was relatively long, considering the hour, and it was filled with a decidedly rough-looking crowd clad in black leather and metal. That at least was not very different from what he had expected.

As he proceeded along the cobblestones, bright with the light from a full moon and uneven beneath his shoes, he kept a wary eye on the smaller, narrower side streets and tight gaps between the buildings. It was at the mouth of one of those alleys that the last body had been found.

Or at least, parts of the body.

A grunt, loud and painful sounding, snared his attention. Two turn-of-the-century brick buildings, built so closely together that the moonlight did little to illuminate the area between them, did a good job of hiding whatever activity was going on in the gap.

Another grunt was followed by the din of metal trash cans crashing together.

Definitely a fight and, judging from the sounds of it, someone was getting their ass kicked.

Jesus pulled out his Sig and advanced to the opening of the alley. He took a step within and let his eyes adjust to the lack of light, revealing the two people locked together in combat. One was tall and much bigger than the other, and as they grappled together, the light from a side-door lamp illuminated their features.

The smaller one was a woman, while the other…

Eerily bright blazing eyes shot a glance his way while long white fangs gleamed under the artificial light of the lamp. The creature growled at him, the sound like the rumble of a mountain lion, but then turned back toward the woman.

Jesus blinked, unable to believe what he was seeing, but

another glimpse of the creature's face confirmed what he was—a vampire. Or at least, someone posing as one.

The much smaller woman had her arms braced against the creature's jacket, trying to keep those wickedly long fangs away from her face, but with the vampire's greater height and bulk, Jesus feared she might be fighting a losing battle.

*No,* he cursed as she continued with the fight, totally ignoring his presence.

The creature spun the woman around and as the light swept over her face, he could tell she was young. Mid-twenties, he guessed before she whirled out of sight again, struggling to break away from the demon's grasp.

With a quick upward jab of her arm, the woman snapped the creature's head back. It emitted a louder growl, but the woman's blow did little to slow the demon. It reached behind to grab the woman by the scruff of her neck and whip her against a brick wall. She hit with a thick thud and fell to the ground dazed, prompting Jesus to action.

"FBI. Stop or I'll shoot," he called out, training his gun on the demon as it took a step toward her.

The thing actually halted and looked at him. What he guessed passed for a smile erupted on its face, but then a second later the demon reeled back, grabbing at its chest with long taloned fingers.

The woman had buried a wooden stake deep into its chest.

Shock filled the creature's face, mirroring Jesus's own surprise as he realized she had just killed someone…

No, make that some*thing*, before his eyes.

Blood leaked from around the edges of the stake, staining the off-white shirt the man-beast wore. It stood, hands flailing, long nails clacking against the stake, disbelief on its face before the look became blank and the creature dropped to the ground.

"One down, too many more to go," the woman said, her voice deeper than what he would have expected from someone so petite. She nudged the creature's body with the toe of her black boot and then bent to examine it, as if to make sure she had finished the job.

One down, huh? He turned his gun on her and warned, "FBI. Put your hands up."

She faced him and just for a moment he thought he saw a hint of fang at her mouth and a glow in her gaze, but then she stepped into the puny shaft of light from the side lamp on the building.

Her face was anything but demonlike.

She stood before him, her hands outstretched at her sides, her totally human face serene and beautiful, reminding him of the pictures of the saints his mother used to have on the wall of their fifth-floor walk-up apartment. Of course, the black leather encasing her slim body was anything but saintlike.

Too beautiful and too young, it occurred to him as she took a step toward him.

"FBI. Stop or I'll shoot." He held his gun steady and aimed straight at her head.

A wistful smile played across her face as she stepped toward him tentatively. "This is none of your business. The FBI has no power here."

"Here? This is New York City, lady, and in case you didn't notice, I've got the gun and the badge." For good measure, he drew aside the edge of his jacket to reveal the silver-and-gold badge clipped to his belt.

She surprised him by laughing, a sexy husky sound that pulled at his gut, confusing him. His confusion only increased with her next words.

"This may be New York, but that gun and badge won't

help you against vampires. Especially ones like him." She motioned to the body on the ground. "Or the ones up the block in the Blood Bank."

Certifiable, he thought, because now that he had time to think, he knew the demon on the ground had to be a man in costume. Vampires were not real and a stake to the chest would kill most anybody. But then the body on the ground did a funny little twitch and began to shrivel up before his eyes.

Following his gaze, she peered over her shoulder. With a shrug she said, "The older they are the faster they dry up. Harder to kill, though. Age makes them stronger."

He shook his head and, for the barest of seconds, closed his eyes to refocus, blaming what he had seen on the lack of light. But when he returned his gaze to the body, it was still slowly disappearing, sublimating like dry ice, and the stake remained buried deep in the middle of its chest.

When he looked back at the woman, he realized she had walked right up to him. The barrel of his gun was barely an inch from her face. Her very young and attractive face.

After she finished perusing him, she wrinkled her nose and said, "You don't strike me as the type to believe in anything that doesn't go by the book."

She was right, which frustrated him; despite his better judgment, her power and self-assurance called to him.

As their gazes met, he detected loneliness in her.

The same emotion that lived in him, thanks to the demands of his job.

Fascinated, he said, "So make me believe."

She smiled and motioned to the entrance of the alley behind him.

"Follow me."

# *Chapter 3*

Michaela watched the bewilderment on his face fade and be replaced by something…

Dangerous, she thought, sensing his attraction to her, sensing the want in him that could make him risky. Somehow that wasn't enough to deter her from fulfilling his challenge. She would make him believe.

When he holstered his weapon, she brushed past him, trying to ignore her response. She wasn't usually the suit-and-tie type, not to mention that he was older than the other men who'd been in her life.

Of course, that was because dead or gone was her typical type. Not old. Especially since old was something she would never become.

Ignoring her contradictory emotions, she put a sexy roll in her walk as she moved toward the Blood Bank. A quick glance over her shoulder told her that he was totally buying in to her challenge. A thrill of anticipation shot through her.

She smiled, pleased that he seemed intrigued, and headed straight to the bouncer. The big man glared at her until she allowed a hint of her gleaming gaze to emerge. He hesitated, maybe sensing the difference in her power, but then she repeated the action and added a bit of fang.

The bouncer relented and, with a broad sweep of his arm, lifted the red velvet rope for her and the FBI agent. As they slipped beneath the boundary, the bouncer emitted a low growl, as if to warn her that the two of them were not fully welcome.

She ignored him and plowed forward, the FBI agent close to her back. After they entered and moved out of hearing of the bouncer, he leaned forward and asked, "Bouncer is a vampire?"

His tone was laced with disbelief, but she nodded as she navigated through the crowd with him nearly plastered to her back. The bar was full tonight, packed with dozens of human Goth and wannabe vampire types, as well as the real deal. Colored spotlights skittered unevenly over the crowd. On the small stage at the far end of the club, glaring light illuminated a band playing loudly and aggressively, half singing half screaming indeterminate lyrics. The strong thumping bass and heavy drumbeats pulsed across the club and incited those on the dance floor to thrash and jump in rhythm.

The lights and noise bothered her senses. She hurried to the back of the club where it was quieter and dimmer, creating a feeling of false intimacy. The area was crowded, but in the farthest corner was an empty table for two.

She sat down with her back to the wall, not wanting any surprises. Unexpectedly, he plopped down right beside her rather than across from her.

When she arched a brow in question, he shrugged and said, "Don't want to have to watch my back, either."

Understandable and yet provoking.

His physical presence was difficult to ignore, and his dark brown eyes seemed fathomless in the dim light.

She hoped he would not prove as fascinating as he appeared.

"So you expect me to believe the bouncer was a vampire and that there are other ones here, as well?" he said, examining the interior of the club.

There were definitely vampires present. She sensed the push of their undead force, but before she got into proving it, she wanted him to buy her a drink. She was low on cash and most men disappeared once they discovered the truth around them.

The truth about her.

Raising her hand, she signaled a waitress.

When the young woman arrived, Michaela said, "Cuervo shooter."

Slipping a glance at her companion, she realized he was checking out the waitress, in a vamp way, not that she expected him to pick up on the signs so quickly. She shook her head.

He understood and ordered a shooter, as well.

The waitress hesitated and Michaela explained, "You're new. You've got to pay up front."

He snorted in disgust, but quickly dug into his pocket, peeled off a twenty from a moderate wad of cash and tossed the bill on the scarred black Formica table. The waitress immediately scooped up the money and walked away to place their orders.

"Must get nice clientele in here," he said as he tucked his money into his pocket. The motion pulled his suit jacket back, exposing the butt of his gun. At an adjacent table, one of the patrons noticed the weapon and quickly scurried away.

Jesus wondered why the man felt compelled to run. In his line of business, it was an obvious sign of guilt, but in here...

For all the patrons' Goth rebelliousness, they were quite uniform in their manner of dress; lots of black, from the leather and jeans to their hair.

"You said you'd make me truly believe," he reminded his companion just as the waitress came to the table with their drinks.

The waitress placed the lime, saltshaker and shots of Cuervo on the table. His companion bit into the lime, skipped the salt and then downed the tequila in one gulp before ordering another.

"Thirsty?" he asked as he paid in advance once again.

"Once guys see how things are, most of my dates don't last beyond the first drink." She fidgeted with the empty shot glass.

"Didn't realize that buying you a drink made this a date," he said, perplexed by her, by the self-assurance on the surface that seemed to hide a well of vulnerability.

"Not your usual type, I suspect," she said and fully faced him.

*Not his type?*

He wondered about that as he sipped his shot of tequila and studied her. Her dark, nearly black hair fell in choppy layers against her roundish face. Cerulean-blue eyes bore an exotic slant and hinted at extreme intelligence, while pale, creamy skin appeared to be as soft as satin sheets.

The black leather jacket she wore fit tight against her body, accentuating both her slimness and slightness of stature, but the tank top beneath the jacket exposed the lushness of her curves.

He imagined exploring those curves. Raising that lean, strong body against his and slipping within.

His type, he thought, fighting back his body's response. Now that they were up close, he guessed her to be at least a decade younger than his thirty-eight years.

"Don't have a type and I'm not the kind to drink and run," he said, taking another sip of the Cuervo to quell the desire awakening within him.

She laughed, the tone of her merriment rich and uninhibited. It had been a long time since he had allowed himself that kind of freedom, but she clearly was not one to hold back.

That only intrigued him more, especially when she challenged him with, "You may be the kind to run after you see what goes on in here."

Elegantly raising her hand, she gestured to the far corners of the club, close to where they sat. He could barely make out the shadows of people engaged in various activities.

Leaning close to him, she said in a hushed tone, "Look carefully if you dare."

Her warm breath against the base of his neck was sweet. He imagined the kiss of that breath elsewhere and decided it warranted the risk.

"I dare."

# Chapter 4

He followed the surprisingly long line of her index finger, which pointed to a doorway guarded by a muscular bouncer. He was another very pale man who exuded a power that Jesus could feel even across the distance separating them.

Yet one more vampire? he wondered before turning his attention to the door.

In the distant corners, so dark they were almost devoid of light, he finally recognized the activity going on.

Sexual, he thought as he watched one woman writhing against someone, her legs wrapped around a waist. Heat raced through him as he imagined his companion riding him like that, but he quickly tamped down the thought.

Beside that couple was another in an intimate embrace. The woman straddled a man's thigh, grinding against it, clearly seeking satisfaction. Her companion had one hand tangled in her long blond tresses. Before Jesus's eyes the man pulled the woman's head back, exposing the long line of her neck. There was a familiar weirdly bright blue-green gleam in the man's gaze and a flash of white fang before the man buried his face against the woman's throat.

Jesus imagined he could hear her sharp gasp of surprise. He saw the jerk of her body, confirming that he wasn't imagining the attack. When the man shifted his head for the barest of seconds, a dark line of blood became visible against the woman's skin.

Instinctively Jesus began to rise, determined to interrupt the assault, but his companion laid a hand on his arm.

"Don't get involved. She came here for that and the vampire knows the rules."

Vampires did not exist and what he had seen so far that night could be explained by…

He didn't know what would explain it, but surely there was a rational reason somewhere.

"The rules?" he asked, sitting back down and picking up his shot glass. He hoped her answer would provide a more plausible explanation for what he had just seen.

"No siring the humans in public. I'm even surprised he put the bite on her like that. Foley—"

"Foley?" He finally downed his shot, wincing as the heat burned down his throat.

"Foley's the owner of this place. He usually has a 'no public biting' policy," she replied easily, but a furrow of worry was etched in the middle of her forehead.

"Not good that they're getting so bold," she added.

The waitress came over at that moment with their next round of drinks and he placed another order.

"Not running?" she asked as she picked up the wedge of lime.

"Not sure. But before I make up my mind...who are you?" He dragged the shot glass close and slowly shifted it between his hands.

She wiped the lime juice from her hands against her jeans and then introduced herself. "Michaela Ramirez."

He eyeballed her hand, then shifted his gaze back to her face as he took her hand in his much larger one. "Jesus Hernandez."

Raking her gaze over his attire, she said, "Special Agent Hernandez?"

"Assistant Director in Charge," he corrected.

"The boss man."

It explained the air of power about him and confirmed what Michaela had already suspected—he was the kind of man who knew how to take care of himself. But it also meant he was the kind of man who would not understand the mission to which she had dedicated her life, and her eventual death.

He played by the rules. Her existence defied such constraints.

Arching a brow upward, he asked, "And what is it that you do? You know, your job when you're not busy staking the undead."

She didn't have an answer she thought he would accept, so she took her time, perusing him once again.

His suit was expensive and well tailored to his big, muscular body. Despite his age, thick dark brown hair showed not one hint of gray. The few wrinkles on his face were the smile lines at the edges of his very sensual mouth and dark brown eyes.

Eyes that twinkled with amusement at her inspection, at her stalling tactic.

Surprising.

"What's a guy like you doing in a place like this?" she asked, wanting to shift the focus back to him.

"Maybe starting to believe."

He downed his shot of tequila just as the waitress brought the third round.

When she reached for the lime and shot glass, he covered her hand with his deliciously warm one. His palm was rough against the back of her hand. She imagined that roughness rubbing other parts of her body and a hot flush erupted within her, dampening the spot between her legs.

"Sure you can handle another? You're kind of…small," he said, dragging his gaze over her figure.

His look lingered at her breasts, yanking a more obvious response from her. Her nipples beaded into tight points, which only convinced her that it had been way too long since she had last satisfied herself.

Way too long, she thought as she turned her hand and grasped his, running her fingers along the fine hairs on the back of his wrist. She stroked his bare skin, edging beneath the cuff of his shirt.

"You'd be surprised at how much I can handle." She grinned when she felt the tremor beneath her fingers.

Jesus held his breath as her simple touch jerked his body to life. It had been so long since he had done this little dance with a woman. He wanted to confirm that he wasn't misreading the signals.

"Just need to make sure you know what *you're* doing in a place like this," he said and half turned in his chair to be certain that he didn't miss a millisecond of her reaction.

"What I'm doing?" She looked down to where her hand still stroked the sensitive skin at his wrist.

He took her question as an invitation and grasped her

hand in his. He noticed the slight chill of her skin and wondered at the reason for it, but he thrust aside the niggle of concern.

"Nervous?" he asked, narrowing his eyes to read her reaction. If anything, she'd been assured, strong and complex so far. He was anticipating experiencing more of the same from her.

"Just…cold," she answered and twined her fingers with his. "As for where this is going… Are *you* sure you're ready to handle all of this and more?"

Jesus shot a look around the club and then back at her. She seemed so much a part of this place and yet removed from it. That might explain the hint of loneliness he had sensed in her.

"If the 'and more' involves the two of us alone together somewhere, I'm ready."

Shaking her head, she smiled, but there was no mistaking the sadness in her voice as she said, "You may be sorry you said that."

He cupped her face with his free hand and explored the soft skin of her cheek. He shifted his thumb downward over her full lips. Her warm, sweet breath exploded against his finger, as if she was shocked by the intimacy of his touch.

"If I promise not to be sorry, can you do the same?"

She sucked in a shaky breath and he saw how her pupils widened with desire. Against the pad of his thumb, her lips quivered before she worried her bottom lip with her perfectly white teeth.

Perfectly white *fangless* teeth. The thought brought some relief that he wasn't about to engage one of the supposed undead in what he hoped to be some very satisfying sex.

"Well?" he prompted, her delay both worrisome and frustrating.

She released her bottom lip and finally said, "I won't be sorry."

# *Chapter 5*

"Good." He rose and stood by the table, obviously waiting for Michaela to choose where they would go for their tryst.

"Where" definitely not being the flophouse where she was staying while she completed her mission. She suspected that Jesus, too, would not volunteer where he lived for their encounter.

Which left only one immediate choice—one of the back rooms at the Blood Bank.

She stood and inclined her head toward the rear of the club. "We can pay for a private room in the back."

Jesus narrowed his eyes, seemingly doubtful, but he didn't hesitate to follow her as she led him to the bouncer by the door. He stood with tattooed and muscular arms across a broad chest barely covered by the metal-studded leather vest he wore. He kept an unwelcoming glare on his face until Jesus reached into his pocket and extracted some cash.

"What will it be for the best room you have?" Jesus asked.

The bouncer looked at her and replied with a snicker, "I guess such a fine *lady* only deserves the best. A hundred dollars until dawn."

"Dawn?" he asked, even as he peeled off the bills and handed them to the man.

"A virgin, are you?" the bouncer said with a sneer, but Michaela shot her hand up to silence him.

"The key is all we need from you."

When he held out the large brass key, she snagged it from his grasp and rushed into the hallway containing the private rooms.

The hall was narrow and relatively short. The walls were painted black and seemed to devour the light from the dated wall sconces located near each door. The floor beneath their feet was carpeted with a thick shag rug in deep crimson. It was matted down in the center, testifying to the traffic that passed this way.

Jesus followed Michaela as she checked the number on the key against the ones on the wooden doors of the rooms. Finally, at the door farthest away from the club and all its noise, a brass number eight marked the room as theirs.

"What did he mean that we had the room until dawn?" Jesus asked, towering over her. His physical presence rattled her calm, causing her to falter while she tried to unlock the door. He immediately covered her hands with his and helped steady her as she turned the key and opened the door.

She had heard about the Blood Bank's private rooms, but she had never been in one. The room was surprisingly more than what she had expected.

A queen-size four-poster bed took up one side of the space, the bed's surface lushly appointed with a satin comforter, an assortment of pillows and remarkably clean sheets.

But it was the accessories on the opposite side of the room that subsequently snared and held both her attention and Jesus's.

He walked to the wall where an assortment of whips, chains, cuffs, knives and other toys were conveniently displayed. Running his index finger along a pair of fur-lined wrist cuffs, he shot her a half-lidded glance as he once again asked, "Why dawn?"

"Why do you think?" She removed the wrist cuffs from the wall and examined them more carefully, even going so far as to undo the strap on one of them.

"It's when the vamps go home after a night of play," he said.

A rough edge tinged his voice. Was it from fear or from imagining their own night of play, fur-lined wrist cuffs included?

"It takes a lot of trust, don't you think?" she asked, slipping on one cuff and holding out her arm the way one might do when examining a bracelet.

It would take a lot of trust, Jesus thought. More trust than existed in their newborn relationship. He reached out and slipped off the cuff, tossed it aside, encircled her fine-boned wrist with his hand and urged her close.

"Tell me what you want, Michaela." He enjoyed the contradictions she presented, but he needed something concrete on which to begin this night, on which to—perhaps—build something more. Because he suspected that with a woman as complex as Michaela, one night just wouldn't do it.

She laid a hand on his chest and stepped so close she had to tip her head back to peer up at his greater height. Softly she rubbed her hand against the fabric of his shirt and said, "I want normal."

The longing in her voice was unmistakable. His own yearning responded in sympathy.

It had been way too long since he had done normal.

Gingerly, aware that she was a little skittish and might bolt, he eased his arm around her waist. Slowly he urged her to move that last little bit, until her body brushed his. But he moved her no farther, not wanting to intimidate or overpower. Somehow, he understood that Michaela needed equal footing.

She needed a partner, he thought as he bent from his greater height to put his face level with hers.

"I think I can do normal," he teased, a playful grin on his face as he sought to begin her night of respite.

Their evening of pleasure.

A smile crept to one corner of her mouth. She cradled his cheek and traced the lines of his mouth with her thumb, shifted it to the dimple beside his lips.

"You have a nice smile. You've done it often during your life," Michaela said. At his puzzled look, she slipped the pad of her index finger across the faint lines on his face.

His grin turned wickedly sexy. "There's something to be said for maturity in a man."

Dipping one hand while bringing the other upward, she placed both on the cotton of his shirt, exploring the gloriously sculpted muscle beneath. As she closed the final distance between their bodies, the hard jut of his impressive erection pushed against the flatness of her belly.

She pressed against him, shifting her hips back and forth. "Maturity doesn't seem to have affected your 'something,' because it's definitely saying—"

"I want you, Michaela. You're…unique." He buried his hand in her shoulder-length hair and cupped the back of her head.

*Unique?*

He couldn't even begin to guess just how different she was, but she had asked for normal tonight. Any explanations could wait until she'd experienced the wonder that he had promised.

"You sweet talker. I bet you charm all the women with lines like that."

The playfulness faded from his face, replaced by an intensity that nearly stole her breath. "Not much for talk, Michaela. I'm an action kind of guy."

At the back of her head came the gentle pressure of his hand, urging her to her tiptoes until his lips were a breath away from hers.

"Are you an action kind of woman?" he asked and his tequila-spiced breath spilled against her lips, creating an intense pull of need within her.

"Yes," she replied.

# *Chapter 6*

A shudder ripped through his body at her answer. He knew then that no matter how much she wanted a normal night, there was one thing he couldn't do…

"I'm not sure I can go slow," he said.

She chuckled and tipped her head upward once again to lock on his gaze.

"That's okay. You can go slow later."

Later, he thought, and groaned as he imagined taking her again and again until the dawn came and maybe even beyond that. But for now…

He slipped his arm beneath her buttocks and raised her until they were face-to-face.

"I think later sounds great." He smiled, which prompted her broad, unrestrained grin. A smile so real and inviting that he had to feel it against his lips. He traced the edges of her welcoming smile with a series of impatient little kisses until the contact wasn't enough for him.

Or for her.

She bracketed his head with her hands, kept him close, as she tasted him and then slipped her tongue into his mouth. Raised her legs and wrapped them around his waist, welcoming him elsewhere.

Jesus kept on kissing her even as he walked with her toward the bed on the other side of the room. When he bumped the mattress with his legs, he dipped down to let her sit on its edge. Michaela grabbed his lapels, the fabric expensive beneath her hands, although she itched to have the more luxurious texture of his skin against her palms.

She urged the jacket from his shoulders, exposing the well-worn and cared-for leather of his holster, the menacingly black grip of his gun and the slick cotton of his shirt. Grasping the fabric, she jerked, sending buttons flying but accomplishing just what she wanted.

As the shirt hung open, she laid her hands on his skin. Hot like a winter fire. Surprisingly smooth since he had little chest hair. The rich caramel color of his skin matched the warm brown of his eyes, which were glittering brightly as he glanced down at her, a deliciously receptive grin on his face.

"I guess I'm not the only one who can't go slow."

"Guess not," she said, wrapping her thighs around his legs once again, imprisoning him tightly. Leaning back against the soft surface of the bed. Challenging him to action.

He didn't disappoint.

He teasingly brushed his hands across her breasts before helping her ease the leather jacket from her body. As the jacket came off, he tossed it to the side, seemingly ignoring the unexpected weight and metallic thud that hinted at some kind of weaponry in the garment. Instead, he immediately grabbed the edge of the black tank top she wore, pulled it up and over her head and exposed her upper body to his gaze.

Between her legs came the jump of his erection. He emitted a low rumbling moan a moment before he put his fingers at the front clasp of her black bra. The slight tremor of his fingers confused her.

"Jesus?" she asked and laid her hands over his.

His name on her lips nearly undid him; it had been so long since a woman had said it with such a mix of need and doubt.

He wanted all doubt gone.

*Needed* all doubt gone.

"Be sure, Michaela."

She slipped her fingers beneath his hands at the clasp of her bra and parted the fabric to reveal herself to him.

"I'm sure, Jesus. Incredibly sure."

He dragged his hands away from her breasts, to her shoulders, where he ran his thumbs across the fragile lines of her collarbone before inching down the straps of her bra and removing it. Then he slowly passed the pads of his fingers down the softness of her skin until he cupped her breasts. He ran his thumbs across the hard peaks of her nipples, intent on savoring all the differences between them: the paleness of her skin against the darker tones of his; the size of him, immense against her slight frame, reminding him of her physical fragility. But as she encircled his wrists with her hands and urged him onward, her actions spoke instead of the strength of her spirit.

He circled the hard tips of her nipples with his thumbs then pulled on them, dragging a response from her as she raised her hips and ground herself against him.

Bending, he replaced his fingers with his lips, sucking and teething. He thrust his hips against her center, building her need. Enticed by the soft gasp of pleasure and the shiver of desire that came beneath his lips, that slipped from her skin to his as his body brushed against hers.

Michaela grabbed hold of his shoulders as he loved her breasts. She rocked his body against the center of her, creating a deep sensual clenching that wanted more.

While he tongued and sucked on her nipples, bringing her to the edge, she reached down and undid her black jeans. Parted the fabric there.

He sensed her motions and responded, lowering one hand down her body until it rested on the gap of skin exposed along her belly. His thumb circled the indent of her navel, while the tips of his fingers brushed the hair between her legs.

She shifted her hips and he raised his head from her breasts, locked his gaze on hers and dropped his hand down the last few inches.

His eyes were dark with emotion when he parted her with his fingers, seeking the center of her. Intense as he slowly circled the nub between her legs, building her pleasure. Warmth and damp erupted between her legs at his caress and she once again urged her hips upward.

Again he didn't disappoint.

He eased first one finger and then a second within her and brought his thumb to her clitoris, the pressure and thrust of his movements sure. Demanding.

She grabbed hold of his shoulders. Powerful. Stable. A solid place where she found purchase as she moved her hips, seeking her pleasure and release.

Jesus loved the look on her face, in her eyes. Part wonder. Part desire.

All woman.

Strong, certain female.

He had warned her that he couldn't go slowly and her actions only made it even more impossible to hold back.

As much as he regretted leaving her, he ripped his hands

from her body and made short work of stripping off her boots, socks and jeans, revealing impossibly long legs and the nest of curls at the juncture of her lush thighs.

He stared down at her, appreciating the beauty she offered.

Fierce femininity, he realized. Sexy strength wrapped around an intensely private and vulnerable soul.

A soul that needed this night's satisfaction and respite.

He intended to give her the evening she desired.

Quickly he undid his belt and pants. He dropped them, but didn't bother to remove them.

He secured her hips in his hands and poised his erection at her entrance. The ripple of her desire beneath his fingers and at the tip of his penis urged him on.

Michaela gasped as he penetrated her in one sure thrust and then waited for her to accommodate the size of him.

So large.

Scalding heat within her, igniting her ardor.

She held her breath, overwhelmed by the sensation of him. Overwhelmed by his barely controlled passion.

Then he destroyed her.

He tenderly brushed his thumb across her cheek as he whispered against her lips, "Let go, Michaela. I'll be here to catch you."

# *Chapter 7*

*Let go.*

It had been so long since she had allowed herself such freedom. Since she had been able to trust anyone enough to permit herself such liberties.

Now, here he was. Promising so much. Unaware of the impossibilities of his promise.

But for this one night, she intended to believe as he did.

With a subtle roll of her hips, she accepted what he offered and took him deeper within.

He dropped his head to kiss her, his mouth open on hers, tasting her. Sucking in her breath while he drove into her, his movements steady and sure.

She cupped the back of his head and played her tongue against his, mimicking the movements of their bodies, but then he shifted away to lick and bite her nipples.

She held him near as her body answered the call of his, rising ever higher. Need tightened into a knot deep within that had her rocking her hips in rhythm to his thrusts and arching her back so that he might more easily savor her breasts.

Then suddenly it came, wrapping around the center of her and stealing her breath. Forcing her ever higher against him as the sharp explosion of passion burst throughout her body. Dragging a strangled scream from her as she dug her nails into his shoulders.

He stilled his thrusts, kissed her lips and whispered, "Let go, Michaela."

She did.

A second later the full force of her climax washed over her, so intense that her body shook from the power of it. Around his erection, her muscles tightened, as if afraid he would leave, but then he slowly pulled out and the slick friction of his withdrawal yanked a protest from her.

Jesus answered that protest, driving in again and again, his forehead leaning on hers. His mouth swallowed her gasps and sighs of pleasure as he drew out her release until unbearable pressure built inside him.

She must have sensed it since she reached down and cupped him, caressing him and dragging a finger along the sensitive gap right behind his scrotum.

Her touch undid him.

With a sharp, swift inhalation, he buried himself so deeply it almost seemed he might split her in half. He spilled his seed in her womb, his body taut. His back arched as he closed his eyes and experienced every nuance of her body, became intoxicated by the smell of her, now marked by his sweat and release.

Michaela watched him as her own climax ebbed around him, the last fluttering motions rippling across his erection as it nestled within her. Milking the seeds of life that could never find fertile soil within her.

His arms were braced at her sides until she laid her hands on his forearms and ran them up to his shoulders. With a gentling touch, she said his name and urged him down onto her. He came willingly, laying his head beside hers, his larger body nearly engulfing her as she lay pressed beneath him.

"Am I too heavy?" he asked and she shook her head.

"No," she replied, welcoming the protective weight of him. She continued her caresses, wanting this tenderness after the intense way they had taken one another.

He brought one hand to grasp her waist, slowly running it up and down her side in a soothing motion. He waited until the tremors had left both their bodies and their breathing had slowed to a regular tempo. Only then did he pull away from her to remove the rest of his clothes. Almost before she could notice his absence, he was back by her side.

He urged her upward on the bed until they were once again lying beside one another. Her head was pillowed on his shoulder; her one thigh tucked between his legs while his arms held her close.

She had wanted physical satisfaction and gotten it.

She hadn't counted on this.

The loving caress of his hand along her back.

The way she was surrounded by him, and not just physically.

There was unexpected security in his embrace. A surprising sense of dependability.

Not that it would last.

Jesus sensed her pulling away from him even though she had barely shifted physically. It was more in the way a slight tension had crept into her body. When she looked up at him, that furrow of worry was back between her finely shaped brows.

"Running already?" he asked softly, but he didn't stop the gentle glide of his hand along her back.

"Is that what you think I do? Hit and run?"

She moved away from him then and he immediately felt the absence as the night chill replaced her warmth.

"Am I wrong?" He spread his hands across her back to keep her from escaping.

She shook her head and looked away, but much as he was determined not to let her leave, he would not abide her hiding her emotions from him.

He cupped the side of her face and tenderly urged it upward. That was when he noted that her eyes were bleeding out to the weird blue-green gleam he had seen earlier that night.

Fighting back the fear he suspected she wanted to see, he injected calm into his voice. "Who are you, Michaela?"

"You mean *what,* don't you?" she asked, a low inhuman rumble in her tone. A slight bit of fang nipped just below the edge of her full upper lip.

He could take a guess at the what, although he was still finding it difficult to believe, even with the proof staring him in the face. He mustered control over his gut reaction to the unexpected, then realized he was neither fearful nor repulsed.

She'd made him feel more than he had ever felt before. Because of that, he was willing to suspend his usually strict approach to learn more about her.

"No, not what, Michaela. Who? Who are you and why are you doing this?"

Christ, she thought, completely at a loss on how to deal with him.

With her vampire powers engaged, there was no missing the slightly hurried beat of his heart and the chill and tension that had crept into his body. Sure signs of fear, not that he was revealing it.

Or giving in to it, she thought, totally puzzled and unbalanced by his reaction.

By him.

"You're afraid of me, but you're not fleeing?"

He laughed harshly. "I didn't get to be an ADIC by shitting my pants and running at the first sign of trouble. So you can cut out the whole creature-of-the-night routine—if that's what it is—cuz I'm not going anywhere."

She morphed back to her human state and realized his response proved what she had initially thought about him—he was a man used to dealing with danger.

A man who might be prepared to deal with her.

So she gave him his answer, praying that once she did, things would return to the way they should be so that she could figure out what to do about him.

"I'm a dhampir."

# *Chapter 8*

He shot her a perplexed look and raised one full dark brow. “A dhampir? Care to explain?”

“Half vamp, half human. Stronger than a human, but weaker than a vampire.”

With his thumb, he traced the lines of her mouth, parted her lips to reveal the now perfectly straight edges of her teeth.

“Do you bite? Humans, that is?” he asked.

She bit down on his thumb with her teeth, making his erection jump against her belly.

“Guess a little fang in a girl doesn’t bother you?”

He shrugged, clearly guarding his reaction. “Depends on the girl. Depends on why she’s busy staking vampires in my city.”

“*Your* city?” As if to prove just how little was truly his, she reached between them and stroked him, fully rousing his erection to life, loving the jerky jump of his body that prompted a sympathetic twitch between her legs.

Jesus knew he'd be hard-pressed to deny he still wanted her despite the discovery of what she might be. She held the proof of his desire in her very capable hands. But he suspected he wasn't the only one who couldn't resist.

Cradling her breast in his hand, he idly rubbed his thumb across the hard tip of her nipple.

"*My* city. My rules," he stressed.

She chuckled and increased the pressure of her hand. She inched upward on the bed until her lips were against his and the spill of her breath flavored his every inhale.

"I warned you before. Your FBI rules have no place in my world and the vampires have no place in yours."

He kissed the edges of her lips. Tasted the sweet straight lines of her teeth with his tongue before he said, "Wrong, *querida*. I came to this place because its violence has already touched my world and I need to stop it."

"Like you may one day have to stop me?"

"Yes. I will stop you if I need to."

Her body went rigid. She ceased her caresses and moved away from him both physically and spiritually. As he met her gaze, the gleam of unshed tears shimmered in her eyes, but she held them back as she said, "I won't let you prevent me from what I have to do. Honor demands that I finish what I've started."

"What have you started? Why did you stake that vamp?"

She shook her head and bit her bottom lip before she finally faced him. "They raped my mother. That's how I came to be born. She managed to escape them, but they came after us."

Jesus grabbed hold of her fisted hands. "They wanted you dead?"

She nodded and a lone tear escaped, tracking down her face.

"They wanted my mother dead. They got their wish," she said, and told him her story.

*New Jersey Shore*
*Twenty Years Earlier*

Her mother was bleeding.

Michaela could feel the warmth and wet of it drip down onto her as her mother held her hand and dragged her through the tall marsh grasses along the edges of the dunes. The stalks, dry from a lack of summer rain, crackled, the noise overly loud in the silence of the night.

Too loud, Michaela thought, recalling the creature that had attacked them. The creature who would surely hear them pounding and crashing through the grasses as they tried to escape.

Suddenly her mother stopped short and shoved Michaela away toward a larger patch of foliage.

She fell to the ground, the sharp edges of the grasses biting into her palms as the tall stalks swallowed her up. The saw edges of the plants cut her hands and arms, but she bit down on her lower lip to stifle her cry of pain, aware the sound would reveal where she was.

Aware that her mother was ready to sacrifice her life to hide her daughter.

Holding her breath, Michaela tried not to move as she peered through the ever-shifting mass of dune grass.

Her mother stood, her chin at a defiant tilt. Blood dripped down the side of her face from a large gash above her brow. The blood looked black thanks to the palette of the night. Her face was washed to a pale green hue by the light of the full moon.

"You didn't think you could run from me again, did you?"

The tone of the creature's voice was low, almost soothing, with an odd rolling sound beneath, like the purr of a cat.

Her mother said nothing for a moment, then picked up her chin another rebellious inch. "You will not take me again. I will not allow it."

The odd rumble in the creature's voice intensified as he laughed and said incredulously, "You will not allow it?"

Something flashed before her mother. A bright white blur so close to her…

A gush of dark liquid erupted from her mother's throat and spilled down the front of her bright yellow sundress.

Her mother brought her hand to her throat, but the creature yanked it away, laughing cruelly. "I will have you now, as you die. I will have you after, as your body cools. But first…"

The creature wrapped an arm around her mother's waist, holding her up as her knees buckled, burying his head against her ravaged throat.

The horrible sounds of his sucking and her mother's moaning carried across the still night.

Michaela covered her ears, but it was too late to avoid hearing him say, "But first I will have your blood."

Curling into a tight ball, Michaela tucked her head against her knees, brought her arms over her head and closed her eyes. She tried to escape from what was going on just a few feet before her. She imagined other places and times. Prayed for her mother to be safe. Thought about the yellow sundress her mother wore and how they had bought it at the thrift store just earlier that week.

The rough shake of the ground beneath her body pulled her back from where she had gone.

Only then did she realize the night was now almost quiet. The only sounds were those of the stalks as the wind moved them and the faraway susurrus of the waves washing against the shore.

She was alone. Or at least she thought she was.

Peering through the brittle green stalks, she saw what had made the resounding thud that had snared her attention.

Her mother's body lay less than an arm's length away, staring sightlessly at the moonlit sky. Her dress was torn, exposing her breasts and the bite marks on them. The cheery yellow was bloodied from the hideous hole where her throat had once been.

Michaela wanted to keen and cry, run to her mother, but instead she grabbed hold of her knees and forced herself to remain still, fearing that the creature lingered nearby. Knowing that her mother had given her life to save her. She could not dishonor that sacrifice with her fear.

A second later the ground shook again and suddenly there were shafts of light piercing the night, moving back and forth across the dark sky. Other tremors came beneath her and she realized they were footfalls. Coming closer and faster as the intensity of the lights increased. Suddenly there were blue pants legs standing before her hiding place.

"Shit. Holy shit," the man said and passed his flashlight over her mother, across her still-beautiful face and sightless eyes.

Michaela cried then, a puny wheezing sound, but it was enough to snare the man's attention.

He parted the grasses before her and the silver-and-gold badge on his chest gleamed brightly against the royal blue of his uniform.

"Jesus, Mary and Joseph," he said as he reached for her.

# *Chapter 9*

"The officer who found us—Joe Santos—had been sweet on my mom." Michaela dragged in a long tortured breath as emotion choked her.

"He didn't turn you in to the authorities, did he?" Jesus asked and swiped away another silent tear from her face, his gaze fixed on her.

She nodded. "He gave me a home and kept me safe. Taught me how to protect myself and use a gun."

"He knew about the vampire?"

Her fists were clenched so tightly they had begun to hurt. She relaxed her hands and he took advantage by twining his fingers with hers as he asked, "Did he know about you?"

She tried to pull away from him, wary of what he made her feel. Of the emotions he had forced her to relive. But he increased the force of his grip. He couldn't have held her if she wanted to escape him.

But she *didn't* want to escape.

There was something safe and secure about his presence. Something that reminded her of the policeman who had adopted her.

"When I hit puberty, things changed. I got stronger. Started needing less sleep. Craved—"

"Blood?" He jumped in.

Regretfully she nodded. "Joe never adopted me, but he was a father to me. He realized something was going on and finally gave me a letter my *mami* had written that he had found and read years earlier. He had put it in a box of things he collected to give me when the time was right. The letter explained about the vampire who had raped her—the one who came back to kill her."

"The vampire didn't know about you?" Jesus asked, caught up in the story she was telling him. Concern for the child who had suffered tangled with his fascination for the woman she had become. As she had promised earlier that night, he was coming to truly believe that vampires were all too real. But even if they were, in his heart he knew Michaela was different.

"If the vampire had known, he would have killed me. Full vamps don't care for half-human abominations like dhampirs."

"And you have no love for them either, only—"

"You can't stop me from honoring my mother by killing the creature who murdered her. By exterminating others like him who care nothing for human life," she urged, pleading her case.

"Honor calls to you, but it does to me, as well. I can't let your violence create havoc with the laws I'm supposed to enforce."

"I don't hurt humans, Jesus. And I promise you that I

won't let the demands of my honor spill over into your world." She laid her hand on the side of his face, stroking the rasp of his evening beard. "But if somehow it did, I understand that this thing between us—"

"Won't protect you from what I'd have to do," he finished, regret already wrenching his gut at the thought of having to choose between her and the laws he had sworn to uphold.

A sad smile crept onto her face, but she inched closer until her lips brushed his. "Then we have a truce?"

A truce, he thought. He confirmed it by bringing his lips to hers, his kiss tentative, tender.

There was none of the urgency of their earlier coupling as he explored the contours of her mouth. Treasured her breasts with his hands. Eased his fingers down to the center of her. Explored the slickness of her lips and the wetness of her vagina.

Her soft, soughing breaths drove him on as did the strong strokes of her hand along his erection.

When he entered her again, he waited, wanting to prolong the union for as long as he could. He needed to experience all the nuances of her as they continued to kiss and caress. This time, their passion grew slowly until they were both shaking.

Rolling onto his back, he urged her to straddle him, letting her set the pace of their loving as he worshipped her breasts. He urged her on with the slow upward lift of his hips, deepening his penetration.

Michaela moaned at the sensations he created as he buried himself deep into her center. Biting her lower lip to control the urge to scream, she rocked her hips, riding him. She sucked in a strangled breath as the climax rose within her and the motions of her hips became more forceful as she sought her release.

He placed one hand at her waist, guiding her as he rose up and licked the tip of her breast. Teething the tip of it gently, the sharp moment of pleasure/pain released not only her climax, but the demon she thought she had tamed.

Jesus sensed the surge of her release as it washed over her, followed by a strange inhuman push of power.

As he met her gaze, the bright blue-green glowed powerfully and a small hint of fang extended beneath her full lower lip.

"You want to bite me?" he asked even as he braced one arm against the surface of the bed and rose up so he could be face-to-face with her.

"I do." The animal purr tinged the tone of her voice and her gaze dropped briefly to his neck before locking back on his eyes.

"What if I bite first?" he asked, but didn't wait for her answer.

He surged forward and laid his mouth on the spot where her shoulder met her neck. He licked up and down before playfully taking a bite that he then soothed with a whispered kiss.

She shuddered against him, bringing one hand up to the middle of his back and the other to cup his head, urging him on.

"More, *por favor,*" she pleaded and rolled her hips, enticing him to finish. To allow his own release to erupt.

He bit down gently and then sucked on the spot once more as he surged upward with his hips.

Against his throat came her rough cry followed by the sharpness of her fangs as they skittered along his skin. He stilled for a moment, awaiting the piercing pain, but the warm wet of her tongue arrived instead, licking upward until she brushed the shell of his ear with the sharp points of her fangs.

"More." The rumble of her voice vibrated against him.

He kissed her throat and drove his hips upward. He gave her another love bite and caressed her breast with his free hand, answering her soft moans of pleasure with tenderness until he was barely able to hold back his own climax.

She lowered her head again and whispered, "Let go, Jesus. I'm here to catch you when you fall."

He groaned and closed his eyes as her strong arms came around him, supporting him. Her hands pressed against his back while her hips pumped up and down, helping him along to his release.

But he had to see her face as he came.

He met her gaze.

Her human gaze, the demon apparently under control, only…

She lowered her head to his throat and gently nipped it with her teeth.

Human teeth.

She sucked on the spot to soothe it, and the tender pull of her mouth sent him over the edge.

A mangled groan escaped him as he drove upward one last time and spilled himself into her. Felt the wash of his climax ripple from deep within and surge through his body.

She wrapped her legs around his waist and her arms around his shoulders, uniting them at every possible spot—hips against hips, her midsection and breasts tucked tight to his. Her heart beat quickly against the wall of his chest as her breath washed over his cheek. Her mouth took his, her kiss tender and calming, restoring something within him that had been empty for too long.

He returned the kiss, burying his hand in her hair to keep her close. His mouth opened on hers, accepting the enticing bite at one corner that prompted his smile. A smile that dragged a playful chuckle from her.

As he looked up at her, her eyes glittered with satisfaction and relief. Somehow he knew his reflected the same.

"Life sometimes brings you unexpected pleasures," he said.

"Nothing says it only has to be tonight," she replied and brushed another kiss across his lips.

He was surrounded by her in every possible way and yet didn't feel trapped. She was a dhampir, inhuman, and yet he didn't feel threatened.

Or fearful.

For the first time in a long time he didn't feel alone.

"I assume you have somewhere to stay while you're in town?"

Shock froze her in place as she considered his question.

*A place to stay?*

She thought of the run-down hotel whose halls smelled of stale urine. Of the indiscriminate stains on the mattress and mustiness of the room that was barely bigger than a closet.

Then she thought of a different place.

A place where someone might be waiting for her at night. Waiting to hold her. Waiting to make love with her. Waiting to share both triumph and disappointment.

But not just anyone, she thought, gazing down at Jesus's handsome face.

She would be coming home to *him*.

Slipping into bed beside *him*. Having *his* arms hold her and keep the monsters at bay.

Those monsters had destroyed her life, but they had also brought her to this place.

Brought her to him.

"Not really, but…are *you* sure you're ready to handle all of this and more?" she asked.

He surprised her by chuckling and shaking his head. "I'm sure of only one thing. I want to explore whatever this thing is between us. Can you accept that?"

Amazingly, she could.

She could accept that uncertain promise because up until now, her life had been empty of any promises except one…

The promise of death.

His vow, unsure as it was, promised life. Possibly love.

Bringing her lips close to his, she said, "I can accept that."

"You won't be sorry," he vowed as he met her lips with his.

Michaela knew she wouldn't be.

Honor had called for her to go on this journey, one that had been filled with pain and loss. But the journey had now given her this night and this man.

A man with his own sense of honor.

As he began to make love to her once again, she realized her journey had offered her another path.

She would no longer walk the lonely road alone.

She had him and the promise of love to keep her company.

She smiled and gave herself over to honoring that promise.

* * * * *

# SHADOW LOVER

*Lydia Parks*

I want to thank my agent, Sharene Martin-Brown,
and editor, Tara Gavin, for making my dream
of writing for Silhouette Books a reality.
And, as always, thank you Bob and Mom,
for making this possible.

***LYDIA PARKS***

grew up in New Orleans, the home of Dixieland jazz, Creole cooking and thrilling ghost stories. She now lives in New Mexico with her own personal hero and writes about sexy vampires and shape-shifters for Harlequin Books and Kensington Books. Her vampire novel *Addicted* is a finalist in the 2008 *Romantic Times BOOKreviews* Reviewers' Choice awards. Visit her at www.lydiaparks.com.

Dear Reader,

I, like so many, have been fascinated by vampires for years. How can a creature who lives forever, lures humans into his grasp and has centuries of experience pleasing women not be sexy? Griffin is a delicious example of just such a vampire.

Dr. Serena Brockman, a psychologist who specializes in explaining dark fantasies, understands the fascination so many of us feel, but she also knows that vampires don't exist. At least, she believes they don't until she meets Griffin.

I hope you enjoy the sensual excitement of Serena's introduction into the reality of dark fantasies.

Happy reading and sweet dreams!

Lydia Parks

# *Prologue*

He heard the sound of her muted footsteps on the wet leaves long before she approached the tree under which he stood. Every evening, she followed the same trail from her sister's home to her own, holding her skirts above her ankles to keep them dry, whistling a soft tune against the darkness. She never tarried on her way, never stopped.

Tonight, he would stop her.

"Who's there?"

He stepped out from the deepest shadows and smiled. "Good evening, my dear. My name is Griffin."

Although clearly startled, she recovered quickly. "What is it you want, sir?"

He strolled toward her, sending forth thoughts of peace and goodwill. "The chance to alleviate my loneliness, dear Molly, even if for only a few hours."

"How do you know…my…name?" Her eyelids drooped as her will to protest faded.

This one he'd watched for months, admiring the way her auburn locks reflected moonlight and her pale skin glistened in the evening dew. He'd retired each morning humming the sweet, sad melody she whistled.

He couldn't spend another night alone.

"You need not worry, my dear, I won't hurt you." He stroked the side of her lovely face, thrilling to the downy warmth of her cheek. "And when I leave, you'll have no memory of what passed between us."

He caught her as her knees buckled. Careful not to bruise her precious flesh, he carried her to his resting place, well inside the damp cavern. Once he'd placed her on his bed, he lit a lamp and watched her wake.

She was truly lovely, a small-framed woman, perhaps twenty years of age, with a heart-shaped face and large eyes the color of wet clover.

He reacted to the sight of her on his bed as any man would, hardening to the point of discomfort. He would have her as his own this night, and then sleep with her in his arms until he woke again at sunset. When he released her, she would remember nothing, and he would have the smell and the feel and the sound of her to carry him through another year or two, perhaps more.

How pathetic his existence had become.

But this was no time to wallow in his pigsty of sorrow. No, he had a beautiful young woman to entertain, to bring to heights of pleasure she didn't know existed.

She watched him without protest as he bared himself to the waist. Then he knelt beside her and unwrapped her from the layers and layers of clothing he found so annoying these days. Finally, she lay naked before him, one arm folded across her small breasts and the other hand cupped between her legs. She shivered, but asked no questions.

He touched her with great tenderness, stroking her arms and shoulders, feeling gooseflesh rise under his fingers and small hairs brush against his palms. He eased her arms to her sides and she complied. Touching again, he moved to her neck and breasts, caressing them appreciatively, teasing the tiny buds of her nipples as they tightened until her breath caught in her throat.

And then he kissed her.

That's when he realized just how much she reminded him of Rebecca. It wasn't her appearance, but her scent and taste. So much like his long-lost love, the memories squeezed his cold, dead heart until he wanted to scream.

But he didn't scream.

With his fingers buried in her hair, he held her close and took her sweet mouth, probing deeper, savoring every bit of it. After a few moments, she began to respond, to draw on his tongue, to moan softly.

"She's yours," the beast whispered.

He ignored the voice as he pulled her under him, pressing his cool flesh to her heated skin. All he wanted was to feel her body submit to his, to wrap himself around her. She writhed against him as he enjoyed more of her, allowing his fingers to slide over her virginal cleft.

Her heartbeat thundered in his ears, loud, steady, the sweetest music.

And the beast spoke louder now. "Take her. She will not resist."

"No," he growled, closing his eyes to fight it.

Her tiny hand came up to his face and the heat of it branded him.

Staring into her sea-green eyes, he realized then that he wanted her with him for more than one day. He wanted her for his share of eternity, to walk the nights with him, to sleep the days away in his arms.

She was so much like the woman he'd loved.

"Remember the glorious taste of her soul," the beast said. "It is yours for the taking."

Unable to fight both the devil and the memories, he let the chains of restraint rip through his hands and felt his fangs descend in a rush.

Molly's hand slid down to the front of his chest.

Her touch felt too good. He couldn't manage this way; the beast would soon take over.

Carefully, but firmly, he turned her over so that she faced away from him and he drew her to the side of the bed.

With the devil again leashed, he ran his hands down Molly's back, admiring her pale, warm skin, her narrow waist, the indentation of her spine, the width of her hips. He reached around her to caress her soft mound, parting her swelling lips, and found her unexpectedly wet.

Pressing his forehead between her shoulder blades, he freed himself from his breeches, aching to bury himself in her. He would control her thoughts to alleviate the pain of her first encounter.

She made soft noises of need and raised her buttocks, opening herself completely, trusting him.

He entered her slowly, intoxicated by the warmth of her, savoring every response as he nuzzled her hair. When tightness became obstacle, he thrust through with a growl of delight.

So much like Rebecca had once been.

Sweet, lovely Rebecca. How could he be expected to resist her?

"Now," the beast commanded. "She is yours. Take her!"

As her muscles began to tighten, and she gasped with approaching release, he succumbed to the beast's demands.

She screamed as he pierced her flesh, but not with pain.

His arm around her waist, he held her close as her body rose against his. His brain exploded with her essence, the intense emotions—love and hate—the needs, and wants and dreams. All of it was his, spiced to perfection with her climax, and he hungered for more. He wanted all.

His body responded as both man and beast, giving and taking.

On and on it went, visions of a short life packed with sunshine and beauty, darkness and pain, dreams unfulfilled. He reeled with the wonder of it.

Unable to stop, he fed and fed, until he'd gone too far. She lay still.

Fraught with terror, he withdrew from her and gathered her onto his bed where he pressed his ear to her chest, listening, straining for any hint of a heartbeat.

He'd snuffed out her life's flame.

No hope of releasing her.

No hope of bringing her into the Darkness.

Caught in an endless nightmare between unbearable pleasure and unimaginable pain, he held Molly's lifeless body and rocked, cursing the beast and his miserable existence. Never again would she walk the dark path in the woods.

Never again would he hear her whistle her haunting tune.

Closing his eyes, he yelled against the misery.

He could not allow one so precious within his reach again.

He'd walk his path alone.

# *Chapter 1: The Illusion*

The first time Serena saw him, she thought she was hallucinating.

He appeared suddenly as a looming apparition directly in front of her when she stepped into the street, and sent her staggering backward. She tripped on the curb and fell back hard, her teeth gnashing together so abruptly she thought she might lose a few.

And then a pickup truck roared past, swerving, speeding through the space she would have simultaneously occupied if not for her strange savior.

She searched the street and sidewalk, trying to recall exactly what he'd looked like. All she drew from her senses was tall, dark and scary.

Sitting there, she couldn't have sworn he'd even had eyes, or any other features. Had he been wearing a mask of some kind?

Another car passed, slower than the truck, and tinny music grated over the empty sidewalk.

As the realization that she'd nearly faced eternity on a lonely Santa Fe street bubbled into her brain, she pushed herself to her shaky feet and brushed off the back of her jeans. And she looked around again, studying the shadows for any hint of movement, but saw none.

With her heart pounding, she picked up her purse, slung it over her shoulder and started home at a fast walk, listening for the sound of footsteps behind her. Once home, she locked both dead bolts, checked the back door and windows, then crawled into an ancient velvet-covered chair and curled into a protective ball.

Had she been wrong all these years? Were there really angels of some kind? Or ghosts? Had an ethereal being just saved her life?

And then she recalled his scent. She'd only caught a hint of it when she gasped in surprise, but it left an impact. Masculine. Leather, smoke and rosemary. And maybe mothballs. Would a guardian angel have an aroma?

But he couldn't have been real.

A memory wormed its way to the surface—a dark memory she'd locked away years earlier. Sometime in college, Serena had started fantasizing about a tall, gorgeous stranger, dangerous yet attractive. He wanted her and she wanted him, but they could never touch because he existed in a shadow world, in another dimension. She'd thought of him when she was alone at night. And she'd thought of him when she walked dark alleys, hoping he was the one she felt watching her. Sometimes, he seemed so real, she could smell him, hear him, even see him if she turned her head quickly. She dreamed he'd eventually take her to his world where they'd live together for eternity.

When she met Robert, she quit thinking about her shadow hero.

That earlier part of life, that dream, must have subconsciously sparked her most recent lectures on the human need for dark fantasies of eternal life in order to deny death.

As she sifted through the event on the street, analyzing memories and possibilities, Serena realized she'd probably only seen a reflection of the approaching truck, and smelled scents from nearby houses. The whole thing had been a fortunate set of coincidences that resulted in her nearly biting off the end of her tongue, but also avoiding one horrific accident.

And she felt better.

Until she saw him again.

Two days later, she had been walking home from an evening seminar where she'd lectured on dark fantasies and denying death, when she caught a glimpse of him standing at the corner of a building, watching her. Although he looked rooted to the spot, she was sure he hadn't been there one second earlier. He wore black clothing, a black cape that left him almost indistinguishable from the shadows, and a black hat, a wide-brimmed 1940s fedora, tilted low and to one side.

Once again she couldn't see his eyes, but this time she knew they were there. She physically felt his gaze, subtle yet definite, like the movement of water across submerged skin.

A shiver ran down and back up her spine.

Fighting flight instincts, she stopped, turned and stared back.

He didn't move, not even to take a breath, and she thought for a moment that he might be a statue like so many found in unexpected places in this city.

The street sounds disappeared under the rush of her

own blood past her eardrums as she walked toward him, forcing one foot in front of the other. She felt as if she were approaching the end of the world, and wouldn't be able to stop until she'd peered over the edge.

When she did stop, she stood less than three feet from the stranger, staring up into his face. He must have been at least six feet tall with broad shoulders and a square jaw. All else about him was conjecture.

Until he nodded and said, "Dr. Brockman."

His voice had the fine quality of an oboe, and although he whispered, it seemed to echo through her chest like the aftereffect of a kettledrum.

She swallowed hard and licked her dry lips. "Who are you?"

His mouth stretched into a smile, then he bowed his head in salute. "A fantasy, I believe."

"Excuse me?"

He laughed, and his laughter was even more incredible than his voice.

Serena shuddered.

And then she jumped when, in a sudden rush, he swept his hat from his head and bowed deeply at the waist like some hammy silent-screen actor.

"Griffin, at your service."

She couldn't respond right away. He was terribly good-looking, in a dark sort of way, much as her youthful fantasy man had been. His wavy black hair just touched his shoulders, and his features were exquisite, almost regal.

But his eyes blew her away. He had blue eyes, so light in color, they seemed to glow as if reflecting a full moon hidden somewhere behind her.

A wave of dizziness washed over her, and she staggered backward to keep her balance.

As quickly as he'd appeared that first night in the street, he materialized at her side, clutching her arm. "My dear, are you all right?"

She looked up at him. "Who the hell are you? And how do you know my name?"

He chuckled. "Well put."

"Huh?"

She was usually more articulate than "huh," but felt as if she'd stepped into a thick purple fog she couldn't explain.

"Now, now," he said, patting her arm, "don't worry. I won't hurt you." Then he leaned close and whispered, "Unless you ask me to."

They walked toward her house, alone on the street, her boot's heels thudding on the sidewalk. Although she was terrified, it wasn't for the usual reasons. She didn't expect him to drag her into a dark alley, rape and kill her, or even to take her purse. Something deeper, more primal, drove her fear. She knew, somehow, that her world would never be the same.

"Would you like to sit and talk?" he asked.

"What?"

"Are you having trouble hearing me? Or is English not your native tongue?"

Serena pushed herself free from him and shook her head to loosen her thoughts.

How had they reached her front porch?

She eased into one of the wicker chairs, and it squeaked under her weight.

Silent, he did the same, settling into the chair to her right, crossing one leg over the other, then placing his hat on his knee.

She sat there, shaking like a leaf in a spring gale; he looked like he awaited delivery of a mint julep.

"Who are you?" she asked again.

"As I've already stated, I'm Griffin."

"Just Griffin?"

"Just Griffin. And you are Serena Brockman—psychologist, orator and writer, born in Atlanta and living in Santa Fe, thirty-two years old."

"I know who I am," she said, anger surging at the one-sided feel of the whole encounter. "How do you know all that?"

"I attended your lecture."

"I didn't say anything about my age or where I was born. And you weren't at the lecture."

His eyebrows lifted in innocence, and he smiled. "I tend to listen from doorways."

"Why?"

"Unfortunately, my appearance causes difficulties."

Her senses seeming to have returned, she studied him more carefully. He watched her with unearthly intensity. Her body warmed in response, but she wasn't sure why. Perhaps it was the sensuous quality of his gaze.

Pale skin gave his fine features the look of marble, then as she stared, his face morphed into something feral.

She blinked hard, found his original appearance restored, and decided that her system must be on overload.

"Look, Griffin," she said as she got up from her chair, "I think you should leave."

He rose in front of her and stood very close to her, as if they were intimate. "Do you really want me to?"

Time stopped, and the air around her disappeared. For some reason, she couldn't lie, couldn't breathe and couldn't send him away. She met his unblinking gaze and shook her head.

"No."

He smiled again. "Good." He stepped back to a reasonable distance. "Do you plan to invite me in?"

Every cell in her body screamed, "No!" She'd grown up in cities and knew the stories, the horror stories. If he stepped over her threshold, past the dead bolts, she had no defenses. She didn't own a handgun.

"Yes," she said.

Holding his hat at his side, he followed her into the house.

"It's quite charming."

She walked around the living room, turning on lamps, taking comfort in the light. Griffin followed her, switching off all but two of the lamps.

"What are you doing?"

He shrugged. "I'm sorry, but my eyes are unable to tolerate bright lights."

"Oh."

He stopped directly in front of her, smiling wickedly, as if eyeing dessert.

She backed away, toward the safety of her kitchen. "Would you like some tea or something?"

"Something, perhaps," he said.

"If you want to wait here," she said, motioning nonchalantly over her shoulder.

But he didn't wait. In the kitchen, he leaned against the tile counter and watched her fill the kettle, place it on the stove and juggle a mug from the cupboard, which escaped her grasp. In a blurred movement, he scooped up the mug just inches from the floor and handed it to her.

"Holy shit," she said, again less eloquent than usual. "How did you do that?"

"I have wonderful reflexes."

"No joke." She placed the mug on the counter beside

the stove, drew in a deep breath for courage, and then turned to face him.

"Okay, I want a straight answer. Who are you and why are you here?"

Griffin dropped his hat on the counter behind him and nodded, admitting defeat. "My name truly is Griffin, and I'm here to erase your memory of me."

"*What?* Why would you want to do that, assuming you could? What are you, a hypnotist?"

He moved forward again, and the lights in the room dimmed as he neared. With his lips not quite touching her skin, he moved his mouth across her cheek.

Her throat constricted and her heart pounded. She couldn't explain or control the erotic excitement tingling in her belly, nor did she want it to stop. She closed her eyes and turned her head, aware of his mouth following the line of her neck, still without touching her.

"No," he whispered, his cool breath caressing her skin. "I'm a vampire."

## *Chapter 2: The Truth*

Serena paced the front of the living room. "You are *not* a vampire. Vampires don't exist, except for those poor deluded souls who get fang implants and run around in capes." She glanced at the cape draped over a chair, and then at the man lounging on her sofa.

Griffin smiled patiently as he slowly rotated the rain stick she kept on the end table. Inside the stick, dried seeds plinked as they tumbled from one end to the other.

"You may think you're immortal—"

"I doubt seriously I'm immortal," he said.

"Oh? I thought—"

"Yes, yes," he said, waving off the rest of her statement. "I hear that one all the time. And you probably think I turn into a bat."

She stopped pacing. "*I* don't think you turn into a bat. I wouldn't be surprised to find out *you* think you do."

He sighed and rose slowly. "No, I don't turn into a bat, and I'm not immortal, but I am a soulless creature of the night."

As he approached, she fought the urge to back away, trying not to show her fear. The man was simply delusional, that's all, and she had been trained to deal with delusional people.

"Griffin," she said, in the least confrontational tone she could muster, "I'm sure you believe what you're telling me. I understand why you don't want to die. I don't want to die, either."

"Oh, but I have died. And I will again, in a fashion." He circled her slowly, then moved to the dining-room doorway and leaned against the frame, folding his arms and crossing one foot over the other, as if posing for the part of Mr. Rochester in *Jane Eyre*. "I simply do not wish to end my existence yet."

He wasn't a typical case, chomping at the bit to prove her wrong. He waited for her to speak.

She decided the best way to handle the situation was to egg him on, then show him the error in his logic. He certainly seemed lucid and reasonable enough.

Except for the vampire thing.

She took a deep breath and huffed it out, then sat in a chair facing him. "Okay. Convince me that you're a vampire."

She was doing all right, until he smiled again, this time as if presented with dinner.

But she wouldn't let him see her sweat. No, she was a psychologist, in control of her faculties. And she wouldn't laugh, no matter how ridiculous it all felt.

"Come to me."

She frowned. "I don't think—"

"*Come to me.*" His voice snapped through the air like

an electric whip, and she rose to her feet, floating out of her chair. She didn't want to, but couldn't help herself.

"Yes," he said, "come to me, Serena."

His dark, rich voice swirled through the room and in her head, making her dizzy, pulling her forward. She took one stiff-legged step and then another, until she stood before him.

"Kneel, Serena."

*Kneel?* She would never—

"Kneel."

She dropped to her knees with the sudden weight of an elephant on her shoulders.

And then, released, she fell backward and scrambled away from the man, who crossed his arms over his chest again.

"How the hell did you do that?"

He shrugged. "It's part of the gift of Darkness."

She shook her head, dragged herself back into her chair and straightened. "Look, I'll admit you're one of the best hypnotists I've ever—"

She screamed when he appeared right in front of her, his face to her face, his mouth open to reveal huge, glistening fangs, and an animal roar emitting from his throat.

And then, in the next split second, he stood in the doorway again, ten feet away, relaxed, as if he'd never moved. "I am a vampire," he said.

Every cell in her body seemed ready to disintegrate as she sat there and trembled. She had no way to explain what she'd just witnessed, and not having an explanation sent her into a tailspin.

"How… Who… I—"

"You have questions," he said.

She nodded.

"Let me see if I can guess what they are. You want to know how old I am?"

She nodded again.

"I always have to stop and count, which is getting more difficult these days, but I was born in 1760. That puts me somewhere close to two and a half centuries, doesn't it?" He shook his head and laughed. "My, my, how time flies."

"Two and a half *centuries?* That's absurd."

"I know, I carry my age well. Of course, I was but thirty when I surrendered to the devil."

"Oh? And where were you when this conversion occurred?"

Her question doused the fire in his blue eyes, and he gazed into space over her right shoulder. "I was on my knees, holding Rebecca, mangled under the wheels of a carriage. Her life's blood warmed my legs as her last breaths shuddered from her breast."

She felt the honest and endless pain in his words, and tears sprang into her eyes.

And that's when she knew it was all true.

She was sitting in her living room, conversing with an ancient vampire.

His gaze slid back to hers and she watched him return to the present.

He smiled sadly. "Long ago."

Serena jumped to her feet, filled with terror, and wonder, and emotions she couldn't identify. Should she run? Would she even make it to the door? And then what?

"Don't run."

She spun to face him.

"You can read my mind?"

He shrugged. "I'm quite perceptive."

"What do you want from me? Why are you here?"

He pushed off from the doorway and ambled toward her. "I told you. I must erase your memory of me."

"But, if you're a vampire, you can just kill me, right?"

She shivered at the soft touch of fingertips sliding up the side of her arm, and he leaned close once again.

"I don't want to hurt you," he whispered.

"I don't understand," she whispered back.

"I like you, dear Serena, and I want you to continue your work."

"What…work?"

He released a deep, throaty chuckle near her ear. "Your work of convincing the world I'm not real."

His presence filled her senses with the threat of inhuman masculinity and preternatural strength. She wanted to hate being near him, but she couldn't.

She'd had men in her life, several who meant a great deal to her, but none affected her the way this stranger did. Her body felt alive, tensed, ready for anything. She closed her eyes to experience his touch.

His cool lips brushed against her cheek as his hand slid across the back of her neck and around her shoulder, drawing her forward. She heard him sniff, animal-like, taking in her scent as she inhaled his. Once again, rosemary and smoke, as from a fireplace, mixed with leather and lavender and the outdoors. And beneath it all, something musty, antique.

Her breath came in stuttered gasps as he drew her closer, brushing his lips across hers, hinting at demands she had no will to resist. Her lips parted, but he ignored the invitation.

And then he wrapped an arm around her waist and drew her up to his solid body, and she realized just how strong he must be. She trembled in response, standing as if with her head in the lion's mouth.

"You fear me," he said.

"Yes." She slid her hands up the front of his silk shirt.

"Good."

His mouth came down over hers and he kissed her. Not a friendly, considerate sort of kiss, but something forceful, demanding, hungry. She melted under his command, unable to do anything but cling to him, thrown into a new world without direction. He encircled her with his body as his mouth opened and he tasted her, offering a taste of his own darkness in return.

She accepted, unable to deny the liquid need welling inside.

She clutched at the back of his shirt and pressed her body against his unyielding lean torso.

His cool mouth warmed as the kiss deepened, and her tongue followed his in wild circles. Desire tingled in her belly and up the backs of her legs, and her knees buckled. He held her up, held her close, offered something she could only imagine. Or thought she could. His hardness swelled between them, and she gasped at the size of him.

A deep rumble vibrated through her ribs—a beastly growl, a panther on the hunt. His embrace tightened. She couldn't breathe, she didn't care.

And then he disappeared, and she stumbled forward.

Serena opened her eyes to find him standing by the front door, hat in hand, staring through liquid silver eyes. "I must go."

As absurd as it was, she couldn't bear the thought of him leaving.

"But...why? I thought you wanted to erase my memory."

He frowned. "Perhaps, but I don't wish to bite you in the process."

With the spell of Griffin's proximity broken, Serena spent the next morning wondering why she had let him touch her. Or, at least, not struggled when he did. He was at best a stranger, at worst a creature, and a dangerous one at that.

But there was something fatally attractive about such danger held in tenuous check. She jotted notes for future lectures.

By noon, she felt lonely. Odd, she hadn't felt lonely since Dave had left five years ago. Until now, she'd always valued her time alone.

As evening neared, she found herself unable to sit still. She cleaned the oven, mopped the kitchen floor, straightened her closet and looked out every window she walked past. Then she showered and dressed.

Once, when she saw someone approaching on the sidewalk, a shadow in the streetlight, her stomach flipped over with excitement, until she realized it was only a man. A mortal man.

Not Griffin.

Had she lost her mind? How could she want him to return?

But she did. She wanted very much for him to return, to hold her in his arms, to continue the kiss where he'd abandoned it.

And she wondered what would happen next.

She jumped at the knock on her front door.

Swallowing hard, she tiptoed to the door and peered through the peephole. Even though she expected to find Griffin standing there, her breath caught when she saw him.

With a trembling hand, she opened the door. "Come in."

He nodded formally and stepped into the living room, wearing more modern attire this time with black boots, black slacks and a dark red shirt. No cape and no hat.

"Incognito?"

He smiled and nodded stiffly.

She closed the door and faced him, clutching her hands to keep them from shaking.

His gaze started at hers, then slid slowly down her body to her feet and back up an inch at a time. She nearly brought her hands up to cover her breasts.

"You look delicious, dear Serena."

She brushed back her hair with one hand and tucked the other into the front pocket of her jeans. Was it obvious she'd worn her best silk blouse, hoping he'd arrive?

"Perhaps a little too delicious." He turned away from her, as if to examine the room he'd already seen.

"What do you mean?"

He didn't respond.

"Why did you come back?"

"To complete my mission," he said over his shoulder.

"Of erasing my memory?"

He nodded. "Yes."

"How?"

In no hurry, he ambled toward her, studying paintings and knickknacks, until at last, he stood close.

He glanced at her with eyes the color of mercury. "I must control your thoughts at the moment when you're most vulnerable, most open."

"What, when I'm asleep?"

He smiled. "No, Serena. When you're at the peak of sexual release. That's when your mind is open."

She inhaled sharply, taken by surprise, then shook herself. She hated the feeling of constantly being caught off guard.

"Oh. So, you're telling me we have to have sex so you can erase my memory. At least that's original."

He sighed heavily. "You'll enjoy the experience, I believe. I've had quite a long time to learn how to please a woman."

"Yes, I imagine you have." She smoothed the front of her blouse, unable to figure out what to do next. She found the thought of having sex with Griffin much too appealing, but couldn't imagine opening herself to a supernatural beast that fed on human blood.

Assuming that part was true, and that he was a vampire.

"Why didn't you just get this over with last night?"

His gaze snapped back to hers and he grinned. "Get it *over with?* Do you not enjoy sex?"

"With a vampire? I don't know."

"No," he said. "In general."

She shrugged. "Sure. I like sex as much as the next person." The conversation wasn't headed where she wanted it to go. "Do you drink tea?"

"No."

She started toward the kitchen door. "Well, I do, and I could use a cup right now."

As she'd expected, Griffin followed her into the kitchen again and sat in one of the old breakfast table chairs. Her mind raced as she went through the soothing motions of pouring a cup of boiling water and taking a Lemon Zinger teabag from the cupboard. She felt him watching her, and flashed on the college fantasy again. Just as she'd imagined then, he liked the way she looked, and that knowledge excited her.

Gripping the steaming cup in both hands, she sat across

the table from him. "How does this work? Am I just supposed to say 'okay' and strip?"

He lounged in the chair, drawing figure eights in the wooden tabletop with one long, elegant finger. "No, I don't think that would be much fun."

"No."

And then she sensed his reluctance.

"If you're so anxious to do this, why are we sitting here?"

He shrugged. "I thought you wanted tea."

"That's not it. What aren't you telling me?"

He shifted in his chair and scratched the side of his neck, exhibiting classic human signs of unease. "Am I so transparent?"

She shrugged. "I get paid to read people."

"Yes." He rose, crossed the room, and turned to lean on the counter and study her a bit too closely. "I find you quite attractive."

"Why?"

"Strange question to ask."

"Is it?" She squeezed out the teabag and dropped it onto a plate. "I'm a realist. I know I'm not gorgeous. I'm not ugly, but certainly not model material. A few extra pounds here and there, and crow's feet around my eyes. Guys don't pant or whistle when I walk by."

He sighed, and she looked up at him.

"You must remember," he said, "I come from another time. Perhaps my definition of beauty is different than that of the average man today. Or perhaps it is my ability to see beneath the outward appearance, as nice as it is. In you, I hear a heart that beats strong and true, feel a soul yearning for knowledge and sense a brain that questions all. Very powerful for one like me." He returned to the chair. "And, you remind me of someone I once knew."

"The woman who was run over by the carriage?"

He nodded. "Yes. Rebecca."

"You loved her." She stirred a spoonful of honey into her tea.

He didn't answer, but it wasn't actually a question.

"Besides," he continued, "erasing your memory could be dangerous."

"How?"

"If I lose control of the demon within, you could die."

Her spoon clattered to the table.

# *Chapter 3: The Touch*

"*Die?*"

He nodded slowly.

Serena shuddered as the impact of his statement hit her. "I don't like the sound of that."

"Nor do I. Unfortunately, I have no choice."

"Why is that, exactly?"

Griffin leaned back in his chair and watched her as he spoke. "The others wouldn't let you live with a memory of me."

"Others?" Her mouth went dry.

He nodded again.

Fighting shaky hands, she raised her mug and sipped the steaming tea, flinching when she burned the roof of her mouth.

"Shit." She carried the mug to the sink, dumped the contents, then turned to her vampire guest. "How about I promise not to say anything and we call it good?"

Griffin rose and floated across the room to stand before her, or at least that's the way it seemed.

"We cannot, dear Serena," he whispered, drawing a slow line down the side of her face with his fingers. "Besides, I want you."

She whimpered.

Gently grasping her chin, he drew her face up to his. All concern, and fear and rational thought disappeared as his mouth covered hers.

His tongue circled and disappeared, then he nipped her bottom lip and she thought she might swoon—something she never imagined she'd do. She felt his desire merging with her own, growing into a live, pulsing beast to fill the shrinking room.

He pinned her against the counter, sliding his thigh between hers, and she not only let him but welcomed the intrusion. She held his shirt in her fists and pulled him closer.

His fingers slid down the side of her neck, stopping momentarily above her pounding pulse, then around to the front of her blouse. He brushed his knuckles over her hardening nipples, and she strained forward against the pleasure.

"I've wanted you since I first saw you long ago," he said, his mouth near her ear. "I want to taste desire on your skin." He pressed his mouth to the side of her neck and nipped.

She raised her head, quivering with excitement.

Suddenly, she didn't care if this was to be her last moment on Earth, she simply wanted more of him.

She wanted all of him.

His arm slid around her waist as darkness closed in, threatening to swallow her whole.

"Yes," she whispered.

And then the world disappeared.

* * *

Serena woke with a start and sat up, confused.

Where the hell was she?

A small light broke the darkness, from a doorway. The hall?

Yes, she knew this place. She was in her bed, in her room. But how had she gotten here? Had the whole thing been a dream?

"Are you all right now?"

She screamed and jumped away from the voice.

"It is I, Griffin," he said.

"That's supposed to make me feel better?"

He didn't respond, but with a sudden burst of light and sting of sulfur, he lit a candle on her night table.

"There," he said. "I much prefer subdued lighting."

She wiped her palm across her forehead. "What happened?"

He rose and walked to the end of the bed where the candlelight barely reached his face. Shadows looked eerier on Griffin than they did on other men.

"I was…swept up in the moment," he said.

"I don't understand."

"Yes."

That damned evil grin reappeared, and she believed she saw fangs denting his bottom lip. A chill ran down her back.

"Cold?"

She shook her head.

He continued around the bed to sit on the side she'd moved to, and she slid to the middle, staying mostly out of reach.

"You see, my mental powers are quite different than yours, as are most of my faculties. Things sometimes become too intense, even unpleasant."

Something about the way he said "unpleasant" made her uncomfortable.

As he spoke, he unbuttoned his shirt. "But I'll be more careful. I want very much to enjoy you, flesh and soul, Serena."

"What if I've changed my mind?"

He froze for an instant, then tore off his shirt and dropped it to the floor, staring into her eyes as he did.

She was more than just a little impressed by his bare torso. Muscles suggested a wildcat of some kind—tight, lean and shaped for speed. A small T of dark hair marked his flawless, pale chest.

Then he turned his back to her and removed his boots. Muscles rippled with the effort, and her mouth watered.

"I'm hoping," he said finally, stretching out on his side to face her, "that I can convince you to cooperate."

"What happens if I don't?"

He studied her face in silence for a long time.

She started to scoot off the bed, but he grabbed her wrist and held her in place. "Don't leave."

"Is that an order?" She glared, angry at the thought of any of this happening against her will, even if his intention was to keep her alive, which she still didn't quite believe.

"No." He drew her hand to his mouth, ignoring her attempt to resist, and held his lips to the back of it. Somehow, his cool, dry lips awakened nerve endings in her hand and sent electric charges tingling up her arm.

She stopped trying to pull her hand away.

He turned it over and studied her palm, tracing its lines with one finger, then he pressed his lips into the middle of it, and his eyes closed.

She barely kept herself from reaching out and stroking his hair.

Still kissing her palm, his eyes snapped open and he looked up at her.

His eyes, now a strange shade of gold, held an eternity of sadness that broke her heart, and she fought back a wave of tears. She remembered the dream of joining her fantasy lover in his dark world.

Releasing her from his gaze, he moved up to her wrist, which he licked and kissed, and then further up her arm, nibbling places that tickled and made her spine rubbery. When he reached her sleeve, he stopped.

"Take this off, Serena," he said, his voice deep and throaty.

With her heart once again pounding, she pulled the blouse off over her head and tossed it aside.

Again, he took possession of her arm, moving up quickly to lick a line up the tender inside of her bicep, snapping loose her bra as he did.

His mouth slid over her shoulder and down to her breast where his velvety tongue circled and teased, and her body reacted with a flood of almost violent need. She grabbed a fistful of his silky hair and held him close, and he suckled as he circled her waist with his arms.

Her head swam.

He dragged her down onto the bed without effort, drawing her under him, marking her stomach with gentle bites. Sharp points pressed against her skin but didn't break it, and she remembered the animal fangs.

Her clothes melted away until she lay sprawled across the bed naked, quivering with excitement. His hands and mouth touched, caressed, teased, soothed and tempted, appearing everywhere at once. She felt as if she would explode into a million pieces if he kept going.

And then he stopped.

Panting, Serena opened her eyes to find him on his hands and knees over her, his clothes also gone.

He stared down with fiery red eyes and an open mouth, and his fangs did more than dent his lip. He raked them with the tip of his tongue as he studied her face and then her neck.

She wondered what he could possibly be thinking, why he waited, but she couldn't begin to guess. She wasn't really sure she wanted to know, anyway.

He growled softly, almost purring, and started down her body like a snake. The gentle friction of his skin against hers sent glistening sparkles through her head; her fingers slid over his body as he went.

He eased her legs apart with his shoulders.

She held her breath, unsure what to expect, but unable to want him to stop.

Slowly, deliberately, he licked a trail up the inside of one thigh, nipping the tender flesh. She clenched her fists to keep from moving.

The sensation of his mouth suddenly covering her most sensitive spot arched her back, and she rose to meet his caress. Fangs pressed to tender flesh as his tongue swirled around her nub, demanding every bit of her attention.

She sucked in a breath between gritted teeth at the intensity of the pleasure.

His mouth pressed harder, sucking, tongue swirling faster.

Her awareness narrowed from the world around her to her own body, focused on his demands.

His hands slid down the outsides of her thighs and under her buttocks, stimulating nerve bundles connected to her back and breasts and crotch, which vibrated with his growl.

Juices gathered, a molten vortex, touching down and lifting away. Darkness swept over her in a heated wave.

He moved faster, deeper, his tongue flicking and plunging.

"Give yourself to me," he whispered, from inside her head.

She opened wider, giving more, wanting all, aflame with need.

The edge approached, a dark void, sucking at her soul.

She screamed as intense spasms of glorious release shot through her, radiating outward, twisting her body. On and on they went, ripping through her muscles. She clutched at sheets, silently begging him to stop.

Too much, too perfect, too intense.

Easing down to the bed as the pulses slowed, she groaned. She'd never experienced an orgasm even close to this and she felt far more than drained.

He moved back up her body, purring again, pressing against stray muscle spasms.

She tingled all over and was a melted mass of useless flesh.

He nuzzled her neck and stroked her side.

Her vampire, her dark fantasy.

"I still know who you are," she said.

"Yes." His voice hissed in her ear.

After a long while, she managed to raise her arms and touch his chest with the back of her hand. He shuddered in response.

"Weren't you supposed to erase my memory?"

He eased a lock of hair from her face with one finger as he smiled at her. Somehow, his fangs didn't surprise her anymore.

"The first one was for you," he said. "My gift."

"*First* one?" She couldn't imagine being aroused again within a week. "Griffin—"

He stopped her words with two fingers. "Hush. My name sounds too sweet falling from your precious lips."

He leaned over and kissed her gently, tenderly—a lover's

caress. Then he drew her into his arms and she rested with her head on his shoulder, her palm pressed to his chest.

It took several minutes to realize what was so strange about him. His heart didn't pound under her hand, and his chest didn't rise and fall.

She gulped.

Griffin tightened his arms around her, nuzzled her hair and made soft, soothing noises she could feel as well as hear.

She closed her eyes to enjoy his scent, which seemed to have changed. Mulled wine came to mind, and late nights at her grandmother's, where cedar and roses spiced the air. Comforting memories billowed over her like a soft old sheet and she smiled.

When she opened her eyes a short time later, he was gone.

The next day, Serena canceled her class at the college, skipped a book club meeting and sat around her house, waiting.

And waiting.

A day turned into a week and then a month. Anticipation collapsed into anger and then blossomed into suspicion. Had she just imagined Griffin? Was he her shadow lover returning in her adult years as a full-blown delusion?

She tried meditating, something she hadn't done in years. She even tried conjuring him from her subconscious, but nothing happened.

Slowly, she gave up waiting for his return and moved on with her life.

She didn't lecture on the mythical beasts that humans created to deny death. Instead, she turned her focus to pubescent fantasies and how family relationships shape sexual desires. Old hat, but at least something she believed in.

Three months after her wild night, she was standing barefoot in her kitchen nuking leftovers when someone knocked. Assuming Jeri had come to say she'd returned a day early so Serena could quit feeding her cat, she carried a half-filled wineglass with her, took a drink as she opened the door—then inhaled it into her lungs.

Griffin stood on the porch watching with concern as she choked and coughed. Serena turned to place her glass on the coffee table as she struggled to breathe.

"Do you require medical assistance?"

She shook her head and pounded on her chest with her fist.

"Are you certain?"

She nodded and finally managed to fill her saturated lungs with air.

After taking several deep breaths, she regained control of everything except, possibly, reason.

"What are you doing here?"

"I thought we'd already established that."

"You mean the memory thing? That was three months ago."

"Was it?"

Actually, it had been three months and two days, but she decided not to point that out.

She frowned at her guest, trying to determine how she felt about his return.

He looked as fantastic as he had before, or maybe even better. He wore jeans, which seemed anachronistic on him but fit perfectly, and a dark blue shirt that showed off his features and made his blue eyes appear even lighter.

She remembered the way he'd looked at her that night as he knelt over her, and a shiver shot through her.

He watched and waited.

She cleared the last of the wine from her windpipe, picked up her glass and returned to the kitchen for a refill. "Wine?"

"No, thank you."

Since he didn't follow, she had a moment alone to gather her wits.

She *hadn't* imagined him; he was real. Or, at least, he seemed real at the moment.

And the memory of the pleasure he'd produced felt suddenly fresh, as if it had just happened. She thought about the night after his visit, when she'd lain in bed longing for him. The only thing she could think about was how incredible it might be to feel his body joined with hers. Would he maintain control? Would he growl like he had before?

His primal strength and the hint of danger had excited her that night, until she'd had to provide her own release. And she'd called on that fantasy many times since. Had she blown the whole thing out of proportion in her mind? Was Griffin simply somewhat better than most men at oral sex?

Just the questions had her nipples tightening under her T-shirt. She took a swig of wine from the bottle, hunched her shoulders a little so maybe he wouldn't notice the effect he had on her, and marched out to face her demon guest.

He stood in the middle of the room, his hands clasped behind his back, watching her approach. He should have been wearing knee-high boots and riding clothes.

She walked past him and locked the front door, then turned to face him. "Why did you wait so long to come back?"

He sighed heavily and took slow steps toward her, one foot placed carefully before the other. She backed to the door, but found no desire to move away. The closer he got, the faster her heart raced, and sweat prickled just under the skin of her face and neck. It wasn't quite fear that swelled in her chest, but something close to it.

"Three months isn't very long to someone my age."

"That's no excuse."

His brow furrowed as he stopped less than a step away, and his nostrils flared. "I smell your desire," he whispered.

Heat rose into her face.

His eyes darkened and he leaned closer. "Lovely, and quite tempting."

She swallowed hard.

He hadn't touched her, but every cell of her skin felt invigorated, freshly scrubbed and alive.

A low rumble filled the air. "You have no idea what you do to me," he said.

She whimpered, wanting to tell him that she shared that sentiment, and the rumble grew louder. Her knees shook violently.

He leaned forward, flattened one hand on the door and then trailed his lips down her cheek and the side of her neck.

She raised her head, offering something she knew better than to give, but she couldn't help it. His lips stopped above her jugular, and she felt her heartbeat against his mouth.

Time froze.

A century could have passed for the rest of the world and she wouldn't have known.

He opened his mouth just a little, and hard points of his fangs pressed to her skin.

She closed her eyes and gripped the sides of his shirt.

Then he locked on to her neck and sucked, and she cried out at the pleasure.

Growling, Griffin wrapped her in his arms, and she felt

his body against hers once again, perfection she'd dreamt of and missed to the depth of her soul.

"No idea," he whispered against her cheek.

She turned her head and he took her mouth as he lifted her from the floor. She wrapped her legs around his hips, wanting him closer. Any second thoughts she might have had dissolved in the force of his kiss.

She tasted his hunger, a flavor like no other, and it shook her. She knew he tasted hers in return. She wanted him at that moment with a longing unlike any she'd ever experienced, and drew him into her mouth, stroking his tongue with her own, thrilling to the familiar strangeness.

His hand slid down her back, and he pulled her hips into his. She felt his erection between her legs and whimpered again, this time with need.

Griffin tore his mouth from hers and turned his head. "Not here."

"My bed," she said between gasps.

He nodded and released her, and she slid her feet to the floor, but before she could step away, he scooped her into his arms as if she was light as air, which she certainly was not.

She clung to him as he carried her upstairs to bed. He moved through darkness with ease, making no sound, tripping over none of the many obstacles.

Staring into his face, she tried to picture him as he'd been before losing his mortality, and wondered what the world had been like for him. She considered pushing him away so they could talk, but found no will to do so.

No, she wanted Griffin, longed for him.

"Yes," he whispered, as if hearing her need.

He placed her on the bed, and she removed her clothes and lit candles without prompting as he undressed.

They faced each other, naked, bathed in candlelight. He

sat very still, studying her, and she took the opportunity to admire his body.

He truly was magnificent. Not in the way male models are, with bulging muscles and perfect tans, but more like a leopard stalking wary antelope on an African plain. He leaned forward with his hands on the bed between them, and she felt as though he were about to spring and drag her down with claws and teeth.

Instinctively, she leaned away.

"Wise girl," he said, smiling.

His smile grew into a wicked grin as he continued forward and kissed her with deceptive tenderness.

She reached out and touched his cool shoulders, and he leaned in for another kiss, this one slow, luxurious, enticing. She pulled him closer and he obliged, nipping her lips carefully, then diving in, swirling into her mouth.

He eased her down under him so gently, she barely noticed the maneuver. As he moved his head away, she opened her eyes to find him stretched out beside her, his arm across her waist, stroking her skin. His leg held her in place, but wasn't necessary.

She noted a flood of emotion she couldn't explain, and sighed. Griffin's touch excited her beyond belief, but she felt more than sexual stimulation. She empathized with what she guessed he must have gone through, losing the woman he loved, and marveled at the thought of seeing centuries pass. She wanted to spend the rest of her life with him, and yet was afraid of what this single night might bring.

"I expected you sooner," she said.

He raised his hand to her face and feathered one finger across her lips. "I couldn't come back right away."

"Why not?"

"Because I wanted you too much."

"I don't understand."

His hand moved down her neck and chest to her breast, where it paused. One finger drew slow, liquid circles around her hard nipple, sidetracking her attention for a moment.

"I wanted your life, Serena. I wanted you with me for the rest of my existence."

She stared up into his steady gaze, understanding that she'd nearly met her mortal end three months earlier, both on the street and in her bed.

As she studied his blue-gold eyes, she found herself wondering if she would have protested the conversion.

"Can you make me a vampire?"

He raised one eyebrow. "I can, possibly. But I won't."

"Why not? What if I want to be one?"

"I haven't offered you the choice."

"I noticed." Unexpected anger flared.

Undoubtedly sensing her emotion, he kissed her again, and her anger faded at the intimate pleasure. His palm slid across her breast, teasing the hard nipple, increasing the ache his fingers had produced.

As he parted her legs with his own, the ache spread through all of her, reaching her limbs. She opened herself to him, trembling with anticipation. He kissed her neck and shoulder, and pressed her to the bed with his weight. She felt his engorged cock, cool between her thighs.

His skin seemed impossibly smooth under her hands as she skimmed his back and sides, and then slipped over his firm butt.

He drew in a sharp breath and rose up on his elbows.

"Listen to me, Serena," he said. "You must do as I say. Do you understand?"

She saw fear on his face for the first time, and realized that she was balanced on a knife's edge she hadn't noticed.

In spite of that, her body responded to his in puppetlike fashion, writhing and lifting to meet his touch.

She nodded, ready to agree to anything as long as he continued.

"We must go slowly," he said.

But she didn't want *slowly.* Her body swelled with needing him. Every inch of her felt ready to explode. After three months, she'd had enough of *slowly.*

She reached between them to stroke his stomach, moving lower. If she could wrap her hand around his swollen cock, he might give up on *slowly.*

Griffin snatched her hand out and pinned it above her head. "No," he whispered.

She grunted dissatisfaction with the arrangement, but he simply drew her other hand up and pinned it, too. He held both hands with one of his without effort, in spite of her struggle.

"Griffin—"

His free hand then did what hers could not and slid between them, his knuckles riding the ridges of her ribs and the trough of her belly, until his hand came to rest between her legs. Soft like silk, his fingers stroked her nub, slipping in the juices welling in her, inviting her to rise up into clouds of desire.

She obeyed, arching her back as he dipped and emerged.

"Yes," he hissed, "so sweet."

Need skittered up the backs of her thighs, tingling inside her belly, pulsing through the muscles in her buttocks and breasts. She'd never felt such strong urges in her life, and could think of only one thing.

"Take me now, Griffin, please."

"Hush," he said, his voice low and threatening. "Don't tempt me."

She raised her knees on each side of him and rolled her hips, offering herself to him, wanting him to mount her with animal urgency.

He growled in response, and her skin rose in goose bumps.

"Hold still," he whispered, with desperation that should have worried her.

She tried to obey, tightening her jaw against the urge to move.

He adjusted his body then to meet hers, and she felt the glorious pressure of his thick cock nudging against her wet vaginal lips.

Years of fantasy collided with unbelievable passion as he started into her, and she thrashed her head from side to side, fighting the engulfing sea of longing. She didn't want it to end yet. She wanted to enjoy the feel of him buried inside her, to know his body joined with hers in bliss.

But her body protested restraint as he pushed deeper, one careful inch at a time, reaching for the center of her soul with his slick hardness, filling her more than any man had, reaching the end and pushing deeper still. His mouth moved across her skin, tasting her neck and lips.

Muscles swelled and tightened, seeking release. Her breath came in quick stuttered gasps.

She needed more, but stretched no farther.

Too much, and not enough.

He withdrew and thrust in steady strokes.

Wet and hard.

Deeper.

She felt the moment approach, felt the blessed relief, and cried out with joy.

And then his thoughts assaulted her brain, and her universe switched off.

# *Chapter 4: The Fantasy*

Serena sat in a sunny green field, wearing jeans and a T-shirt, her bare feet tucked up under her. Insects buzzed and birds sang, and somewhere nearby, water gurgled around boulders.

"Where am I?"

"You're with me," he said.

In spite of not being able to see him, she took comfort in Griffin's voice.

"Where?" She rose, brushing grass from her palms. The air smelled impossibly sweet.

"We're in the void, Serena, in a place where only the two of us exist. Your mind is open to me now. Here I control your thoughts."

She spun around and found him standing behind her, smiling. A soft breeze lifted his hair from his shoulders and danced strands across his forehead.

He didn't look like a vampire now, and for the first time she realized what he'd looked like as a man. His blue eyes, though still gorgeous, were much darker than she'd seen them, and his skin had been bronzed by the sun. With his fine features and wide shoulders, he defined male beauty in any century.

He wore a loose white shirt with sleeves gathered at his wrists and tight black pants that ended in knee-high leather boots, much as she'd pictured when he stood in her living room.

"I could simply wipe clean your memory, but I don't wish to do that. I want to show you the truth," he said. "Once you've seen it, you'll understand. I want you with me, Serena, but I can't risk it. Once you've experienced the Darkness, you'll understand why I refuse to try."

He offered her a hand, palm raised.

She felt no fear now, as she slipped her hand into his, surprised by the human warmth.

He laced their fingers and drew her close. His breath brushed across her cheeks and lips as he lowered his mouth to hers.

With human longing, he kissed her, holding her in his trembling arms. She clung to his shoulders and savored this impossible embrace, opening her mouth and heart to him.

When he ended the kiss, she rested her head on his shoulder, as he soothed her hair and hugged her.

"Hold on to me," he whispered, "with all your strength."

She nodded.

Suddenly, she was plunged into an abyss of darkness, falling.

Images flashed before her eyes as something of a blur, but it was the emotions burning in her soul that told the story.

A woman ran into the night, and Serena screamed in horror as steel-covered wheels rolled over her. Such sorrow, a deep gash in her heart as she held the broken body in her lap and rocked.

Rebecca. This was Rebecca!

Serena felt Griffin's horror as her own. She realized he was showing her his past as more than just pictures. She *was* Griffin.

"Do you truly wish to save her?" An old man with white hair and white eyes stood beside him, wearing tattered clothes that had once belonged to a gentleman.

"Yes," Griffin said.

"At any price?"

"There's no price too high. Please, I beg of you, show me how."

As the old man sank his fangs into Griffin's neck, Griffin realized he'd been tricked. He knew he would die, but he didn't care. He'd wait in the afterworld to greet his true love.

And then he woke to excruciating pain, but it quickly passed.

He knew he must use the Darkness to save Rebecca, that he could not exist without her. He drained her of life, and watched as the old man brought her back.

Death without death. Life without life.

Rebecca stood before him, reborn, beautiful again, but angry and sad at the need to kill. "Why have you done this to me?"

Years of cruelties together, hunting for food, taking life to survive, led to anguish. And the roar of loss ripped through him for the second time, when he woke to find her gone, no longer feeling the connection. *Rebecca.* Gone to the sunlight, this time truly forever. How could he go on without her?

The visions whirled around, faster and faster, like lights from a crazed merry-go-round.

Decades passed, and he wandered alone, untouched, unfeeling. Everywhere he went, death surrounded him. A woman with auburn hair lay dead beside him. And another, a blonde. Too many to remember, yet each impossible to forget.

He craved the light, just one blinding moment of sunshine to ease the sorrow.

The visions slowed as he saw a young woman walking alone through an alley.

Recognition came with a start, and Serena realized he had watched her. Not now, but years ago. *He* had been her shadow hero, the one she thought was only a dream. And later, from the shadows, he watched again on a different sidewalk, an empty sidewalk in Santa Fe, where he had to act to keep her alive.

He felt a tenderness, a love of sorts. He wanted to be near her, to hold her.

The visions faded, and all emotion sank down to a point of quiet despair, replaced by hunger—all-consuming hunger. Hunger clawed at every pore, driving him against a hurricane of resistance. He heard a heartbeat so loud it nearly burst his eardrums, and he smelled the coppery scent of blood, as heavenly to him as any flower.

No more! She couldn't take feeling his infinite loneliness and hunger. She'd fly apart and lose her sanity.

She tried to scream, but couldn't.

And then, like a rubber band snapping back, she was flung into her own body, back to the present in her own bed with Griffin's arms around her, and she cried out with joy.

Waves of thick, pure pleasure washed over her, and she

clung to him as he drove her to release, his steely cock stretching her, offering more, demanding all, plunging deeper.

She rushed up to meet each thrust, her mouth open against his cool chest, her fingers digging into the muscles of his back. Too much, too intense, she rode out the waves, drowning in the troughs, exalting in each crest.

Slowly, the waves lessened and eased into swells. His urgent thrusts slowed to long, sensuous strokes, then stopped.

She enjoyed the peace of their bodies entwined. Her senses felt raw and abused, but her soul seemed at peace, perhaps for the first time in years.

"You see now," he whispered. "I can't have you."

"But you brought Rebecca into the Darkness."

"With help. I've lost others." He nuzzled her neck, sending goose bumps in waves across her back. "I can't take the chance of losing you, or making you miserable. You're so much like her, and the hunger is more powerful than you know."

"Don't you see? Griffin, I'm not like her. Not at all. I can handle it, as long as we're together. There's no reason either of us has to be alone."

He raised himself up to his elbows and smiled down at her, his eyes once again glittering gold. He still filled her, and he seemed in no hurry to end their link.

"I'm willing to take the chance," she said.

He studied her face as if to memorize it.

She realized it was pointless to argue. "Why have you followed me all these years?"

"The years have passed like hours for me."

He rolled them over then, withdrew and urged her head to his chest. "Sleep," he whispered.

"But I don't want to forget."

"Hush, my sweet."

* * *

"In summary, death is the one great mystery of life, the feared unknown that each of us must face. That's why we invent creatures such as vampires."

Serena scanned the audience before her, a sea of college kids scribbling notes.

"Any questions?"

One young woman raised her hand. "And you're sure they aren't real? Vampires, I mean."

Laughter tittered through the crowd, and the student slumped in her seat.

"I know it's tempting to believe in these sensual, immortal creatures created by Hollywood and a multitude of authors, but I assure you they're completely fictitious."

Her gaze slid across the auditorium and stopped on the far door, which was now opened a crack, as if someone were peeking in from the unlit hallway. A shiver ran through her, but she didn't know why.

"They do, however, make wonderful fantasies," she added.

Several of the women nodded, a few blushed and most of the young men made immature noises of disgust.

"Okay, you have your assignment. Find a copy of *Dracula,* the original 1931 movie, not a remake, and be prepared to discuss the lesson about immortality we're supposed to take away from it."

Two of the guys did a high five as they stood. Watching horror flicks for homework never failed to meet with approval.

"See you all next week." Serena closed her notebook and shoved it into her bag as she watched the students leave, then she followed them out into the darkness.

As much as she enjoyed her students' exuberance, something about their wide-eyed wonder made her tired.

Every semester seemed to be the same as the last, and that thought depressed her. Maybe if she were returning home to a family or a husband, she might feel differently.

But she wasn't. Her house would be cold and dark, just as it was every Wednesday evening.

Her heels clicked on the asphalt as she cut across the parking lot.

Two blocks from her house, she passed an office building set back from the street where the shadows were deep, and she thought she saw someone standing outside the door watching her. With her heart suddenly in her throat, she stopped and stared, but found no one there.

She glanced around the empty street, swallowed hard and hurried on. "You're seeing things again," she said, wondering if she should worry about talking to herself.

Her house was exactly as she expected, and she switched on the closest lamp as she locked the door. After tossing her bag onto the sofa and kicking off her shoes, she turned on two more lights on her way to the kitchen.

What she needed was a nice, hot cup of tea, and maybe a good book. She nodded to herself as she placed the kettle on the stove. If she were married, she couldn't just curl up with a cup of tea and good book whenever she felt like it. She should be happy to be alone.

As she stared at the dancing blue flame, she considered the moment a short time earlier when she'd thought someone was watching her. She'd been terrified, of course, but there was more to it than that. It was as if she'd expected someone she knew to be standing in that shadow.

That was absurd.

Wasn't it?

Something prickled at the back of her mind. Something

vague. Was it the old fantasy of her secret lover, the one she'd dreamt of as a teenager?

Serena filled her cup with hot water and dunked the tea bag as she carried the drink carefully to the living room.

Maybe she needed a cat. At least a cat could greet her when she came home in the evening, and sit on the sofa with her while she read. Not a bad idea. Something to consider.

As she waited for her tea to steep, she closed her eyes, listened to the silence, and tried to remember what her fantasy man had looked like. He'd been tall and dark, and most definitely handsome. That was the cliché, wasn't it? But there'd been a quality to him that was both frightening and exciting. Funny that she couldn't quite remember.

With a sigh, she opened her eyes and drew her teabag from the cup.

Time to face reality. No man could ever measure up to her fantasy. She needed to forget about her shadow lover. Otherwise, she just might end up spending her entire life alone.

She glanced at the empty end of the sofa. "Definitely. A cat."

# *Chapter 5: The Choice*

"To put it simply, your heart has suffered a great deal of damage and is still enlarged. We can repair the valve problem causing the murmur, but the infection left scars we can't easily fix, and the size is a serious issue." Dr. Thorpe gave her the same sympathetic smile she'd grown used to seeing since first being admitted to the hospital two weeks earlier. "Don't worry. We aren't out of options yet. I'll go ahead and put you on the waiting list."

"Waiting list?" Serena noted the familiar flush of terror sliding up her neck.

"For a transplant."

"A heart transplant?" She closed her eyes and swallowed hard. "Oh, my God."

Dr. Thorpe rested his hand on her covered foot. "Dr. Brockman, medicine has made great strides in this field in the past few years. People with transplanted hearts can live quite a long time. There are risks, but we'll deal with those as they arise. The main thing is for you to rest and conserve your strength so we can keep you with us while we wait for a donor."

Serena nodded. "Yes. Thank you, Doctor."

She listened to his soft footsteps leave her room and the door squeak shut behind him, and then she let the tears fall.

How could this be happening? She was only forty-eight. One minute she's feeling a little achy, the next she's in the emergency room trying to figure out where three days have gone. If not for her teaching job and a handful of students wondering why she'd missed her class, she would probably have died in her home and no one would have known for who knows how long.

Taking her time, Serena eased her legs over the side of the bed, sat up and wiped her eyes as she looked outside. Evening sparkled in the fading sunset, and car lights snaked through a quiet neighborhood beneath her window. Everything looked just as it had two weeks ago when her world had been normal and the future had spread endlessly before her.

The one thing Dr. Thorpe hadn't said was that she could die at any moment, but she knew it. And if she didn't die suddenly from a massive heart attack, chances were good she'd fade away while waiting for someone else to die. What a horrible thought.

She glanced down at her left hand where a purple bruise marked an injection sight. Why was her skin so wrinkled and thin? She was too young to look so damn old.

More tears fell. She knew they were tears of self-pity, but she didn't care. There was no one else to pity her at this point. A few of her students had stopped by shortly after she'd been admitted, and two members of the faculty had dropped off books and magazines, but no one had been in to see her for days. She had no friends or family. That fact hadn't really bothered her until now.

"Dinnertime." One of the orderlies, a young man who always seemed unflappably cheerful, breezed in with a tray of food.

Serena let him adjust the bed for her and slide the bedside table into place. She felt weak and helpless, and annoyed by his good cheer. "Gruel, again?"

The young man laughed. "How'd you guess?" He placed a cup on the table and dropped a straw into it, then lifted the cover off the plate. "Here you go. Best gruel in town." He smiled and turned to leave. "I'll be back for the tray."

After he left, she stared at the food until she couldn't look anymore, then she lay back and closed her eyes.

No one really cared that she was about to die. She longed for someone to sit beside her, hold her hand, kiss her fingers and cry at the thought of losing her, and tell her that everything would be all right.

Why had she let her life slip by like this?

Scenes flashed in her memory, scenes from her youth. She remembered days of sunshine with her parents when she was a child. And she remembered their funerals, less than six months apart. She remembered the men in her life, with all their flaws and shortcomings, each walking away. Was she really so hard to love?

The orderly, Mr. Happy, interrupted her memories, and then a nurse arrived to chatter at her while taking her vitals and changing IV bags. The window acted as a mirror now, reflecting her bedside light against darkness.

Finally alone again, she closed her eyes to continue where she'd left off. Tears burned down the sides of her face, and sleeping aids pumped their way through her bloodstream without effect.

The door opened again and she groaned. Couldn't they just leave her alone with her terror and her thoughts? She opened her eyes, turned her head and frowned.

"Serena." A man swung a black cape from his broad shoulders, draped it over the visitor's chair and carefully sat on the edge of the bed at her side. He took her hand in his and smiled into her eyes.

She stared up at his handsome face, into eyes the color of a cloudless sky.

"Do I know…you?"

Even as she asked the question, sensations flooded her mind: the feel of his arms around her, his mouth on hers, his voice low and sexy in her ear. She remembered the excitement of his cool body against hers, and the joy of sharing his thoughts. Her neck suddenly tingled with the long-lost memory of his bite.

"Griffin," she whispered.

After sixteen years, he hadn't changed a bit. No wrinkles, no hair loss, no paunch. If she'd ever doubted his claim of being a vampire, this was the proof.

She studied his face, his fine features, full lips and strong jaw. How could she have forgotten him? It was like forgetting she had arms.

"What are you doing here?" she asked.

He stroked her face, easing strands of hair into place and ignoring her question. As fresh tears of joy spilled from the corners of her eyes, he wiped them away with his thumb.

"No flowers or chocolates?" she asked, trying to smile.

He shook his head. "No."

He closed his eyes and cocked his head for a long moment as if listening to distant music, then opened them again and looked around the room. Kissing the back of her hand, he rose.

"Don't leave," she whispered, her voice barely working at the terrible prospect of losing him again so soon.

At the door, he held the handle and leaned against the wood, and strange wrenching sounds of metal on metal and splintering wood screeched in the relative quiet. He must have wrenched the door into the frame so that no one else could get in. Then he hurried back to her bedside.

"I'm not leaving," he said.

She nodded. "Good."

He held her hand again.

"Why did you stay away so long?"

He shook his head. "I've told you before, Serena, time is meaningless for me."

"But not for me. Now I'm all wrinkled and ugly, and my heart isn't working right. I don't have the strength to swat a fly. You could have picked a better time to stop by."

He leaned forward until his mouth was inches from hers. "You could never be ugly. I explained that to you before. Don't you remember?"

She saw his fangs and for a moment was back in her bedroom, looking up at him straddling her with hunger burning red in his eyes and his wild hair framing his gorgeous face.

Emotion balled in her throat, choking off all possibility of words. All she could do was look at him.

Griffin sat up and studied the machines hooked to her body. He carefully removed the IV, but left the heart monitor leads taped to her chest and stomach. Had he removed those, nurses and doctors would probably have come running from all directions.

Moving the wires out of the way, he stretched out on the bed beside her and wrapped his arms around her. His scent, for so long a forgotten memory and yet still familiar, made her smile as she rested her head on his shoulder.

"I'm here to give you a choice, Serena."

She rolled her head back to see his face.

"I've shown you the truth before, about what I am. And I've told you how much I want you with me. Now you must decide. If you come with me, you will never again see daylight, and you must constantly fight the drive to kill. It won't be easy."

Did he really think there was a choice to make?

"There is," he said, once again answering her unspoken question. "For one thing, I might lose you. This doesn't always work. You might live many more years as a mortal."

"Or not."

"Yes, or not. Life is uncertain, which is what makes it precious. When you become a vampire, your existence changes. Meaning becomes something you must search for."

"Is that why you followed me years ago?"

He smiled and pressed a kiss into her hair. "I've followed you since you were a child, Serena. And I've been here every night to check on you. I've watched over you."

She drew in a difficult breath. "You should have told me."

"Not until the time was right."

He must know what Dr. Thorpe had told her. Could he hear the erratic beat of her heart?

"Come with me, Serena."

She'd decided to go with him sixteen years earlier and no decision in her life ever felt more right. Funny that he didn't know that.

She nodded against his shoulder.

Griffin rolled up onto his elbow and gazed down at her. "Are you certain?"

She nodded again and reached up to clutch his shirt.

His smile revealed lengthened fangs, and his eyes glistened red, blue and silver. "Good." He leaned over and kissed her, groaning softly as she opened her mouth under his. Their tongues met in a dance of seduction, and his fingers traced a line down the side of her cheek.

In spite of everything, her body reacted to him by hardening and tingling. She slid her arm around his neck to hold him close.

He raised his head and she looked up into the terrible beauty of a beast with red, feral eyes. His ravenous gaze ran down to the side of her neck.

This was it, the moment she'd dreamt of years ago. Would there be pain? Or joy?

It didn't matter. There had never been anyone else in her life, and she suddenly realized why. She'd been waiting for him, waiting for her shadow lover to return. Somewhere deep in her subconscious, she'd known he would.

Steeling herself, she slowly raised her chin, baring her neck to him, willingly surrendering.

He leaned forward until his mouth was near her ear. "Everything I have is yours," he said, his voice low and deadly, "and you will be mine."

As she drew in a stuttered breath, he lowered his mouth to her neck.

She cried out at the momentary sting as he sank his fangs into her neck.

Pain faded to pleasure, and she clung to him, holding his head to her. Orgasmic joy drew her up against his body and into his embrace.

He sucked hard, drawing out the pain, and fear and sorrow. She shook from head to toe, unable to stop.

And then she lost her grip on him, and her hand fell

uselessly to her pillow. Cold crept up her legs to her torso and arms.

Her world darkened and faded to nothing.

Her last thought was his name.

"Serena."

A voice drew her from sleep.

Was the nurse waking her again? Had it all been a dream?

She opened her eyes and found Griffin looking down at her, his body bare and his eyes silver in flickering light.

She smiled at the rush of giddiness. "You're real."

"Yes," he said.

She glanced around at the unfamiliar room. Candles illuminated dark corners, and artwork adorned the walls. "Where are we?"

"Our home."

"*Our* home?"

He smiled. "For as long as it pleases you."

She thought back to the room full of monitors. "How did you get me out of the hospital?"

"Through the window."

"But won't people be looking for us?"

His smile widened. "You're in my world now, Serena."

Yes, the shadow world.

She sat up and looked at her hands, no longer wrinkled and thin-skinned. She appeared as healthy as she felt. "This is amazing."

Glancing down, she realized she was naked. "You undressed me?"

He grinned. "For the sake of saving time, my sweet."

"Oh? So, what, now you plan to have your way with me?"

In a movement so fast she barely saw it, he drew her under him and into his arms.

"Indeed I do," he said, "and I can wait no longer."

Serena sucked in a breath of surprise when he pierced the flesh of her neck as he entered her. Erotic pleasure swept over her in massive waves.

Griffin moved his shoulder to her mouth and instinct took over.

Connected, both as humans and vampires, her thoughts reached out and swirled into his, taking his past as her own, giving her future with joy. As one, they rose into a haze of perfect delight.

She knew it then. He had always loved her, and he always would, just as she loved him.

"Forever," he said, his thoughts as clear as words.

She agreed. "Forever."

* * * * *